TRICK MOON

THE WILD NINES
BOOK 5

A.R. KNIGHT

1

CELEBRITY STATUS

Davin had the target in his sights. The lighting a perfect golden white, no wind to disrupt his aim. No cover, no crowd getting in the way.

"Got you," he whispered, striking.

The toothpick skewered the shrimp clean, Davin lifting the snack off its ice bed and popping it in his mouth. Salty, succulent, just like the last ten he'd devoured off the buffet. He ditched the toothpick, grabbed a new one, and took aim at his next victim.

The late—or was it early?—hour meant the buffet neared empty, the stocks similarly low save for the shrimp serving as Davin's after-drinking dessert. Four long serving aisles bled right into a sparkly seating area where robots and workers rushed around cleaning for the morning crowd.

One which, if Davin had his way, he'd never see. Dreamland called, a destination pushed off by a rumbling stomach.

A destination all his crew must've already found. Normally the earpiece would've been bustling with chatter, most of it insults slung back and forth. Good-natured ribbing, the conversation he'd hoped to hear after several days on the *Galaxy's Song*.

Sure, they'd left Freestar with a pressing commitment: find Alissa, figure out why she refused to strike a peace deal with Eden before all the people on the outer planets became fodder for that company's marching war machine.

But, you know, they didn't really have any leads. So in the meantime, why not get some R&R?

The *Song* had been gliding along in Saturn's outer orbit —the best views without snarling shipping traffic—and offered a sublime opportunity: Davin, hero of Earth, could make a surprise appearance, delight the wealthy interstellar tourists.

Provided, of course, his crew received a few comped amenities in return.

"These are really good," Davin said, chewing shrimp number twelve, to a passing cook. The woman blinked at him, kept moving. "Really good."

When you'd lived for so long on nutrient goop, any real food qualified as really good.

The cruise ship's captain took Davin's deal and, so far, was making the Wild Nines leader work for it: Several appearances a day, though none before noon, and private drinks after. As Phyla put it after the first night, when Davin came stumbling in near dawn—at least, the ship's programmed dawn—this was the first real job Davin had held in a long time.

Well, if all real jobs came with three a.m. shrimp, maybe Davin had been doing it wrong all along.

Leaving the buffet line with a crostini-filled plate and a much-needed water, Davin settled in at the first table he found. In the table's center, Davin saw his own face staring back at him, a grinning, fresh-printed slip showing times and requesting interested parties inquire for more.

"That's me," Davin said, pointing at the thing with a fork, glancing around to see if anyone happened to be nearby.

A vacuuming robot didn't reply, continued its resolute search for crumbs.

"You know, I've fought androids," Davin said to the vacuum. "They're, like, the worst version of you."

The robot ignored him. The crostinis, thankfully, did not. They indulged his fork with little resistance, a crunchy delight. One he enjoyed until he felt two palms on his shoulders, fingers kneading through his light shirt.

"You got up just to give me a massage?" Davin said, glancing to see Phyla, hair pulled tight, racing uniform on.

"They're opening the circuits early today," Phyla replied, slipping her arm around to steal Davin's fork and the last crostini. "Guess who's the star challenge?"

"You?"

Phyla nodded as she munched. She'd been enjoying the cruise as much as Davin, burning hour after hour in the bullet sims. She took cash off of one mark after another, most happy enough to get a shot at a real racer, a real pilot.

"Still, it's like three thirty," Davin said. "No way things open this early."

"They don't, but Viola asked me to come find you, and I was too excited to sleep much anyway."

"What's the kid want?"

Phyla flicked her eyes around, changing the conversation's tenor. Davin blinked, put his celebrity persona in a mental box and refocused. Not every member of the Wild Nines treated this like a joy ride.

"She thinks she's got a lead," Phyla said. "A guy on the ship that's had connections with Alissa in the past."

"Connections? Like what, they met at a bar?"

Phyla shrugged, "Ask Vi. Point is, she swapped the guy's lunch to put him at your gig. When it's over, you sweet talk him and maybe we get somewhere."

Davin tried to lean back, sprawl his arms out in a shrug, and nearly fell out of his chair. Flimsy things.

"You want to ruin this good run so fast?" Davin asked.

"For once, not really," Phyla quirked a smile. "But it's not just you and me anymore, Davin. Some people are on a mission, and they're our friends."

"Our crew."

"Exactly."

A big sigh, a mournful look at the empty plate. "Guess that means I should probably get some sleep."

"Wouldn't be the worst idea."

"Want to walk me back? Still a few hours to kill till those races start, right?"

Davin tried a wink, Phyla laughed.

His pilot dumped Davin in their bed and left him there, telling the ship's AI, Fournine, to keep things in absolute darkness till ten at the earliest. No interruptions, no chance for Davin to get messed with.

Their rumpled mattress served as a soft, jelly-like home for those hours. Nestled in a metal frame, the bed jutted into the room's middle like a blunt spatula. Random memories crowded the leftover space: artifacts, clothes, weapons. Some even bought legally. To Davin's left, stuffed safe in a locker near the door, sat the one relic left for him by the *Jumper*'s former captain.

Davin looked at Melody first when Fournine nudged him awake—a blaring trumpet solo—and indulged in a cursory inspection. The energy shotgun's charge was topped off, its parts all registering in the green. If need be, Davin could take the thing and, even half asleep, blow his way off the *Jumper*.

"Not going to need that today, are we?" said a hard bass tone as Davin's door slid open.

Mox, the metal man, leaned against the door frame. Not that he could lean all that far: the man's bulk, all those carbon fiber lines running along his arms, back, and legs filled the space.

"Completes the picture, don't you think?" Davin scooped out the shotgun, twirled it and caught the grip in his right hand. The move staved off a hangover's attack, just enough potential action to keep his body in the game. "Been thinking we should add this in."

"Do it on Merc's turn, not mine."

"Scared?"

"Don't want to be there when you blow a hole in the ceiling putting on a show."

"Me?" Davin put on his hangdog face, held Melody up like she was some harmless toy. "Never."

"Remember that night on Titan?"

"Apparently you're never gonna forget it." Davin stuffed the gun back home, started for the door. "How was I supposed to know they made the drinks stronger for every bullseye?"

"Ask?" Mox put up a hand as Davin came close. "How about some clothes, captain, or is this a new show you're putting on?"

Davin glanced down at his ragged t-shirt, his underwear.

"Give me five."

Mox chuckled, "You got three, boss."

Davin made it out in four, stomping into the Jumper's rectangle center. The ship had two levels, the top for the bridge, most of the cabins, and the mess. Down below sat the cargo hold, access to the engines, and a small docking bay, currently empty, where a one-man fighter could sit.

Most mornings walking out felt a little like striding across a tiny town. Davin would see various crew, the occasional vendor walking through chatting about this and that. Fournine might be testing some system or another. Motion apart from himself, the whole thing feeling alive in a way it hadn't for far too long since he and Phyla went off on their own.

Today, with twenty minutes till showtime, dolled up in his swarthy knee-length black trench coat, blast-scarred pants, and a shirt telling sordid stories in stains, Davin embraced his home.

"Looking disgusting, captain," Mox said when Davin emerged.

"Clean is boring, my friend," Davin eyed Mox, who wore a t-shirt and pants get-up better for the gym than an expo. "And you're one to talk."

"People want to see the steel, so that's what I show them."

Truth. The first couple days, Mox had donned his Centurion red and nobody gave a crap. Lunar cops had their own aura, and nobody wanted a reminder of the law on a ship like *Galaxy's Song*. Since then, Mox had gone natural like Davin, much to everyone's approval.

Including the woman waiting for them on the Jumper's lower floor, arms folded as Davin and Mox stepped off the open-air platform. Viola, one eye looking at a her comm, always seemed like she was about to explode. So much twitchy energy, a thousand ideas clustered inside waiting for their chance.

Whenever he needed a night off, Davin would just buy Vi a couple drinks and let her go on, the most fascinating, cool inventions spilling out.

Too bad she'd flipped and worked for Eden instead of her dad.

"You know, it's a real drag waiting this late for you," Viola said to Davin, pointedly not to Mox. "It's my day too."

"Paid for by my nights, Vi," Davin said. "Phyla dropped your message. You want to ruin the fun?"

"Fun for you, maybe." Vi frowned towards the Jumper's repair room. "I came along with you because we were going to stop the war, not to get free margaritas."

"Ah, but have you tried the strawberry?"

"Pretty good," Mox added.

Vi rolled her eyes, smiled, "'K, point. But unless you think we're gonna get this free ride forever, maybe it's time we make a move?"

"Could be, could be," Davin said, stretched out his shoulder. "Throw me the details. I'll see if I can't sweet talk something outta this guy."

"Already did it." Viola blinked, her glass overlay folding up and clearing her eyes for a good look at Mox. "When Davin's playing host, keep an eye on things, okay? I found this guy by comparing the *Song*'s passenger list against Eden's wanted database. He shouldn't be on this ship, but someone put him here."

"A little smuggling for some R&R?" Davin asked.

"No clue, but Davin, he's not some broker shaving off cents for Alissa. Eden thinks this guy slaughtered a few transports worth of civilians."

Davin felt Mox stiffen beside him.

"Is it true?" the big man asked.

Vi shrugged, "Couldn't tell. Eden doesn't advertise that stuff."

"Looks bad when you can't keep your own people safe," Davin said. "We'll be careful. Keep a line open?"

"Fournine's all over it." Viola stepped aside. "Good luck guys."

"As if we'll need it," Davin replied as he and Mox headed for the boarding ramp.

"Hey captain," Viola called as the two hit the ramp's top. "Might wanna get some mouthwash, your breath smells like shrimp."

Davin blew on the back of his hand, took a whiff. Crinkled his nose.

The engineer had it right.

ALL THE YEARS Davin spent blasting his way from one planet to another did absolutely nothing to prepare him for a room flush with fans. Today marked the third straight morning the mercenary captain spiced his coffee with adoring onlookers, so the fake smile came easier. The bags beneath Davin's eyes, the stubble, all seemed to add authenticity. This here, Davin tried to say with his cocky slouch, this here was a rogue who meant business.

And today, that business was brunch.

"We're not here to hunt scrambled eggs," Mox whispered as Davin lead them through the crowd towards his reserved table and the entree already gracing it.

Eat first, then crowd surf.

"I've tackled too many fights—hey, good morning—to do it on an—Davin Masters, at your service—empty stomach, you get me?" Davin's hands worked magic, stretching out and gracing fingers as he slid past seats.

Mox drew fans too, but the exoskeleton cast a different spell, its hard metal reality clashing with exotic fantasy. Better to look, not touch.

"Admit it, you like this," Mox said when they settled into their folding chairs, backs against the wall so their audience could watch them stuff their faces. "All of it."

"Hell yes I like it. We've worked so long, so hard, not to enjoy a gift."

"Gifts have strings, Davin."

"Yeah, well, you see any on this one, you let me know." The eggs partnered with some greasy bacon. All grown, Davin would bet, in the ship's cell spinners. "Meantime, I'll smile and eat for free."

Mox, forking his way through some buttery, jam-coated toast, didn't argue any further.

Every table had a mic dragged onto it, so as brunch burned on the various guests had a chance to tap in and ask a question. Most were simple: what was Davin's worst fight, fastest ship, and so on. The first time through Davin had thought about sugarcoating answers, adding verve to this and that, but these jokers, these silver spoons, they'd lived so far from any real threat that the basic day-to-day of mercenary life proved incredible enough.

Rattling off mechanical answers gave him, and Mox, time to pick apart the crowd itself. Scan the faces for the one Vi had picked out. She'd beamed a picture to them on the walk here, a gaunt guy who didn't look at the camera so much as through it.

"Table four," Mox said as Davin finished up talking through the fight with Fournine on Europa. "Middle-back. Looks confused."

"Guy wasn't supposed to be here. I'd be confused too."

Davin snuck a glance while guzzling another mug of the black stuff. Always strong in space, where water was put on a premium. Not a bad thing.

The guy did indeed look perturbed, and his outfit put him apart from the other diners. For one, he dressed for business, not pleasure. For two, he didn't seem to be sharing a word with anyone else nearby, an odd one out and not caring to remedy the situation.

Worse, the guy made Davin's spying. A clear eyes-meet-eyes situation. The gazes held—Davin wasn't one to look away, that showed weakness, doubt—but with the man's piercing pupils, an escape would've been lovely. An escape provided, thankfully, by the coffee bot, trundling by to refill Davin's mug.

"Thanks," Davin said to the robot. "Mox, dude saw me."

"Hate to break it to you, captain, but everyone here sees you."

"Not like that."

"Then like what?"

"Like I was being examined. Haven't felt that way since Bosser used to give me the stare-down. Felt like I was being calculated."

Mox huffed, threw a straight-up glare at the guy himself. Davin would've reminded him to be discrete, but the word didn't mean much to Mox, didn't mean much to the mission either. Even if the guy got up and ran, the *Galaxy's Song* wasn't gigantic. They could find him anywhere.

"Bet I could snap him in half without breaking a sweat," Mox muttered as Davin told another story—Melody, pirates in the asteroid belt, bloody chaos. "Man might die before I touch him though. He's sweating already."

"Why?" Davin glanced down at himself after wrapping

the tale to more scattered applause. The heat stuck right in temperate's middle, a pleasant breeze gliding by on the ship's vents. "What's he got to be nervous about?"

"Us."

"Now, Mox, we just want to have a little chat. Nothing to be scared about there, right?"

But the guy evidently was scared. As soon as the Q&A wrapped, he shot up from his seat and made for the exit. Randoms in the crowd went for Davin's table, hoping for a bonus conversation. A swarm that'd make tailing the guy too hard. Unless...

"You owe me," Mox said as Davin dished him the plan and scooted away.

The Centurion announced, loud and bold, that he'd be sticking around for autographs, photos, the like, but that Davin had to beat it. The hangers-on apparently valued a picture with the metal man as much as a chat with Earth's greatest hero, leaving Davin with a few waves as he hustled past the tables and through the glass double-doors into the ship.

Galaxy's Song offered top-level views, its main deck using cameras and massive displays to let passengers sit just about anywhere and look into space. Its levels were latticed, eschewing the hard, claustrophobic space on most ships for a skeletal look. Sight lines were preserved, each level seeming to float on the one below it thanks to disguised struts. Ceilings had the display coating, so even on the ship's lowest open floor you could look up and see Saturn's brilliance. Only individual cabins and special rooms, like the one Davin used for his brunch shindig, were closed off.

Despite the infinity views, *Galaxy's Song* wasn't about taking in the zen. Announcements followed Davin as he followed the guy, the man's lithe form slipping between people in a determined walk. Buzzing drones weaved overhead, bringing ordered food and drink to lounging passengers reclining in soft yellow viewing chairs lining every level's edge. Those same drones burbled schedules, hailing potential activities to anyone in earshot. The idea, Davin supposed, was that you'd either wear your own earpieces to filter out the noise or embrace the chaos.

Going by the placid faces around him, Davin figured the former. Little nodes, some sporting neon colors, lingered in the ears around him. Viola and Merc had pairs, and Phyla had a special set geared for racing simulators.

Davin? Davin had a single one, an oldie slotted into one ear. Not much good for filtering out noise, but plenty capable of getting Vi's updates.

"The next thing on his schedule's a massage," Vi said, her voice coming in grainy. "Maybe that's why he's walking so fast?"

"Gotta hurry up and relax," Davin replied.

The captain shrank the distance with longer strides, a willingness to nudge people aside. His target didn't have the same weight, instead swerving around interlopers.

"What do I do when I catch him?" Davin asked.

"You're asking me?"

"Anyone else on the channel?"

"Davin," Vi said, "aren't you the experienced fighter? Deadly mercenary captain and all that?"

"You must have the wrong guy. I'm a full-time celebrity now."

Vi snorted through the mic. Someone else, another Nine listening in, laughed.

"That you, Opal?" Davin asked.

"Good to know your head's not too big," the sniper,

former rebel leader, and current badass said. "Tell you what, get the guy back to the ship and we'll have a chat."

"I'm guessing he won't want to come."

"A sweet talker like you can think of something."

Well, he'd have to come up with an idea soon, because Davin had closed the gap to a few meters. This near, Davin watched the man's clothes, searched for hidden weapons and saw none. Then again, if the guy was going to a post-brunch massage, arms probably weren't in the cards.

Various opening lines danced through Davin's head. None seemed to fit the situation. If he hadn't left his coffee back at the brunch site, Davin would've tossed it on the target, offered to take him back to the *Jumper* for a clean-up.

He'd just wing it. That never failed him, right?

"S'cuse me, buddy," Davin said, matching the man stride for stride. "Have a minute?"

The man glanced at Davin without stopping, did the usual double-take at the scoundrel's grin. Still, the footfalls continued.

"Sorry, I'm going to be late," the man said. "Another time."

As if Davin could be dismissed like a salesman.

"It'll only take a minute," Davin pressed.

"What'll only take a minute?"

"You remind me of someone," Davin said, free-wheeling now. "Ever been to Mars?"

"Once or twice." The man kept walking. They'd passed the halfway point on the ship now, not too long to the spa, a spot dumped near the engines to suck some bonus vibration into the sessions. "I'm sorry, I'm really in a—"

"Helluva planet, Mars," Davin interrupted, put a hand on the man's shoulder. Put just enough pressure on the grasp to slow the dude down a hot step. "Think I remember where I saw you there."

The man's eyes closed for a long second, but he slowed, stopped. Turned to face Davin as the people and drones flowed around them, a few sending annoyed glares their way for clogging the main conduit.

"Why is Davin Masters stopping me?" the man asked, what little congeniality he had dead.

"Like I said—"

"Don't care what you said. What do you want?"

All right. Straight up? Davin could play that way too. The smile vanished. His eyes narrowed a bit. Hands drifted to coat pockets. Sure, Davin had nothing more than a pen in one, a crumpled napkin in the other, but imagined threats were often as dangerous as real ones.

"I want to talk. Somewhere private." Davin nodded to the left. "My ship."

"My cabin," the man countered. "It's closer and more secure. Trust me."

"Don't trust you yet, but fine, lead on."

Vi and Opal exploded in his ear as the man resumed walking, same pace, same gait. The sniper and the engineer wanted to know why the hell Davin was changing the plan. A question Davin couldn't answer without words, so the two just railed on.

"Didn't expect you to be here," the man said, tone shifting again to a curious calm. As if they'd played their first match, found it a draw, and could now be casual friends. "A ship like this isn't where the action is."

"The food's free, the drinks aren't bad," Davin replied.

"You just happened to be near Saturn?"

"When you're a spacer like me, you take what luck you

can find," Davin said. "Seeing this beauty show up on the radar was about as lucky as it gets."

The man kept probing as they walked, ditching off the concourse for less-traveled walkways, the ones heading for cabin clusters. Unlike those big earth-bound boats, the *Galaxy's Song* set its cabins in big blocks near the ship's middle. Screens offered great views on the walls inside the small spaces while giving everywhere else on the ship a huge feeling, as if you were wandering free among the stars.

Not that Davin paid much attention to the aesthetics. His eyes crawled for potential threats, his mind kept making up new generalities to answer the man's questions. Questions that were getting awfully targeted.

"Last I heard, you were spotted on Freestar," the man said as they took a lift down several levels. "Right when that station had some big problems."

"Coincidences," Davin said.

The man opened his mouth for a follow-up, curiosity playing on his face. The follow-up never came: as they went down the black-and-blue hallway, passing an intersection, a red-haired racer came from the right and wrapped Davin in a hug.

"Vi said you might need some back-up," Phyla whispered, following the words up with a peck on Davin's cheek. She backed off a bit, threw the man a smile. "Who's this?"

"Roxley Jones," the man replied, giving Phyla a nod. "I think I know who you are."

"Doesn't everyone?" Phyla rolled her eyes Davin's way. "He put us all on the map."

Davin blinked. He'd never seen Phyla put on this routine before. She'd always been the blunt cannon, ready to get the job done without any fluff. Someone must've put her up to it.

"Still want to talk?" Roxley asked Davin. "I'm on a schedule."

"Would love to," Davin replied. "Mind if she tags along?"

"Don't mind one bit. My cabin's right up here."

Roxley's cabin claimed the hallway's end, its door grander than the ones they'd been walking by. Viola said the man had money, and he must've been dropping it in big amounts to claim this room. Roxley put his finger on the door's scanner, the device beeping a hello after a short second.

"After you," Roxley said, guiding them in with a hand.

"Thanks," Davin said, leading the way, ready for anything, Phyla on his heels.

The suite made his captain's quarters on the Jumper look like yesterday's dump. Glittering clean counters, couches, coffee tables sprawled through the space. The wall screens showed Earth scenes, skipping stars for waterfalls, oceans, mountaintops, a dizzying array that threw Davin, kept his attention one moment too long.

Phyla grabbed his wrist, tearing Davin away from the images, put his eyes on the suite's doors. The ones opening on all sides. Two women came from the right, a man from the bathroom on the left. All decked out in gear meant for something worse than a cruise ship. All holding sidearms.

"Now," Roxley said from behind, and Davin turned to see the man pull his own gun from a stand near the door. "You said you had something to talk about?"

2

A PERFECT VIEW FOR PLANS

Some people might stare down the barrel of a gun, or two, or three, and find themselves blanching. Might find their legs go a little weak, sweat beading just about everywhere, and the first words out of their mouth slide straight into groveling, whimpering nonsense.

Davin, separating himself a careful bit from Phyla, gave the foursome a long turning look, scoundrel's grin held firm the whole way. No panic, no quivering lip.

Once you'd had an android coming for your guts, humans didn't quite register the same on the ol' threat scale.

"Talk about?" Davin asked, responding to Roxley's question. "Actually, yeah—"

His earpiece shrieked, a sharp buzz breaking into static. Davin winced, shook the thing from his ear as Phyla did the same.

"They're cut," said the man at the bathroom door, a cup-sized saucer in his left hand, red light blinking. "We're good."

"Continue," Roxley said to Davin.

"Right," Davin straightened, tried to ignore his ringing ear. "First thing, she's not involved in this. Let her go, Rox."

Phyla caught on quick, gave Davin more room and pressed her back against the wall, hands up. She looked a little too hardened, a little too savvy to act the damsel with much success, but Davin didn't have another card to play.

Without their earpieces, nobody on the Nines would know if they needed help, if they were moved or shot.

"My name's Roxley," the man waved Phyla back to the middle with his gun. "She stays. Ask your question."

"You going to give me an answer?"

One of the women laughed.

"I'll answer it, one way or another. Ask."

Sometimes, the old charmer guise fell on its face. Sometimes Davin had to cut straight to it to survive. The truth shall set you free, wasn't that the line?

"You know Alissa Reinhart. We're trying to find her," Davin said. "Simple as that."

Nobody moved. Davin didn't have to look around to know the threats were watching Roxley, waiting for the order.

"What side are you on?" Roxley asked.

"The side that doesn't want to wind up dead," Phyla replied. "The side that wants to get out of this apartment and go back to our ship, please and thank you."

"I'm still deciding if that's going to happen. One more time. Who's side are you on?"

"Look," Davin said, "this war's going to leave a lot of bodies behind unless we can stop it. Eden's willing to talk, but Alissa's gotta answer, or everyone's going to start shooting again."

More laughter, this time from all three. The derisive kind. Davin found his fingers wishing they could hold some steel of their own, show these bums who they were threatening.

"You think anyone can trust what Eden says?" Roxley shook his head. "Only an idiot would think they're coming to the table with anything real."

"Someone's a cynic," Phyla muttered.

"Someone has other things to worry about," Roxley replied. "You two take a seat. My friends here are going to take a look at you, see where we can wind up."

Davin ran a quick check. Roxley stood before him, maybe two meters away. Double that to the doors and the people on either side. Minimal cover. Not one of these people looked shy on the trigger either, the guns all holding steady.

The Nines had gone up against Alissa's handpicked people before. Bakr and his crew outside Neptune. They weren't idiots, weren't greenies fighting with ideals and nothing else. A surprise wouldn't make them miss, wouldn't get him and Phyla out alive.

"Sure," Davin said, "We're all playing for the same team here."

The team, as Roxley explained it to Davin and Phyla on the room's only couch, under the shadow of guns, wanted money. Needed money.

"We're not running on charity," Roxley concluded his opening statement. "We're not running a business. We take what we need."

"By going on a cruise?" Phyla countered.

"Exactly," Roxley replied. "Nobody on this ship expects anything other than their afternoon margarita. A show by the pool. Quiet. We're not going to ruin that for them either. They'll only notice something wrong when they disembark, by which time we'll be long gone."

Davin leaned back into the cushions—they were a damn sight more comfortable than anything on the Jumper—and gave Roxley a two-fingered wave to go on. "Don't you have a massage to get to?"

Roxley's return smile was all teeth, "One I'm missing thanks to your poor timing. But if you are who you say, and who my friend is confirming, then I think you can help."

"We're soldiers, not thieves," Davin said.

"And racers," Phyla added.

"Looks like you have a lot of talents already," Roxley held that upturned maw. The look of someone who knows they've already won and was relishing it. "Time to add another to the list." He hunched forward, the conspirator about to unleash the conspiracy. "Everyone on this ship handed over their accounts before they boarded, all so the ship can charge expenses when the ride's over. We know the ship has the account data on here somewhere. If you can find it, get it, and give it to us? I'll get you your meeting with Alissa."

"What," Davin said, "you think they have the numbers printed out somewhere, on paper sheets?"

"If they do, great," Roxley shrugged. "I don't care how they have it. My guess, it's stored on a secure server onboard. Now, that's not my problem. It's yours."

"Or we could turn you over to the ship's security if you don't contact Alissa."

Roxley nodded at the drawn weapons, "Two things happen then. We kill you before security finds us, and you damn sure don't get your meeting."

Phyla flicked a look Davin's way, the reasonable slight shrug she used whenever Davin ought to agree with an offer. A stance Davin wasn't particularly thrilled with—who liked getting press-ganged into anything—but there didn't seem to be an easy way out. The Nines could just up and leave the ship, but that'd put them back in space with zero leads.

Time ticked away.

"Fine," Davin said. "You want your accounts, we'll get you your accounts."

"Perfect," Roxley said. "My friend here will send along what we know, but it's not much. This ship isn't the easy egg to crack we thought it would be." For once, the sly criminal's vibe slid away from the man, his slight features looking less like a choice and more like battered exhaustion. "We're disembarking at Titan. It's all we can afford. So you have two days. And please understand how many lives depend on this."

"What a noble ass," Phyla said as they walked towards the Jumper, back on the ship's concourse. "Lives depend on him robbing a bunch of tourists? Please."

"You gotta buy weapons somehow."

"No, you don't," Phyla had her arms folded, an icy fixture in her eyes. "They don't have to keep shooting. They don't have to put turrets on their ships. It's escalation without an end."

Davin threw an eyebrow at her, "You want'em to just give up?"

"I want them to be smart. There are better ways to fight Eden than shooting."

"Like embarrassing them on the race track?"

Phyla rolled her eyes, "You know what I mean. The Solar System's a big place. Lots of ways you can make a point without open warfare."

"Maybe that's what they're doing here."

"Excuse me?"

Davin pulled Phyla over to a poolside bar, a place lathered in soft-whites and playing a jaunty sun beat. Kids ran after each other in a hectic tag game, forcing chair huggers to save drinks lest they be knocked over.

"Shrink all these accounts, get the money good and gone, then pump out a release saying they'll give it back if Eden gives up the fight? Not the worst play."

Phyla turned on a skeptical look as Davin ordered up a couple mojitos. The synthetic mint looked real good on the iceberg blue bar counter.

"Roxley didn't mention that at all," Phyla said.

"He didn't *not* mention it."

"Okay, so I'm arguing with a toddler?"

"You're arguing with the savviest captain this side of Saturn, is what," Davin replied.

"You mean the one that just got ambushed?"

"I mean the one buying you a wonderfully delicious drink."

Davin handed over Phyla's mojito, took a sip of his own. The chilled gin hit just right, a soft kiss of summer a billion kilometers away from any place with the season.

"Okay," Phyla said after her own taste. "I'll give you that one."

You want to be a mercenary captain, Davin found, you had to realize a few fundamental truths. First and foremost, everyone on your crew had their own objectives: some wanted the cash, the credits, the gold. Others aimed for reputation, skills, maybe a chance to see somewhere new. Still others needed to shoot something. Acknowledge those goals without pandering to them and you'd have a crew that'd stick around, even if they all desired different things.

Second, give'em a chance to breathe. Davin couldn't have been a taskmaster if his life depended on it, and the thought of micromanaging his team's every move filled him with a kind of nausea only a bad bender's morning could compete with.

And third?

Earn their respect.

Davin, mojito in hand, left Phyla to get herself cleaned up post race and hostage adventure. He headed towards *Galaxy's Song*'s bridge and the docking bays near the ship's bow. The folks taking siestas on board tended to be the type that might need to fly away any day, so three bays dedicated themselves to shuttles and ferrying out the needy.

While Phyla found her kicks racing and Davin by flashing his mug, signing autographs, Merc parlayed his passage by playing pilot. The man sucked up shifts down here, dashing to and from surrounding stations, moons, and ships.

"It's crap work, but it's better than nothing," Merc said when Davin found him outside bay two, having just landed a jaunt to an Earth-bound cruiser passing by. "Don't have to smile all day, anyway."

"Not as bad as it sounds," Davin raised up the mojito glass.

"Point, I guess," Merc squinted at Davin. "You sloshed already captain?"

The fighter pilot had a small frame, one always seeming like it was about to bound off in any direction. A fast hand with most weapons and cocky enough to use'em, Merc also had the guts to fall in love with the most deadly patient woman Davin knew. The two equalized each other, a killer harmony.

He and Phyla could and should take a page from their book.

"Sloshed? Nah, this is only number one," Davin noted the passengers, the maintenance crew bustling around them. The broad hall had its walls overlaid with signs advertising deals on current and future voyages, enticing newbies and departing veterans alike. A singsong jingle played through idle speakers.

Privacy was not a concern.

"You have time to step away for a minute?"

Merc glanced at one of the digital clocks hugging the walls, soft green lines hard to see, as if to say time didn't matter while you were out here coasting.

"Have an hour before my next one." Merc seemed to realize Davin wouldn't normally be down here, nodded to a side room. "C'mon, bet there's nobody in there."

The small break room wasn't quite deserted, but Merc threw the only other occupant a look that said she ought to take a walk, and the scrubber shrugged, left. Davin and Merc settled into rail-thin chairs across a card table swamped with coffee stains.

Without waiting for Merc's invitation, Davin spilled the details. Roxley, the guns, the mission for the meeting. At the end of it, Merc threw up a single hand.

"So whaddya want me to do about it?" Merc asked. "Sounds like this is Viola's bag."

"Wanted to see if you had any ideas?"

"Yeah, just gave you mine. Ask Vi. If someone can hack into this place, she and her bot can."

Okay, so Davin had already thought of that. It was the obvious answer, but if you wanted a fourth rule about being a good mercenary captain, getting input from your whole crew was usually a good idea.

"We need a lead on where to look," Davin said.

"The ship's network, maybe?" Merc still looked confused.

"Roxley said the numbers weren't that easy to access.

They have their own computer expert with them." Davin caught sight of some bagels on the break room counter, stood up and snagged one. Cinnamon raisin. "He didn't say so, but I'm betting if these numbers were right there on the network, Roxley would have them already."

"Again, Davin, you're asking the wrong guy."

To toast or not to toast? Davin looked at the bagel, flipped a mental coin, the mojito's mint still dancing in his mouth. Toast it was.

"You pick up new passengers on these flights, yeah?" Davin asked.

"Sure?"

"New passengers mean new accounts?"

Merc twisted in his seat as the bagel fried in the small silver toaster. "They put in the information when they arrive. There's a terminal right there in the bay."

Davin popped a nice fridge, found some cream cheese. The package had a *Galaxy's Song* wrapper. The blade-less butter knife had the ship's logo on its hilt.

"But Davin, if you're thinking what I think you're thinking, buddy, that terminal's watched," Merc said. "Not by some bribable flunky either, but by a bot. It's a friendly one, all dressed up like some bellhop from a couple hundred years ago, but I bet it'd turn you into a pretzel if you tried to crack that machine."

"Pretzels," Davin nodded. "Those do sound tasty."

The bagel popped. Davin commenced the spread. Just the right layering.

"Sure you're not sloshed?" Merc asked.

"Fine. Thinking." Davin plopped back at the table, fresh bagel ready for consuming. "We need to get Vi access to your terminal."

"Cool, yeah, sounds good," Merc watched Davin take a

bite. The bagel melted in Davin's mouth, delicious. "I'll just walk her right in, have her take a look. Nobody's gonna mind. Or, you know, maybe they'll just kill us."

"Nobody's gonna kill you on a cruise ship," Davin said, his words mushy with the bagel in his mouth. "Bad for business."

"Yeah? How much sympathy we going to get from these passengers when they find out we're trying to take all their accounts?"

The break room door popped open, another two workers coming in. Davin raised his bagel in welcome while they stared, no doubt looking for a *Galaxy's Song* badge that wasn't there.

"Play with it for a bit," Davin said, standing. "Maybe something will come to mind."

On his way out, the captain grabbed the bagel's other half. He had a long walk ahead, a good snack was necessary.

THE *GALAXY'S Song*'s center coalesced into a spire jutting from the ship's hull like a crystal thorn. If you bought a ticket, you could take a special lift right up to the bulb at the top and join a dozen other guests for thirty minutes of stunning views. The hardened glass, wrapped with a radiation-deflecting energy shield, gave a no-frills, all thrills look at Saturn's rings.

And a particular mercenary captain, signing autographs and telling stories for the rest of the afternoon.

"See that one right there?" Davin pointed at a random dot, one little larger than a dust mote. Eyes, most glazed with wine or liquor's lacquer, followed. "That's Europa, and I'll tell you now it's the best place to go to feel better about every place you've ever been."

A couple pity laughs. Davin would have to work on the delivery. Nevertheless, he bled the awkward transition into the story about Eden Prime, about androids and conspiracies and a runaway girl.

A runaway girl, Davin noticed, who'd snuck her way off the last lift. Viola's bot, Puk, floated with her, the little thing hovering like a balloon in the background. They deadlocked on Davin, Vi's scowl deepening every time Davin tacked on an embellishment. She'd descended into a full glare by the time Davin stood triumphant atop the ruined terramorpher.

"Thanks for listening," Davin said. "Going to get myself a beverage and be back, you all enjoy yourselves."

A small automated bar sat near the lift at the center, its selection available in precise amounts for anyone with the cash to spend. Viola, sadly, parked herself in front of the machine, keeping Davin away from the refreshment such a story doubtless deserved.

"Really?" Vi asked when Davin tried to get around her, press the button for something, anything. "You're that desperate?"

"Look, you try telling the same stories every day. It takes stamina."

"Know what else takes stamina, Davin?" Vi moved aside, let Davin hammer home a request. "Keeping up with the crap you throw my way."

Cabernet acquired, Davin took the plastic cup and its rosy red contents to an empty table. Vi followed. Most tables were left alone, the guests choosing to squash their noses up against the glass, probably deciding where next to spend their infinite bank balances.

"Crap? Vi, one, they had guns in our faces," Davin said, swirling the wine. Wafting it, as these people might say. "If I hadn't struck a deal, you'd be reeling in our frozen bodies out there. Two, I said a deal. A deal! We do this, we get Alissa. We get answers. Maybe we even get peace." Davin sat back in the chair, raised the wine in a mock toast. "Think that's pretty good."

"So we're thieves now. Not mercenaries, not people trying to help save the solar system, just thieves."

"Gotta break a few eggs to make an—"

"If you say omelette, Puk's going to shoot you right now."

The bot made a curious noise, "I'm what?"

Davin sloshed his wine at the floating machine, "Puk doesn't have a gun on him."

Vi's scowl turned into a nasty grin, "Not that you know." She faded back, straight-lined, strait-laced. "Look, my point is, we don't know who all these people are. We don't know what this guy's going to do with the money either."

"He told us the rebels need it," Davin shrugged. "Feel like that's an answer."

"One you believe?"

Oh, yeah. Guess there's something else you had to do to be a good captain: put up with your crew.

"Who cares, so long as we get that meeting," Davin said.

Vi countered, spun off dire scenarios where, flush with cash, Roxley bought and unleashed hell on small outposts. Hired and deployed other scams, or created a mercenary force of his own and threw the solar system further into chaos.

"Okay," Davin said. "You're pushing hard. I know you well enough to guess you've got something else in mind?"

Vi's crusader look faltered, "Not something totally different. Just, like, playing it safer."

"By?"

"We still get the accounts, right? But we don't hand them

over, not till we talk with Alissa and confirm what this guy's saying."

"So we get the meeting and keep our scruples?" Davin made a show of drinking the wine, mulling the idea. "How about we go one step further?"

Vi leaned forward. Puk, too, drifted in. Conspiracy's sweet, sweet temptation.

"How about we take all the money for ourselves and forget the meeting with Alissa?"

The girl reeled back. Puk gave an indignant squawk, one covered up by the lift announcing time's up for the current viewing crop.

Davin laughed. Felt good to mess with the kid.

"Look," the captain said, "we're gonna get those accounts, and we're going to get that meeting. Whether Roxley's telling the truth or not, what he does with the cash, that's on him. Not us."

"Then I'm not going to help," Vi said. "Good luck getting those accounts without me."

Davin downed the rest of the wine. In a few minutes the next round would be here, and he'd have to start the spiel all over again. Viola ought to know by now that life out here was messy, compromises needed making.

"Roxley's not going to come with us to find Alissa," Davin said, forestalling the inevitable 'how do you know' with a single raised finger. "If he gives us anything, it'll be a location and a contact number. Then he'll disappear." Davin kept the finger raised. "But more than that, Vi? We made a deal, and I'm sticking to it. You don't like it, you're free to buy your own way off ship."

Vi's glare returned. She pushed back from the table.

"Maybe you forgot who I am," she said to Davin. "You

don't get to push me around. I give Eden a call and they'll be here as fast as they can. So what's it going to be, captain?"

Davin stared. The clueless girl on Europa wasn't so clueless anymore.

"Okay," Davin leaned on his elbows, trying to draw them in again, but this time Viola and Puk kept their standoff distance. "I pulled this trick once back on Phobos. Thinking it's time for another spin."

DAVIN RAISED his second cabernet to Vi and Puk as they disappeared down the lift. They'd bought the plan, and Vi was on her way to Merc's shuttle bay to get a peek at the terminal. Hopefully she'd find a key to get the accounts. If not, Davin would get Mox and they'd go in the hard way.

Until then, Davin would have to decide who he'd lied to: Roxley, or Vi. You'd think it would be an easy choice, but as soon as Roxley realized the charade, the Nines would be screwed six ways from Sunday.

But, really, if you were going to be captain, the crew topped everything else.

At least, that's what Davin told himself as the last pre-dinner crowd left the thorn's tip. Davin waved them good-bye, then soaked in a solo view while the lift ran its trip.

Saturn held up its end of the bargain, its rings fuzzy this close and more beautiful for it. A moon—Davin couldn't tell which one—made a clear appearance off to the left, its bulk eclipsing some golden stardust. Below and to the right, engines marked another departing craft.

"Davin Masters?" asked a voice, just after the lift's chime signaled its return.

The captain turned 'round, expecting some last minute autograph seekers. Instead, three crisp white uniforms, seams marked by the *Galaxy's Song*'s gold and blue colors, the Saturn patch on their chest, greeted him. The closest man, the one addressing him, held a relaxed smile, hands free, but Davin paid more attention to his pals and their own mitts just about hugging their stun batons.

"You found me," Davin raised his fourth cabernet in a boozy salute. "Don't think I have a dinner engagement today, but hey, I could be wrong."

"You do now," the man said, "with the captain."

Davin nodded, as if this was the most expected thing. He put some extra spin on it, his foot sliding a little with the move. The cabernets had him buzzing a bit, but something about these guys sobered him up fast. Better to make them think he'd left sense and sensibility far behind.

"Sorry, my friend," Davin said, playing up a slur. "Don't think I'll make good company."

The man's smile thinned, "She won't mind. If you would?"

On his way out, Davin left his last glass on the bar, cabernet still inside. Where he was going, he wouldn't need it.

3

———

VACUUM TWIST

For a ship as big as the *Galaxy's Song*, the bridge left no questions about where the profit was. A narrow lift shrouded behind bright, friendly, *authorized personnel only* signs took Davin and his three-man escort down, down, and then down some more.

"They really don't like you guys, huh?" Davin asked as the lift sped beneath passenger quarters.

Nobody answered. Davin had been sticking them with jabs the whole way, most of the jokes verging on too stupid to tell. But not without purpose: every pun, every slight he said was picked up by Davin's earpiece, sent along to the crew.

If Phyla and Opal didn't have the Nines ready for a fight, a run, or something worse by now . . .

"Captain Parvi!" Davin announced as the lift doors opened, revealing the dim workstation collective making up the bridge. A narrow slit gave a real view into space, one washed out by the twenty monitors crowding a room not much larger than Roxley's suite. "Hear you want to talk to me?"

Parvi, as she seemed to do whenever she saw Davin, sighed about as deep as it was possible to sigh. Her uniform, as crisp as the others, had only a spiffy hat to differentiate it. She stood, too, while her fellow bridge crew sat at their stations. Most wore headphones and took zero notice of Davin's arrival.

Committed, or perhaps briefed in advance that this wasn't a public conversation.

"Captain Masters," Parvi replied, not bothering to force the smile she'd played when the 'Nines first landed on her ship. "I'm sorry to call you here on short notice, but there's been a development."

Davin shuffled on his scoundrel's grin, plopped his hands on his hips. If he'd had a toothpick to gnaw on, that would've been perfect.

"A positive development?" Davin asked, hearing the guard trio splay out behind him, covering the route back to the lift. "Because, Parvi—can I call you Parvi?" She shook her head, Davin kept going anyway. "Parvi, I appreciate the heck outta what you've given me and my crew, but I want you to know, the mojitos at the pool bar?"

"The mojitos?" Parvi's eyes about bugged out of her head.

"Yeah, I think it's the third bar back from the bow? The bot's watering them down. You ought to have his circuits checked."

Parvi blinked, "Uh, no, Captain Masters, I—"

"Davin. We're both captains, right?"

"Davin then. You know we welcomed you onboard out of our generous spirits—"

"Uh huh."

"With every intent of letting you off at the end of this journey," Parvi gathered strength, like a storm building.

Davin could've interjected more, thrown her off her game, but the wine had worn away. Time to get this show going. "But it seems Eden has declared you an enemy of Earth."

"Funny, I seem to recall saving that planet."

A pitying smile, "As it is, I can't have a criminal on my ship, much less one with your notoriety."

"Give me a few hours and we'll be gone, Parvi. No harm, no foul."

Provided, of course, Viola and Merc could get those accounts by then. If not, stall stall stall.

"You won't have a few hours." Parvi, for just a moment, seemed to show genuine sorrow, the irritation drifting away into worry. "This all came up because an Eden frigate is approaching. They seem to have followed you from Freestar."

"They want to tango?"

"Perhaps. They've sent a shuttle, one that will be boarding us in five minutes."

Oh, Parvi. Nasty move waiting until right now to tell him.

"Parvi, I thought we were friends," Davin put on a pout, letting his mind race. "This is what you do to me?"

"Most of our passengers come from Eden territory, Davin. I need to stay on their good side. I'm sorry."

"I'll bet." Davin glanced over his shoulder at the guards. "These boys meant to keep me here till Eden arrives?"

"I'm hoping you'll choose to wait politely. I can get you one of those mojitos, if you'd like?"

Parvi had genuine hope in her expression, earnestness in those eyes. Maybe cruise ship captains could keep themselves sheltered from the dismal outcomes Davin saw so often. Like the one he was about to deliver.

"Sure, I'll take one," Davin said. "No sense getting arrested sober, right?"

Parvi, doing exactly what Davin hoped she would, nodded to one of the trio, who called the lift, deputized into running beverages.

"So do I just stand here till the goons arrive, or you got a chair for me?" Davin asked.

Parvi pointed past Davin, to the lift's left where several seats sat locked to the wall. Meant, probably, for visitors or tourists wanting to see some maneuver from the captain's perspective.

Davin gave Parvi the slightest of winks, turned 'round, flashed a grin at the lead guard. As Davin took the first step towards the chairs, the lift arrived, doors dinging open.

Wide open.

His left foot planted, Davin broke for the open lift. With his left arm, Davin shoved the back left guard aside, right into those chairs. The right one, the mojito man, started to turn back at the shouting, just in time for Davin to shoulder-jack the man into the lift. Something, someone grabbed at Davin's coat, the captain's black leather, but the fabric proved too slippery.

With his jacked guard on the lift's floor, Davin spun as he went through the doors, hand hitting the keypad, pressing any button that'd take him away from here. Looking back out towards the bridge, he saw the lead guard dashing towards him, Parvi behind, with her hand on her forehead.

Good, a headache was the least she deserved, setting Davin up like that.

The lead man's stun baton proved a more immediate problem, especially since the lift didn't want to shut with something in the way. Davin backed up against the lift wall to dodge the initial flail, then darted forward to grab the lead guard's arm and pin the baton out wide.

"Let me go," the guard said, his clean-shaven, far too neat face and minty-fresh breath right up in Davin's business.

"Nah," Davin replied, and gave the man a good headbutt.

Now, smashing one's head into another was a risky move. Do it wrong, and Davin would hurt himself as much or more than the next guy. The key, as Davin had learned over far too many failed attempts, was to connect his hard skull with the fleshy bits on his opponent.

In other words, Davin went for the nose.

The captain's forehead delivered the blow, crushing some cartilage and sending the lead guard back a few steps, shiny red staining that oh-so-nice uniform. The stun baton dropped, hit the floor as the guard brought his hands up to staunch the flow.

Bad moves all around, proving the *Galaxy's Song* didn't put much money into its security forces. As the lift doors, clear now, swung shut, Davin waved goodbye to the wide-eyed bridge crew. After this, they'd probably be happy to go back to dealing with pool deck drunks.

A searing pain shot up Davin's left leg, numbing it as soon as the shock ran through. Davin kicked out on instinct, smashing the guard's head into the lift's wall and knocking the man senseless. Falling to one knee, his left leg no longer interested in straight-up work, Davin tore the stun baton free and gave the guard a good shock too.

"That sounded fun," Phyla said, her voice pouring into Davin's earpiece. "I assume you're not getting that mojito?"

Davin glanced at the lift numbers, the climbing floors in

fluorescent blue on black, "Heading to the bar now, you want one?"

"How about we rain check and you get your ass back here?"

Davin tested his leg, almost fell on his face.

"About that. They were a little handsy with a stunner. My left leg's going to be out for a bit."

"You saying you need help?"

"I can limp with the best of'em, but I'd appreciate a ride."

"Got you," Mox's baritone rode on in. "Hold your position."

The lift hit its mark, stopped and swung doors open to show the crowded main deck. Sitting behind the *employee's only* signs meant not a soul bothered to look away from their beers to see Davin lurch his way free.

"Yeah, I'll hold it," Davin said, collapsing against the wall to the lift's left. The doors swung shut again, the lift probably heading back to pick up bloody nose and his buddy. "How's our hacker?"

"Not a hacker," Vi said, her signal scratchy. "I'm an engineer, thank you very much."

"And?"

"And if Merc can keep sweet-talking these people for another few minutes, I think we're in business."

Davin leaned his head back against the cold metal. Felt good. A drone buzzed by bearing a flier with Davin's name, picture, an advertisement for a dinner with Earth's hero.

"Phyla, you still there?"

"I am. Opal's getting the Jumper ready."

"Parvi said an Eden shuttle was inbound. Can you confirm?"

"It's past inbound," Viola's voice again. "It's one bay over, but they're ignoring Merc and me."

"Talk about star power," Davin muttered. Beside him, the lift hummed its approach. "Mox, my man, where are you?"

A pointless question: if Davin had spent a breath looking, listening, he'd have heard and felt Mox's approach. The metal man rumbled on the main deck, tourists and staff scattering at his sprint. The lift chimed its arrival. Mox barreled through the signs.

With a whoosh, the lift's door swung open as Mox stopped in front of the thing, Davin watching as his friend folded his arms, put on his best mean mug.

"Think you were going down," Mox said to the people inside, ones Davin couldn't see, ones who heard Mox's words, ones who hesitated. "Now."

A button clicked, the lift door shut, and the elevator zipped away. Mox pivoted, picked Davin up as easy as Davin picked up those shrimp back at breakfast.

"Spineless, aren't they?" Davin said as Mox, holding Davin like some fairy tale princess, dashed across the deck.

"I'd call 'em smart," Mox replied.

Merc and co ran shuttles from the lower levels, but the *Galaxy's Song* gave its high rollers—and celebrity guests—special slots along the main floor, easiest to get the coin off-board and into Parvi's pockets. The five bays hung near the ship's aft, where the big cruiser's engines marred the otherwise perfect view.

"They're still open?" Davin asked, enjoying his ride in Mox's arms. The left leg wouldn't be coming back soon. "The bays?"

"The *Song*'s engines aren't on," Phyla replied. "Better get your asses moving so they don't think to close 'em."

Mox grunted, his breathing otherwise even as he dodged some, bulldozed others on the trek across the ship. Tourists gawked, staffers swore, and drones spun away. Davin threw grins and winks, knowing every one of these jokers would take this story back to their pals, grow his legend ever further.

Those appearance fees would be going up.

A growing light drew Davin's face from the viewers towards the glass view above, where several spacecraft shot overhead in a close brush with the cruiser. Close enough for Davin to recognize the green colors, the needle-like build favored by everyone's least favorite company.

"Pick up the pace, hoss," Davin said to Mox. "They're going to pin us."

"Davin," Phyla cut in. "We gotta jump, or we're not getting off. If those fighters get an angle, we're toast just leaving the bay."

"They'd better not shoot my ship."

"Mind asking them not to?"

"I will, just not the way they might like," Davin said, then he poked Mox, a finger jab right between the black metal claws wrapping the man's chest. From a centimeter away, Davin saw more than he cared to about the dark nodes buried in Mox's skin, transmitting signals from the man's brain to his metal limbs. "Change of destination, my friend. We're going to the thrusters."

"You sure?" Mox replied between breaths, no breaks in stride.

"You hear doubt in my voice?"

As Mox swerved to the right to dodge a beverage cart, Davin snaked an arm out, grabbed a can of something. Popped it and took a swig. Cherry soda.

Could've been something stiffer.

Behind Mox, Davin looking over the man's shoulder, an even, bouncing forest green cadence bobbed. Eden's shuttle soldiers, up and out, pursuing with slow and steady confidence.

"Vi, give me some good news?" Davin asked.

"So we're getting there," Viola's comm crackled. "Merc's in here with me. We barred the door."

"What? Thought you were being ignored?"

"I know a guy," Merc jumped in, sounding sweaty, tight. "Or he knows me. Back from the Earth days, so we're scrambling a bit. But don't worry, cap. Vi's bot has us covered."

"How're you getting out of there?" Davin peeked over Mox's shoulder again, saw they were still gaining on the Eden soldiers. Good. "Don't like your shooting odds."

"Got ourselves a good shuttle stuck in with us," Merc replied. "If Vi gets those accounts in the next five, we'll be fine. Unless this cruiser's got any weapons."

"Merc," Opal, as dead serious as Davin could never be, cracked in, "you dodge anything this bloated whale can shoot, or you best not be coming back."

Merc laughed, "Challenge accepted, love."

Before Davin could think up another question, Mox turned, lowered his shoulder, and rammed through two white-clad staffers and the door behind them. The thin portal led right to the engines, or rather, the monitors banked one on top of another controlling the *Galaxy's Song's* big thrusters.

Most ships this size would run everything from the bridge, just like a human didn't have brains in their feet, but a foot, unlike an engine, wouldn't explode if something went wrong, so the cruiser kept its manual controls back here. Babysitting them was a man sucking on a caffeine stick, a man who looked, saw Mox crush through the door and made the smart decision to step aside.

"Davin, you got an idea, now's the time," Phyla said as Mox set the captain down in the man's chair. "They have us blocked in."

"Watch the door," Davin said to Mox, who went back out, ripped the stun batons off the nervous staffers and sent them packing. "Phyla, you get the Jumper ready. You'll have a small window."

Reaching up to his ear, Davin dialed down his comm as he flashed teeth at the engine flunky.

"How about you help me turn these boys up to full blast?"

"Full?" The man looked like he was about to start an argument, so Davin cut him off by reaching for the console and pressing buttons. "Holy crap, man!" The dude lurched forward, grabbing for Davin's hands. "You'll kill us all. You want the engines going, just do this."

The man took over, punched up several levers. A calm announcement rang through the ship, telling everyone to pay no mind to the rumbles, the ship was just making a slight course change. Davin watched the man's choices, waited till he was done, then the Nines captain took out his stun baton and jabbed the poor sap.

"Nothing personal, bud," Davin said to the numb body on the floor. "Can't have you ruining our grand escape."

"Time's ticking, Davin!" Mox called from outside.

"You heard the man, Phyla," Davin said. "Those fighters gone yet?"

"They ran, but I'm not flying into that wash," Phyla replied.

"You won't have to. Count to five, then blast outta there."

"What're you going to do?"

"Mox and I'll get creative, don't you worry."

"Wasn't worried, just curious."

Ah, Phyla. Always showing her love.

Davin did her the favor of counting out loud, getting to five and sliding the controls just the way the body on the floor had done it a minute ago. The engines stuttered, their full thrust dying fast, but the ship, big and slow as it was, gave zero notice.

Vacuum, a beautiful thing.

"We're out!" Phyla shouted and Davin, the faintest tingling coming back to his left leg, pushed himself from the console.

"Mox, go time," Davin called.

Mox didn't answer, forcing Davin to spin around in the console chair. Outside the busted door, *Galaxy's Song* was a war zone. New alerts blared, an urgent Captain Parvi telling all guests to return to their cabins until the disturbance could be resolved. Abandoned drinks, confused drones, staffers hiding behind food carts provided the backdrop for an Eden squad engaged into a cautious, one-sided firefight with Mox.

The exoskeleton man had himself hunched behind a stolen, overturned popcorn cart. The thing's metal counter, likely made for deflecting butter's stains, proved an adequate defense against sporadic fire.

Guess Eden wanted to keep things controlled.

Davin, scooting into the doorway's corner, glanced out. Figured the company wasn't too keen on putting more bad publicity on its plate by shooting up a civilian vessel, particularly one carrying Eden's political allies, the Earth fat-cats bankrolling its expansion.

So instead the twelve soldiers fanned themselves out, using the occasional popped shot to keep Mox down. In another few seconds they'd have Davin and his friend encircled.

"New plan, Mox," Davin said.

"New plan? When has any of this been a plan?" Mox said, twisting to put his back to the cart and his angry eyes on Davin.

"You know how we do it," Davin replied, then wheeled himself back to the console.

Straight acceleration wouldn't do much in a vacuum, but a hard stop? A reversal? Physics would be his buddy.

"Don't suppose you'd help with that," Davin glanced down at the stunned engineer. "No? Oh well. Mox, get in here!"

The metal man took the advice, ignored Eden's calls for surrender and made a laser-splashed dive into the engine control room.

"Hold that door up and buy me a minute."

Mox obliged, lifting the busted panel and holding it as best he could to fill the gaps in the rectangular portal. Davin turned back to the console, tried to read the numbers, the screens.

Piloting the Jumper was pretty simple: a flight stick, a single lever controlling thrust. Reverse, a far less powerful option using just the maneuvering jets, required a single toggle.

Galaxy's Song looked to have something similar, a weak option highlighted to help with docking maneuvers, meant for when the big cruiser was already puttering along. That wouldn't generate the force he needed, so—

"Hurry up and do something, man," Mox growled, "They're melting away my panel."

"Always complaints with you."

The engines didn't have a way to pilot the ship either, as

expected. Which meant Davin would have to be creative. First, he slapped at the section running the *Galaxy's Song*'s maneuvering jets, kicking on the group towards the ship's aft. A thrum started up beneath Davin's feet, the cruise ship going into a slow tumble as its forward velocity burned along unchanged.

"Give yourselves up," a new voice called out, a woman whose tone said she believed the Nines would do no such thing.

More worrying was how close the call sounded: the Eden fighters must've been just outside the door, waiting, hoping to avoid bloodshed. And, perhaps, needing to take Davin and Mox alive.

Wouldn't do PR wonders either to have Earth's former hero gunned down, unarmed, in the public view.

"Gotta love being famous, right?" Davin said. Before Mox could reply, the captain turned his head and shouted out the door. "We're unarmed! Don't shoot!"

Buying time.

Galaxy's Song hit a perfect ninety degrees, its engines not quite where they needed to be. The maneuvering jets kept on kicking, not yet pushing back on the ship's momentum.

"The hell you doing?" Mox asked.

"One more time, Captain Masters. Come out, hands free," the squad leader called again.

"Throw the door aside, let'em see us," Davin said.

His earpiece buzzed, Phyla describing how they'd blasted out the back, how she and Opal were engaged in a firefight with Eden's craft. Viola had better news: they'd cracked the database, the accounts now on her drive. Merc was powering up their escape.

Everything going good for the Nines, except this right here.

Mox launched the door aside, put himself in the doorway with his hands up. Blocked the Eden squad's view.

The cruiser continued its tumble.

"Don't shoot!" Mox called. "What do you want with us anyway?"

"We just want Davin. You can walk away," the squad leader replied.

"My crew doesn't mutiny," Davin shouted back. "Gotta say, this is an aggressive way to get an autograph."

The squad leader didn't take the bait, instead launching into a rambling series of offenses, charges, crimes against whatever, who cared. The cruiser hit its goal, completing a full orientation, its butt where its nose used to be.

The console flashed. Someone from the bridge trying to take control. They'd finally realized, maybe when Saturn went upside down, that things weren't sanguine anymore. The station's comm hissed, Parvi asking the engineer what the hell he was doing.

"Captain Parvi," Davin answered, the Eden squad leader still listing her demands. "I recommend you sit yourself down."

Parvi cursed.

"We're coming in if you don't leave now," The Eden squad leader said.

"Okay," Davin replied. "You win. We're comin' out."

He pushed the engines on, full thrust, and hoped Mox was ready to play catch.

4

SHUTTLE SLAM

The poor Eden fighters had nowhere to run, nothing to grab onto. Davin chose to go, chose not to grab onto anything as he launched back off his chair towards Mox. The *Galaxy's Song* juddered, a full on firing in the opposite direction sending everyone shooting end over end.

Mox, being Mox, pivoted, held against the doorway just long enough to wrap his arms around Davin and let the force take them. Like a slow motion ball, they tumbled into chaos.

Every loose object on the main deck flew. Plates, cups, whole carts, water in the pools shot free, spinning to splatter against the ground, each other, or hapless crew that hadn't secured themselves.

The Eden squad went right along with them. Davin, safely wrapped in Mox's arms as the man's exoskeleton ground along the floor, sparks shooting, laughed as the hapless soldiers bounced all over, ramming into this and that.

"Ride it," Davin shouted to Mox, even as the friction began slowing them down.

Mox did what he could, keeping his drag isolated to the metal ridges on his back. Mox's feet bounced in the air, Davin's legs entangled with them like some bad dance. They cleared the restricted section near the engines, hit the concourse looping around the cruiser's main deck. A drone, its jets confused, smacked off the ground next to them, still blaring the evening's drink deals.

"Flip it," Mox said, letting Davin go, pressing his arms over his shoulders.

Davin flew off, rolling as he hit the conduit. The Nines captain tried to look as good as Mox, punching his hands into the walking track's springy faux-wood and pushing off, trying to stand. His still-numbed left leg didn't want to, causing Davin to shamble a half-step before falling forward.

Only for Mox, flip completed, to snag Davin by his jacket and hustle him on.

"Do I have to carry you like a baby?" Mox asked, holding Davin up by his jacket.

"Would be nice," Davin replied. "Angle for those life boats, mid ship."

"Figured."

Mox scooped Davin back into his arms, indeed carrying his captain like a baby. The exoskeleton didn't make for the most comfortable bedfellow, but Davin wasn't going to complain: it beat an Eden cell.

The scattered squad seemed to be getting itself together, as a few shots spat after Mox, but their heart didn't seem to be in it. Davin glanced over the big man's shoulders, saw again the Eden fighters falling behind, stumbling around.

Another successful getaway.

"Pretty good idea, Davin," Mox said between breaths. "Even for you."

"Think you mean, *as expected for me*," Davin countered. "Great ideas are kinda my thing, you know."

"Sure, except you always seem to get us into spots where we need one."

"Remember how much you hated your boring life on the Moon?"

"I do not."

"You did," Davin said, "I could tell. All over your face. Any excuse to get away."

"False."

The life boats came up on their left, nestled into a red-bannered, emergencies-only alcove. If anything qualified, this would be it.

Davin and Mox made for the left most of six, each a sturdy, narrow craft able to hold up to a hundred people. The boats hung like lampreys off the *Galaxy's Song*'s side, angled down so that, in the slightest gravity, they could drop away without any thrust needed. Beyond the spiral door into the lifeboat, a circular platform waited to whisk people to their seats, each one loaded with straps to keep people alive.

The Nines didn't care one bit, with Davin sliding himself right into the pilot's chair and slapping the launch sequence. The artificial gravity made Davin feel like he was resting on his back, staring straight up, but, as the life boat kicked off with nary a protest, microjets flung the cylinder away and righted Davin the way he ought to be: facing a solid, perfect Saturn view.

"See?" Davin said as the cruise ship moved off to their right, the life boat rolling through its pre-programmed instructions in a pleasant voice. "Smooth and simple."

Mox sighed.

"Smooth and simple?" Phyla's voice crackled in his ear. "You want to tell that to these Eden pilots?"

Davin leaned back in his chair, looked around for his ship among the stars and didn't see it. The lifeboat's simple scanners picked'em up, though: the *Jumper* swarmed by five fighters, little dots circling a larger square.

"Phyla, Opal, I thought you'd have them dealt with by now?" Davin said.

"I've downed three. They don't take a hint," Opal growled."Tenacious bastards."

"Pick us up and we'll help you out," Davin said.

"I slow down for a docking and we're going to lose this ship," Phyla shot back. "Take care of yourselves."

Frowning, Davin turned to Mox. They were adrift, the life boat's minimal thrust just enough to get them to a habitable moon in, say, a few days. No weapons, just distress signals.

"Ideas?" Davin asked.

"Hope they win," Mox replied.

"Better ideas?"

His earpiece crackled.

"How about a rescue?" Merc's voice came in clear, no longer muddled by the docking bay's magnetic shields. "We're free. Have you on the scanners and heading your way."

"Tell me you've got the accounts," Davin said.

"Oh we got'em," Vi replied. "They'd better be worth all this."

Davin chose not to say Eden would've chased them out anyway. Accounts or no accounts, the Nines would've been blasting off the cruiser.

"Helluva job, Vi. Grab us, then let's see how we can help Phyla."

That would prove to be a tricky question. Phyla and Opal kept up the dance, downing another Eden fighter while the *Jumper* suffered laser burns and blown subsystems. Merc had, of course, taken an unarmed passenger shuttle. Precisely zero use in combat. The craft, a long cube with a couple bulbous wings for cargo storage off either side, wasn't built for atmosphere. Wasn't built for anything except ferrying people stuffed into its row upon row of lightly padded blue seats.

With *Galaxy's Song* rapidly receding, Merc had the shuttle on an intercept course with the *Jumper*, a twisting and turning journey as the latter juked and jousted with the fighters.

"And that's their home?" Davin asked, taking the co-pilot's seat in the cramped confines. The shuttle's priorities were not the pilots, but space. Mox, Viola, and Puk squared up the passenger seats. "The Eden frigate?"

"You got it," Merc said, both glancing at the radar's biggest blob other than the *Galaxy's Song*, and the only one heading their way. "We get to the *Jumper*, we'll have a few minutes to get away."

Four fighters now circled the Nines' ship, Opal pegging another with the *Jumper*'s turrets. Good work, but the *Jumper*'s existence posed a different question: six fighters should've been able to turn Davin's ship into shrapnel by now, especially without a full crew aboard to man the *Jumper*'s weapons.

"So why isn't she gone?" Davin muttered.

"What?" Merc asked without looking away, his hands on the shuttle's clunky flight wheel. "You ask something?"

The Eden squad leader's words came back. Demands, patient ones, to take Davin alive.

"They don't want us dead," Davin said.

"Why?"

"Because Eden doesn't want to kill you?" Davin shook his head. "Me, maybe. But Phyla? The *Jumper*? Those fighters are just playing games, trying to slow Phyla down."

"Don't think it's Phyla they want, boss," Merc said. "Opal's on that ship."

Opal, at one point a rebel leader. Someone who'd know where their bases were, what ships they might have left. Who could tell Eden whether these peace overtures were worth making, or whether the rebels were a sneeze away from collapse.

"We're a valuable bunch, aren't we?" Davin said.

"Two of you. Maybe Vi." Merc shrugged. "I'm happy without the spotlight, easier to shoot Eden in the back."

"Now there's an idea."

Davin tapped open the comm, tied its signal destination to the *Jumper*. They couldn't see the ships, not themselves, but against Saturn's bright backdrop laser flashes showed their goal.

"Phyla, how about you flip back our way?"

"Case you haven't read your radar, Davin, there's an Eden frigate coming up your ass," Phyla replied.

"I've got a plan for that, but we need to reel 'em in first."

"You're asking me to trust you?"

"You know I am, Phyla."

A curse, a click.

Davin grinned at Merc, "Tell me, you and Opal talk like that?"

"Not quite. What're you cooking, captain?"

"Slow up, let's bring everyone nice and close."

Davin shot from the seat, scrambled back to Viola and Mox. Delivered the idea, let Mox and Vi poke holes in it, holes they filled up together. By the time Davin returned to the cockpit, the *Jumper* and her fighter pests were closing in hot. The frigate loomed in the rear view, visible when Davin swiped a cockpit screen to the aft cameras.

"Give me the open band," Davin said.

"Done," Merc replied, flipping a toggle.

If the comm to the *Jumper* went straight to Phyla, the open band went everywhere nearby. The fighters, the frigate, anyone else—maybe Captain Parvi?—who happened to be listening.

"Hey there, folks," Davin opened, leaning back in a seat that had no flexibility. "This here's Davin Masters speaking, hero of Earth and general good guy. Seeing as we're all about together, I was thinking we could put a stop to the shooting and have ourselves a chat?"

A glance at Merc, a shrug in reply. Cold. Davin figured that was a decent opening, cool the mood and let the Eden punks know who they were dealing with. Silence ran for five solid seconds, but Davin noticed the fighters stopped lighting up their lasers, gave the *Jumper* some space. Opal was smart enough to accept the ceasefire, the *Jumper*'s top and bottom turrets going quiet.

"Davin Masters," came a gritted teeth voice. "Good to see you're coming to your senses. Power down all your vessels and prepare for boarding."

"Can do, good buddy," Davin said. "Except, I gave you my name. How about you give me yours?"

"Heath Swane. You don't need to know more, and I know you don't care. Power down."

The man was right that Davin didn't care, but the name helped. Soon as they made it away from this little inconvenience, Davin would have Vi do some digging.

"You heard the man, Phyla. Merc. Let's play nice."

Merc made one last maneuver, orienting the shuttle

towards the frigate. Arrayed the ship for docking, then killed the power. Davin swapped spots with Viola, let her put in place some shenanigans, and joined Mox in the lifeboat.

"Bet you didn't think we'd fly this one again," Davin said.

"Knowing you, I expected it."

"Am I predictable?"

"Better hope not."

The shuttle's lights went out, Merc doing as Swane instructed and shutting all the systems down. The pilot and Viola, with Puk floating behind, joined Davin and Mox in the lifeboat. Vi's wicked grin told Davin enough. The plan was a go.

Davin flipped the lifeboat's comm on, changed the frequency to the Nines' band. With the *Jumper* less than a kilometer away, Phyla and Opal should pick it up.

"You ladies paying attention?" Davin asked.

"Do you have a plan, Davin, or are you just giving us up?" Phyla responded real quick.

"Because I will not go to an Eden prison," Opal added.

"Me either," Merc said.

"Nobody's going to an Eden prison." Davin checked the scanners. The frigate was close. They'd sent out a couple small automated tugs to snag the shuttle, and the *Jumper* after it. "You ready to pop back on and catch us?"

"If they don't blow you out of the sky," Phyla answered. "Let's hope Swane's not that smart."

Swane went by the Eden playbook. The tugs found the shuttle, latched on, and carried it towards the frigate while Phyla settled the *Jumper* in behind, cutting the power and waiting for her turn with the tugs. A turn that would, hopefully, never come.

Davin had his finger up, watching numbers crawl on the lifeboat's screen. Specifically, the distance between the lifeboat and the frigate, the meters separating Davin's cocky half grin from Swane's no-doubt angry face. The Eden captain sounded like someone who'd murdered their own sense of humor.

When the digits dropped beneath a third of a kilometer, Davin dropped his finger.

"Go time," Davin said as he slapped at the lifeboat's release.

The vessel popped off Merc's stolen shuttle, ejecting parallel to the frigate, straight towards the *Jumper*. Davin's hands didn't stop there, flipping a toggle and pushing up the small lever controlling the lifeboat's engines. The little ship didn't have much fuel left, but it would be enough. It had to be enough. The stolen shuttle, the frigate fell away as Davin oriented the lifeboat towards his ship. The *Jumper* burst into life: turrets aimed and fired, knocking two tailing Eden fighters away as Phyla accelerated towards Davin.

"Now we see what kind of guy Swane is," Davin said.

The comm crackled. Davin ignored it.

"We're starting up," Vi said. "Five seconds."

Davin set the lifeboat on a collision course with the *Jumper*'s docking port, a small circle to aim for in all this space. Lines splashed up on the screen, screaming at him to alter his trajectory, lower his velocity, pray the *Jumper* would lower its own.

Not yet.

A bright green bolt lanced out from the frigate, splitting the path between Davin and the *Jumper*.

"A warning shot," Davin said. The comm crackled again. "Vi?"

"Here we go," the engineer said, and the whole group turned to watch.

The stolen shuttle ran a particular program, several

steps coded in a hurry by Vi. She didn't have the time to do something complicated and she didn't need to: the shuttle sparked to life, its engines powering on to full blast. She had less than a hundred meters between her and the frigate, far too close for turrets to find an easy target. One green bolt skimmed the shuttle, torching off a roof panel. No time to dodge. Orange blossomed. Debris flew. The frigate seemed to shudder, its course veering off as the explosion rippled from the docking bay and died as oxygen vanished. Eden's, Swane's spotless frigate looked like it'd taken a sucker punch in its side.

"Slow us down!" Merc shouted, pulling Davin away from his handiwork.

The captain yanked the lifeboat's thrusters to a halt, kicked up the maneuvering jets to kill velocity as the *Jumper* drew close. Eden's remaining fighters kept their distance, apparently not feeling like risking their lives against Opal's marksmanship.

"That was beautiful," Mox said to Vi.

"Glad it worked," Vi said, and Davin noticed she kept staring at the wreckage.

"Hey," Davin spoke up as the *Jumper* initiated the dock, clicks and clanks sounding throughout the lifeboat. "Eden's got hostile protocols, right? Bet there wasn't anyone in that docking bay when she blew."

Viola hesitated, then nodded back at Davin. "Sure, you're right."

Davin heard the chime, a successful link. He slapped the button, the lifeboat's one hatch opening into the *Jumper*'s beautiful confines. Playing the captain's part, Davin let the others off first, only Mox hanging back. Expecting a congratulations, maybe a pat on the shoulder from the big man, all he saw were glowering eyes.

"You can't keep protecting her," Mox grumbled.

"She'll see it when she's ready," Davin replied. "Till then, what's the harm?"

"You'll need her to pull the trigger and she won't be able to." Mox pulled himself past Davin, launched into the *Jumper*. Davin sighed, followed, and ejected the lifeboat as soon as he was inside.

THE EDEN FRIGATE was little more than a dot when Davin climbed into the *Jumper*'s cockpit, easing into his usual seat alongside Phyla. Much more spacious and broken in than the lifeboat or Merc's stolen shuttle. Little mementos graced the space too, artifacts from around the solar system gathered on their journeys: a Galaxy Forge post card from Mars, a picture of the whole Nines crew—including Erick, Trina, and Cadge—back on Eden Prime's icy wastes. Davin's favorite, though, had to be a full size metallic hand.

"Hey buddy," Davin waved the hand at the center console. "Miss me?"

"About as much as I miss those fingers," Fournine, the former android, the current ship AI, replied. "Which is to say, not at all. Bodies suck, my friend. You should lose yours."

"I'll get right on it," Davin leaned back, arms behind his head, looked at Phyla. "Where are we off to?"

"Nowhere yet," Phyla said. "Vi's getting the accounts ready to send to Roxley, so until that's done I'm trying to stay in *Galaxy Song*'s transmission range."

Fournine took Phyla's words and splashed a diagram on the Jumper's windshield, one showing Eden's frigate, the *Galaxy's Song* moving away to the right, and Phyla taking a looping turn in the same direction. As the overall diagram faded, Davin saw a thin blue line extending out into the dark.

"Is it even piloting when you're just following the rail? Davin asked.

"Tell me who just outflew six Eden fighters by herself?" Phyla countered.

"Ouch," Fournine quipped.

"Okay, computer, you can get some credit," Phyla said. "Fournine did keep our energy shields optimized."

Davin flipped through his console's screens, getting to a damage assessment, any systems knocked offline. Nothing there.

"Cosmetic only," Fournine chirped. "An expert job, if I do say so myself."

"You just did say so," Davin replied. "Not to take any wind out of your sails, but I don't think they were trying to kill."

"Davin, they sent a whole frigate after us," Phyla said. "That's a warship. Dozens of Eden soldiers. Six of us."

Fournine issued a robotic cough.

"Seven," Phyla corrected. "Sorry."

"Yeah, we're important," Davin said. "Obviously."

"More than that, they have to think we're dangerous. Really dangerous."

Davin held back another sarcastic shot. Phyla was doing her thing, the serious talk meant to pull him from dumb bravado. Maybe he should listen, just this once.

Vi saved him, coming into the cockpit and knocking her head against the sloping roof. She cursed, looked up from her wristlet and rubbed the bump.

"Couldn't you guys make this bigger?" Vi said, sitting in the chair behind Davin. Puk, ever-present, drifted his spherical self into the spot behind Phyla. "It's a real hazard."

"Only when you're glued to that screen," Davin said. "Have good news?"

"It's packaged up and ready," Vi said. "Encrypted too. Nobody snooping is going to know what we're sending."

Davin rubbed his hands together, reached for the console, "Then let's get chatting. The sooner we get away from this frigate, the happier I'll be."

Roxley answered the call, Fournine splashing the video feed up on the *Jumper*'s windshield, such that Roxley's bluish head had Saturn for a beautiful backdrop. His suite looked like a disaster, overturned furniture being set right, his flunkies busy sweeping up shattered glass. The man himself had what looked to be a developing shiner beneath his left eye.

"You morons," Roxley said by way of an opener. "I suppose it was too much to ask of you to keep things quiet?"

Davin grinned, "Is that one of my qualities? Stealth?"

"Apparently not. If you're calling to beg me to get you in touch with Alissa, you can shove off, because—"

"We have the codes," Davin interrupted. "All the accounts you could ever want. Packaged up real nice too."

Roxley hesitated, tilted his head, "How did you get them so fast? We've been on this boat for a week without cracking security."

"Trade secrets. But trust me, they're genuine."

"Then where are they? My inbox is empty."

Davin clicked his tongue, "Now now, Roxley. That's not how the deal works. You give us the details, we give you the accounts."

"There's no trust between us, is there?"

"Zero."

Roxley nodded, "Understand, if these accounts are false, if you're cheating me in any way, Alissa's going to know before you ever talk to her. You won't get what you want."

Behind Davin, Viola sucked in her breath between her teeth. Roxley wasn't dumb enough, apparently, to get fooled by simple tricks.

"All right," Davin said. "Send us the details, we'll get the accounts going your way." He looked away from the camera, threw a frown on his face. "Sorry, looks like Eden isn't done with us yet. Expect the accounts ten minutes after Alissa's info hits our box."

Roxley glowered, "Don't die first."

The call clicked off and Davin felt weird looks coming from his pilot and engineer. Rather than explain himself, Davin turned back to Vi.

"Do you just have the numbers, or did you get more information with those accounts?"

Vi tilted her head, "Fare class. Their cruise packages. Corporate sponsors if they had any."

"Well, isn't that perfect?" Davin said. "Sort the list, dump all the Eden flunkies on top. I bet Roxley's going to drain the accounts in order, so give him a bunch, then scramble the rest."

"Won't he figure that out?" Phyla asked.

"If we're lucky, not before we find Alissa."

"You're risking this for Vi to save some cruise passengers their cash?"

Vi, hard at work throwing in Davin's suggestion, ignored Phyla.

Davin offered a slight smile as an answer. "They don't all deserve their cash going gone."

A ding sounded throughout the cockpit, Fournine announcing a digital package had been received, downloaded to his servers, and cleared of any nasty viruses.

"Read it out, my friend," Davin said, turning back to the stars, Saturn, and the *Jumper*'s blue line.

"You want to reach Alissa, send the message Earthward on the following frequency." Fournine read the note in a passable imitation of Roxley's voice. "Use the attached code. After that, she'll get in touch if she wants to talk."

A bit paranoid, but doable. Davin's stomach rumbled and the buffet popped into his mind. Succulent shrimps, fluffy rice, mangos by the dozen . . . until he remembered where he was. "Nutrient goop it is," Davin muttered.

"Poor you," Phyla replied, punching in the coordinates. The blue line shifted as Fournine picked the optimal path towards Earth, the faster to get Alissa's response. On the radar, the Eden frigate made a slow turn their way, but the big ship had no chance to catch the *Jumper* in a free race.

"They're going to follow us the whole way," Phyla said. "And if we stop, they'll catch us."

"When they do, they'll regret it," Davin said.

"Why's that, big shot?"

"Haven't you heard? You're flying with Earth's biggest hero. We can't lose."

Only Vi gave him a pity laugh for that one.

5

———

ON THE SOLAR ROAD

A shower, a snack—nowhere near cruise ship quality—and Davin felt just about normal. The stun baton's lingering effects gave his left leg a twitchy sting, and Davin had the usual bruise and sore muscle collection earned after any fight, but hey, he stood onboard his ship, his crew intact.

Hard to argue with that.

The *Jumper* hummed with life. From his cabin, Davin heard Opal and Merc chatting down the hallway to the left. Below, Mox worked on himself in the cargo bay, Vi's bot Puk running an assist in cleaning Mox's exoskeleton joints. Vi herself, going by the occasional clank and clink, burned time on another project in the workshop.

And Phyla?

Phyla hadn't left the cockpit, crunching numbers with Fournine. She'd shooed him and Vi out after the Roxley chat, angling for privacy to concentrate, get the ship oriented for the long-range comm blast. Which, fine, Davin could use the wash-up.

And he owed people some thanks.

Mox came first, the big guy too hard to miss right there

in the middle. Rags littered his space, along with a couple greasy cans. Puk, the floating sphere, dipped an extended syringe in the oil and drifted around, squirting it into the flexible fiber joints.

"Realize how gross that is?" Davin said, walking up and putting his hands on hips, face arranged in faux disgust.

"Wasn't in the brochure," Mox said, looking to his left and scrubbing one black band there.

"What was?"

"Revenge."

Sore subject, that. Time to veer away.

"Thanks for back there," Davin said. "Felt like old times."

"Rescuing your ass? Yeah, it did."

"Hey, feel like the saving went both ways."

Mox showed a couple pearlies, "You always find an out."

"More like a win." Davin floated his back against a nearby wall, watched Puk spray another joint. The slight hiss followed by a splatter was real ugh. "But I'm not getting many happy vibes off you right now."

Mox flipped shoulders, met Davin's look with a weary one of his own. "I have a job. It's back on Luna, not getting chased around out here."

"You'd rather do that than chum around with us?" Davin's flippant air struggled. "Really?"

Puk retreated a meter as Mox spread his arms back, creaking out the exoskeleton to its full span. For a moment it looked like Mox might be about to give Davin the heaviest hug he'd ever earned.

But no, just another systems check.

"We did our time, didn't we?" Mox said. "I'm in it for this. Can't let Eden run over everything, but I'm not scrapping for bad jobs anymore." He brought in the arms, Puk started in on the back's lower half. "Aren't you tired, Davin? Or does this still get you going?"

"We tried retiring. It didn't go so well."

"Phyla found her thing."

The unasked part: what would Davin do with himself if he wasn't getting blitzed and beat up?

"You're saying I ought to get a hobby?"

"Maybe even two," Mox glanced back at Puk. "Almost good back there? This man needs a shower."

"You're not wrong," Davin said.

"'Bout which part?"

The workshop looked, as it always had whether Vi or Trina ran it, like some torture chamber. Chains hung on rails across the ceiling. A long workbench bedazzled with tools stretched the room's length. Hoses, saws, emergency cut-off valves lingered everywhere. Enough crap to build a new engine from scratch, not that Davin would ever dare.

Some things you paid the right people to do.

Vi bent over a funky orb, a magnetic monstrosity designed to kill power across ships for kilometers around. Unless, of course, you happened to block its frequency. A trick now known to both the rebels and Eden, making the device useless.

"Right?" Davin asked after a few seconds trying to figure out what Vi was doing. "It's useless?"

"More a one-time play," Vi said. "Swapping the frequency's easy. The encryption too. But if we use it again, ships will just cut off their transponders."

"Not a bad effect." If the enemy couldn't talk to each other, the advantage went in Davin's favor. "What's not to like?"

"They have'em too," Vi said. "We make this a thing and everyone's fighting in silence. It's like going back to the dark ages, trying to use flags or something to signal what we want, only the battlefield is a million kilometers wide."

Davin sat on the workbench, watched Vi use a screwdriver like an artist might wield a paintbrush. "So in this scenario, you're saying we have friends?"

"I'm saying," Vi replied without looking up, "that there's going to be another fight, and the best way to stop it before it starts is this thing right here."

"Back there, you didn't want the rebels to rob all those people. Before that, you went and invented a device that can stop a fight, and now you want to guarantee it works. When did you become a pacifist, Vi?"

"Always was."

"Your family makes a lot of money on weapons, you know that right?"

"I don't like seeing people get hurt, Davin. Is that a problem?"

"No, so long as it doesn't keep you from helping us out."

Now Viola looked up, goggles glaring in the harsh workbench light. "Has it so far?"

"I had you do that dance with the accounts for your conscience. It's risking a meeting with Alissa, the shot we have to get her to see sanity, find a deal with Eden. I did that for you." Davin patted the workbench, slid off of it. "You're a good kid, you're damn smart, and I'm lucky I ran into you in that Europa bar too many drinks ago, but in our world, the risks catch up to you."

"In your world, Davin," Vi said. "Not in mine."

"Then I hope, Vi, your world's the one we're running toward."

. . .

THE *JUMPER*'S true power couple snarfed in the kitchen, a moment Davin interrupted after hearing their voices on his way to the cockpit. Merc and Opal had their dinner laid out before them, a delicious-looking pasta-and-veggie dish not normally found on the Nines' ship.

"Took a few after lunch back on the cruise," Opal said at Davin's look. "Figured we'd want something other than nutrient goop. Want a bite?"

"Very much," Davin said, but he waved off Opal's offered fork. "It's yours, enjoy it."

"I am, thanks," Merc said. He joined Opal in glancing at Davin. "Back to Earth again?"

"Boring, isn't it?" Davin slipped himself into a chair. He hadn't seen Phyla leave the cockpit yet, which meant she might still be crunching numbers. "All these cool planets and we're always going back to that one."

"Earth's not so bad," Opal said. While Merc hunched over his food, tearing through it, Opal ate with strategic elegance, sniping one noodle at a time and savoring the bites. "They like you, Davin."

"Hah. Last I checked, most of Eden comes from Earth, and they don't seem too fond of me."

"Especially since you joined up with us," Merc said. "Bad move for your public image, cap."

"Davin doesn't care about his image," Opal said. "He's a money man. Bought and sold for a good price."

Davin wrinkled his nose, "Uh, thanks Opal."

She slid him a smile, "Not everyone needs to be a saint."

Davin laughed. "Are you saying I'm a devil because I don't like being broke?"

"I'm saying you and I have different ideals, and I'm okay with that."

Davin leaned back in his chair, an easy move in the *Jumper*'s zero gravity.

"Are you compromising yours to fly with me?" Davin asked.

The words brought a different edge to the conversation. Not one Davin really intended, but so be it. Every Nines member had gone off their own way after Earth and the androids, every one had changed. Opal, always so haunted by her past, seemed to have lost the merciless loner drive that made her such a good sniper.

What'd she traded it for?

"So long as you're hurting Eden, I'm in."

Revenge, then? Joining up with the rebels not to help their cause but to burn as much of Eden as she could? Cold stuff, even for her.

"That's the idea," Davin said, then turned to Merc. "How about you, hotshot? Happy you're here?"

"I just go where she tells me." Merc shoveled in more pasta.

"That's all there is to Merc now?"

"All there is."

Davin waited, expecting the pilot to elaborate, but Merc just threw a wink at Opal and kept his focus on the food. Then again, how surprising was that, really? Wouldn't Davin follow Phyla wherever she went? Especially if it had a seafood buffet?

"When we find Alissa," Davin said to Opal, "are you going to be okay if she wants peace?"

Opal put her fork down, folded her hands, "Davin, she's not going to want peace."

"No?"

"She's like me. Eden's hurt her too much. The only thing Alissa wants is blood."

. . .

PHYLA WAS INDEED STILL CRUNCHING numbers in the cockpit, talking with Fournine as Davin joined her. Navigation charts splashed across the windshield, ways to get to Earth via different stopping points, each with their own risks: Eden patrols, possible pirates, or so isolated any problems with the *Jumper* would be fatal.

"Pick one yet?" Davin asked, retaking his seat. The *Jumper* had turned away from Saturn, leaving a star field dominated by the far-off Sun as the view. "I vote the shortest."

"That'd get us killed," Phyla said as she continued swiping on her console screen. "From what I can tell, Eden's not resting. They're hunting."

"Could've told you that. That butterball Swane and his frigate gave a pretty good clue Eden wants to take territory."

"Right, which makes going towards Earth harder. We'll be running through a crowd and we can't hit a single person."

"Thankfully, we've got a good pilot."

Phyla rolled her eyes.

"What we need is a fighter for Merc. We need to restock hard rounds so we're not relying on the lasers after a fight or two. And the shields could use a retrofit: they collapsed too fast in that fight."

"All I'm hearing is cash falling from my pocket." Davin reached out, put a hand on Phyla's wrist. "We don't have enough to re-arm. Dodging's our game. Keeping quiet."

"Something you do so well."

"If I have to keep this face under wraps for a while, I'll do it," Davin let loose an extravagant sigh. "It will be so hard for all my fans."

Phyla shook her head, "How'd I ever wind up with you?"

"Fate, I'm afraid." At last Davin earned a chuckle. Phyla sat up from the console, stretched.

"Fournine, keep us on the quietest course for now." A look Davin's way. "I could go to sleep, but . . . " A sparkle in those eyes. Davin raised an eyebrow. "I've been in this cockpit too long," Phyla continued, the sparkle bringing out a mischievous look. "How about it, captain? Want to take a ride in the sims?"

Davin's face fell, but only for a moment. "You sure, Phyla? I've been on a roll today."

"Oh, I'm very sure. C'mon, big shot. I've got the perfect course in mind."

A CROSS-SECTIONED SKY shone down on ramshackle stacks, towers built from scrap and maintained with spirit. Cook-fire smoke cluttered the air, winding up before getting sucked into ceiling vents. Looking down, Davin could see crowds shuffling along, could hear barking calls as merchants tried to find deals with people too poor to afford them.

"This is really close," Davin said. The sim even sprayed a smokey scent. "How'd you make this?"

"I didn't," Phyla replied. They both sat on their virtual bikes, resting on a platform well above Vagrant's Hollow. "Some fans of mine did when they found out where I'm from."

"Wait, you have fans that made this?"

"What's more surprising, Davin, that my fans did this or that I have fans at all?"

Davin hesitated, realized he didn't have a ready answer for that question. Phyla, clad now in her slim racing suit, hair and head bundled beneath a helmet, saved him with a laugh.

"Relax, this is supposed to be fun," she said.

She threw her leg over her bike, looked ready to get the race going, but Davin squinted down at the town instead. Now that he looked more closely, he saw imperfections: towers standing where there were none in reality, the crowd repeated the same people every couple meters, and nobody actually went anywhere, they all shuffled along an endless loop. Punching a hole in the scene let Davin wrench himself from the memories always waiting in Vagrant's Hollow. He hadn't been to Miner Prime in a while, felt no need to go back. Ever.

"Is that some introspection I see?" Phyla said, looking over from her bike. "The great Davin Masters looking back into his past and wondering how he made it here?"

"Nah," Davin shook into a smile. "Just studying the course so I can show you up on my home turf."

"Your home turf?"

"I'm older than you, so yeah, it's all mine."

Phyla laughed. "You can't prove that."

True, Davin had no record of when he entered this life. Neither did Phyla. Nobody really gave two bits about what happened in Vagrant's Hollow, save their parents, and they were long gone.

"You can't prove I'm wrong either." Davin slipped his leg over the bike. "How many laps?"

"Just the one," Phyla said. "It's late enough, and some of us have to keep this ship on course."

"One lap's plenty."

Davin settled his hands on the throttle, the brake. Ahead, the track streamed off the platform, a purple strip running away from them and spiraling around, through, over and under the towers. Real courses couldn't send blitzing racers near so many people, much less their homes, but here in the simulator?

The more thrills the better.

Three dim red dots appeared over Davin's vision, hovering in the virtual air. They went green one at a time, in a slow sequence. As they ticked off, Davin held down the brake and revved up his throttle, waking the bike up from its slumber. The simulator vibrated his seat, the grip beneath his left hand. A scratchy whine buzzed. The final green flashed. Davin let the brake go. The bike flung forward, a beast unleashed.

The course dropped before him, speed pushing Davin along its contours. Phyla paced him to the right, the opening a straight shot, their identical digital bikes matching each other. Skill would come into play in moments. The first left brought a wide swooping turn, letting the bikers bank high and come sliding down with momentum. Phyla slid to her right to do just that and Davin let her, nudging the brake and slacking the acceleration to get a sharper turn. See, the course dipped lower just after the bank to rustle the virtual crowd, and Davin meant to take advantage. As his bike nosed left, while Phyla shot up the embankment, Davin crashed the accelerator, cutting across the corner and flying off the course.

"Wooooo!" Davin shouted, because why the hell not.

He landed with a soft thud on the downward slope, comfortably ahead and zooming. Davin glanced behind him as a straight-away gave them a breather, and saw Phyla shaking her head. As if she expected anything different. Those tricks didn't keep coming though, and Phyla chipped away at Davin's lead as they wove through the scrap city. Every turn brought her a little bit closer, the finale more or less a certainty, until Davin swung around the far end of a hairpin and found himself staring at something he'd all but forgotten. He slammed the break, let off the accelerator, then let the bike coast until it came to a stop in front of a particular shop, a stacked spot with a few too many memories. Phyla zoomed past, saw him, and took her bike in a lazy turnaround.

"Thought you said they were fans," Davin said, numb, looking at the store where his life's first love, Lina, had worked, had grown up. "Why would they know about this?"

The building had all the right details. It wasn't the copy-pasted sameness Davin saw elsewhere. Someone had taken the time to create this thing, make it right.

"They didn't," Phyla said, sliding off her bike to stand next to him. "I asked them to, gave them pictures. Told them the details."

"Why?"

Phyla glanced at him, "We always joke that we don't have a home, Davin. I wanted to show you that we do. We always will."

Davin reached towards it, but his hand flickered as it went beyond the course, beyond the program's ability to render.

"Just like a memory," Davin muttered. "It's not really there."

"But when you need a minute, when you want to remember, you can come back and look at this. You can hear and smell home."

Davin stared. Counted the few windows, confirmed they were right. Saw the dusty path leading by the house, where they'd played so many stupid games. Immaculate. And not something he wanted to drown in right now.

"Guess you won the race," Davin said finally.

"I won ten seconds in. That maneuver you pulled was illegal. No leaving the course, even for cool jumps."

"This sport sucks."

"If you were any good, maybe you'd see it differently."

The sims didn't have programming to let you hug someone, hold their hand or give them a kiss. When Phyla moved next to Davin, they both flickered, the game trying to figure out if they'd crashed into one another. Romantic? Not quite, but then, for Davin and Phyla, not quite romantic was about as good as it got.

6

GIVE PEACE A CHANCE

Post-sim, Phyla escaped to the showers and bedtime. As the person keeping the *Jumper* from slamming into an asteroid or a wayward ship, Davin didn't contest her decision, even though the others had decided to celebrate survival with a nasty poker game in the *Jumper's* center. Fournine kept a pulse on Alissa's frequency, but nothing had come back yet.

Compared with the sims, with other games and movies stacked in the *Jumper's* drives, pulling out the raggedy cards always felt a bit low-tech, but in the best way. Mox excavated a table from Vi's work room, set it up square in the empty cargo hold. Merc mixed a round from liquor pilfered off the cruise ship, laid out the glasses, and Davin slid into the last spot.

The stakes were simple: ship responsibilities. Davin had a grid drawn on the wall outside the cockpit, with names and jobs written all over it. Whomever wound up with the most chips at the end of the night could pick their tasks, with the worst player getting stuck, inevitably, with the toilets.

Merc's stiff drink, a sweet-sour combo pack loaded with

a fiery whiskey, brought Davin's energy to a rascally level. He opened with hard bets and bluffs, pushing around the table and enduring the insults flung his way.

"Next time, I'm not gonna shoot the guy before he blasts your back," Opal said after Davin forced her to fold before a tasty flop. "See how you like it."

"You've been sitting in the commander's seat for so long," Davin countered, "do you even know how to shoot anymore?"

"There's four Eden pilots back there who know the answer."

"But were they good pilots?" Mox asked Merc while Vi shuffled, dealt the next hand. "Or typical Eden garbage?"

"Are you asking if my wife could blast me in a Viper?"

Davin threw in a low whistle, while Opal locked eyes on Merc and his snarky grin.

"With one eye closed," Opal said.

"You'd miss by a click," Merc shot back, "with both eyes open and Fournine telling you when to shoot."

That hand, Opal took Merc for a ride, almost emptying him out in a single shot as she rode pocket aces to glory. After, she waved Merc off, told him to get another round, and the pilot acquiesced without complaint.

"I see how you climbed the ranks," Mox said to the sniper.

"Confidence and skill are a lethal combination," Opal replied.

"One the rebels don't have much of," Vi spoke up while Davin shuffled, waited for Merc. "Roxley had been on that ship for days and we stole those accounts in a few hours."

"We're just that good," Davin said.

Opal didn't echo the sentiment, instead pointing a single finger in Vi's direction.

"You have the right idea. The rebels are a bunch of ragtag outliers who don't like getting told what to do. We're not organized, we're not trained to fight. Eden should be squashing us, we're just hard to find."

"They'll find you eventually," Vi said.

"Hey," Davin interjected, "none of that bummer talk. Not after we pulled out a win today."

"A small win," Vi said, but her face spoke something different, a slyness as she picked up her cards.

Chips, a cheap set that'd been on the *Jumper* since before the ship fell into Davin's hand, splashed around the table. Vi, Davin, and Mox stayed in.

"You thinking something, Vi?" Mox asked, flipping a card.

Davin's hand was crap, but he kept up with the betting anyway. Vi'd been a mix of disinterested and shy all night, but this time she came out firing. Raise after raise, so ludicrous both Mox and Davin should've folded. Should've, but the next card gave Davin's hand a glimmer.

And the final one? Now here was a chance.

Vi hadn't responded to Mox's question, letting the chips do the talking as the hand blazed on. She met eyes whenever Davin or Mox needed to match a bet, her look that of iron excitement.

They flipped. Davin's last ditch hand wasn't enough. Neither was Vi's. Mox toasted them both, looked as confused as Davin felt. Vi had wiped herself out, doomed herself to toilet scrubbing.

"I'm thinking we have to go for it all," Vi said, sitting back from the table, accepting Merc's second round as the pilot came back. "Cass said she didn't know what Alissa was thinking. What if she's not thinking anything? What if she's ditched the cause? By the time we find out, Eden might've already won."

"Spit it out," Mox said.

"We send a message," Vi replied, then looked at Davin. "Not just anyone, but him. Earth's hero. The big guy. Have Davin say that the people won't be crushed, that we're together in this fight."

Davin dug into Merc's second drink. Considered Vi's announcement. Opal shook her head, Merc fiddled with his glass, and Mox gave Vi a curious stare, as if she'd announced she could fly by flapping her arms.

"Don't you get it?" Vi continued. "Right now Eden's the only voice out there. They're calling us all criminals and nobody's saying otherwise. That's going to twist Earth in Eden's favor, it's going to make us hunted, just like on the *Galaxy's Song*. They'll stamp us out like bugs."

"What's Davin's ugly mug going to do about that?" Merc asked.

"Who you're calling ugly?" Davin said. "This beautiful face graced the cover of Mercenaries Monthly back in the day."

"Magazine doesn't exist," Mox noted.

"Yeah, well, I would have if it did, and you all know it," Davin said. "Vi, I see what you're saying. We get the spotlight back on the people, maybe Eden can't go murdering us all without thinking twice."

"Exactly," Vi said.

"My question is," Opal said, "where'd you get this idea? You're not a marketer."

Vi flushed, "The cruise ship. Davin's face was everywhere, and his events always sold out. Yeah, captain used them for free drinks, but what if we did something useful? He's popular."

"Deserved or not," Mox said.

Davin finished Merc's drink. The whiskey gave a cinnamon burn boost to his confidence, as if Davin needed it. Vi had it right, the Hero of Earth was pretty damn popular, and he might as well use his fame for something worthwhile. He stood up, pushed the chair back from the table.

"Vi? Let's go have a chat with the solar system."

DAVIN FELT the slap through his dream. Felt it worse in the bleary seconds after, when his eyes opened to see a furious Phyla standing over him. In the cramped confines of his captain's quarters, Phyla's looming made her look larger, angrier, and altogether not what he wanted to see.

"Hey," Davin mustered, throwing up a weak smile.

"Hey? Hey?" Phyla looked like she was about to laugh for a second before Davin's hopeless grin did its work and she slumped on the bed. "That's all you can say?"

Davin reached for a water glass, found it, and poured the stale recycled liquid down his throat. His mouth felt dried out, cotton balled. Otherwise, though, a hangover seemed well at bay, a sign he'd slept longer than intended.

"Vi had an idea. We ran with it," Davin said, lurching up to sit next to Phyla. "What's wrong?"

"Just get your ass to a turret."

Turned out broadcasting a message wide attracted attention. Turned out too, in a detail Parvi didn't provide, that Eden had substantial bounties on the Nines. Particularly Opal, Merc, and Davin. Capture all three and a scum-running spacer might find themselves set for a good long time.

Beaming out Davin's overture for everyone to get along was like shining a light all around Saturn and Jupiter saying hey, here we are, come find us. The quartet pursuing the *Jumper* now, closing from multiple angles, didn't seem to care about Davin's message either.

"It's like they didn't even listen to it," Davin said as he settled into the *Jumper*'s top turret. Opal had the bottom, while Mox, Vi, and Merc played support. "Here I am, saying give peace a chance, and they're coming in guns blazing?"

"They aren't blazing yet," Vi corrected from the engine room.

"But they will be," Phyla said, the voices pulling into Davin's earpiece as he reacquainted himself with the turret's controls.

First he slid goggles on. The screens before each eye transported Davin into outer space, using cameras nestled around the turret on the hull to give Davin a clear targeting picture. Red highlights sprang up around the four approaching craft, only two of which were in Davin's firing line. The others would be in Opal's, or Phyla's, who had a front-facing gun and missile launcher.

Oh yeah, the *Jumper* could defend itself. Even with their cargo running stint, neither Davin nor Phyla wanted to scrap the weapons. Call it intuition, call it nostalgia, but the ability to blow something up always seemed to come in handy.

Davin couldn't see his hands, but they each gripped a soft-padded gray stick, a rotating gimbal that'd slide around with his vision as he pulled, nudged, or swung his hips.

"We just shooting them?" Davin asked, the nearest ship about in range.

"You were too busy dreaming, but they all sent their ulti-matums. Surrender or die," Phyla growled back. "Guess Eden's cleared the bounties for dead or alive."

Merc whistled, "Really is just like the old days."

"Those were good times," Davin said.

"Let's not make these the bad times, gentlemen," Opal interjected. "Focus up."

Davin's first target took a modder's attitude to space-faring, claiming a cheap, ugly vessel and jacking it up with crap. Guns, jets, extra shield generators and who-the-hell knew what else stuck out from the box on all sides. The lack of subtlety continued to its approach: a straight line inter-cept, easy to lead, easy to blow up.

Space combat didn't happen all close and cuddly-like, so when Davin started holding down the trigger and spitting lethal energy, he aimed for an outline, one now lined with green to show the ship had ventured within shootin' range. The craft and its mottled metal weren't visible to the naked eye, but as Davin fired a 3D model appeared in his virtual space, hovering in the lower-right corner.

Just in case Davin wanted to scope out his enemy, the *Jumper*'s computer gave him a picture.

Most ships would take evasive maneuvers when lasers came their way, but this one stuck straight to its stubborn path. Davin's shots bounced off, each one glaring a purple-blue on impact as its energy fizzled out on the ship's shields. Weirder still, the enemy didn't bother firing back, streaming in on its assault course without, well, the assault.

"My guy's packing defense," Davin said. "How's our stocks?"

"Refreshed on Freestar," Phyla flashed back. "Have at it."

Davin flicked a switch with his thumb on the turret's control stick. A soft clicking series finished with a gleeful chime, letting Davin know he was good to go, so he went, holding down the trigger. The turret shook, forcing Davin to level out his stream, a recoil effect not present with lasers. Very present with his new fire, though, were bullets.

If lasers were cheaper and easier to cart around due to, well, their lack of a physical form, bullets had the mass advantage. The conical shards zipped through space to slam into the approaching ship, gliding clean through the craft's energy shield and biting into its hull. The lasers prompted the blue-white flashes, the bullets earned Davin a sparkly show followed by his target's engines as the pilot broke off his attack.

"That shook him," Davin said, spraying a few extra rounds at the man.

"Both of mine are taking it slow," Opal said. "They don't like the heat."

Oh, right. Davin had a second one to deal with. He swiveled the turret, flipping back to the lasers, and found his new target coming in from the *Jumper's* back. The *Jumper's* engine wash made the target judder, flicker.

"Guy's smarter than the other one," Davin said. "Phyla, need you to swing up, on three."

Phyla clicked an acknowledgment, started the countdown as Davin leveled his turret. Green lines bounced through the engine wash, laser strikes swallowed up by the *Jumper's* hefty shields.

See, Davin had been at this game for a while, and the *Jumper* even longer. This wasn't some easy snack for would-be bounty hunters. A grin found its way onto Davin's face as the lasers bit into nothing. Four on one, and the Nines had the advantage.

Phyla swooped the *Jumper* up in a hard swing, one stealing away the engine wash cover. The enemy, sitting at near-max range, couldn't adjust, which left Davin with a perfect opening.

Yellow energy poured from his turret, an almost-solid

stream slamming into and chasing the sleek hunter craft as it tried to dive away.

Unlike the hefty mod monster Davin shot first, this thing had speed in mind. That speed and agility, as Phyla would've said, needed a pilot to use, and while this one had the smarts, they didn't have the skill to react fast enough. Davin's lasers hit shields for the first second, punched through a moment later, and blew the arrow-like ship's engines apart in the third.

"Got one distress beacon," Phyla said. "Three to go."

"And all three are on my side," Opal cut in quick. "They're grouping together. Think they understand how we work."

"Should've kept that Viper, Davin," Merc interjected.

"Should've stayed with our crew, Merc, and I would've."

The starfield in Davin's view yanked. Not the gliding twist from a Phyla-induced turn but a sharp reel. Being stuck between Jupiter and Saturn made it difficult to find stellar landmarks, but Davin could read the little white and blue dots well enough. That, and Phyla's curse confirmed something had gone wrong.

"That damn box grappled us," Opal said. "I'm going to fry his—"

The comms fizzled. Davin's headset died, the goggles going black. Static poured into his ear as he ripped the headset off, took a breath in pure darkness.

"Fournine," Davin said, feeling around him, uncoupling his seatbelt, "is life support still on?"

There was no reply.

The *Jumper* shot through space, dead and on a reel. Davin climbed down from the turret, feeling his ship shake as their captor tugged them closer. Shadows played tag with scattered yellow diodes, the emergency lights so crucial on any space vessel proving their money's worth now.

Shouts and callbacks echoed throughout the ship as the Nines confirmed their health, their frustration. Davin dropped onto the second level, looked towards the cockpit. Below him, Mox, Vi, Merc and Opal were arming up. Whomever felt cocky enough to board them wouldn't be getting a kind welcome.

"Blast grapple?" Davin asked as he crouched into the cockpit.

Starlight washed out the yellow, highlighting Phyla in a smeary gray as she hunched over a dead console, fiddling with manual levers beneath.

"Stuck us good," Phyla replied. "My own damn fault to get three of'em on a single side."

"They flew too. You can't control everything."

"Thanks Davin, but I know when I've messed up."

Davin pressed his lips together. A blast grapple would've hit the *Jumper* with a power surge, one delivered straight to the ship's innards via the sharp hook. Nearly all systems, including Fournine, fried to a short dead zone till things restarted.

"How bad is it?" Davin asked.

"Go to the engines and check," Phyla snapped back. "Fournine's not responding, so it's not great. And because of your stupid message, there's going to be more coming."

Sometimes it was best to leave Phyla to her own devices. Give her space.

Davin retreated to his own quarters, popped open the locker with Melody and readied the weapon as the Jumper made one final lurch. Clicks sounded near the hatch. A hatch that wouldn't open without the manual release.

"Mox," Davin called, heading back out to the cargo hold.

His crew stood in various covered positions, overturning tables, chairs from the card game to make a slapdash defense. "Open the hatch."

"Say again, boss?"

"They blow us open, we're stuck with this barnacle. I don't want that, do you?"

Mox took the advice, clomped across the cargo hold in two long strides to the main hatch. As Davin jumped down, pushing off with his hand to get himself lower in zero gravity, Mox yanked on a hefty switch on the hatch's right side.

Four valves disengaged with a protest groan, the door swinging up. With a novice crew, Davin might've issued some strategy, might've called out who ought to fire first.

With these old folks, Davin spoke with his shotgun.

The door swung open and, as soon as he had a clear spot, Davin poked Melody around and pulled the trigger. The shotgun spat a concentrated energy ball, a blue-burning orb careening away down the docking tunnel.

"See anything?" Davin said, his back to the Jumper's hull, no vision down the corridor.

"You put a real nice burn on their hatch," Merc, crouched behind the poker table with his laser pistol in one hand, his stun baton in the other, said. "They're too scared to come out."

Before Davin could come up with a second crack, Puk, Viola's spherical bot, buzzed into the room.

"They're coming in through the bay!" Puk announced, his bot voice doing a nice job conveying panic.

"Merc, Opal, Vi, hold here," Davin said, strategizing on the fly. "Mox, with me."

The big guy curled across the open hatch to follow Davin as they kicked their way across the cargo bay to the shallow slip on the *Jumper*'s side, just big enough for a one-person fighter.

Nowadays the docking bay served as a junk repository, extra foodstuffs and belongings shuffled in here. A couple yellow diodes hung above the entry, a square door leading right into the stacked crates, bags. None in the bay itself, leaving things dark.

Dark except for a bright glow coming from the far right corner. Morons thinking they would cut their way in.

"Suit up," Davin said, pulling a similar lever next to this door. The manual release did its job, slamming the bay door shut tight enough to seal air in. "I'll take the smaller suit."

"Obviously," Mox replied.

Nine emergency space suits hung in the docking bay, the only spot with enough extra space to store them. As the glow outside grew brighter—as the attackers cut in further—Davin and Mox threw on the suits. A little awkward, meant for survival instead of gunfights, the ghost-white suit made Davin feel a bit like he was coated in jelly. Everything a bit slower, a bit heavier. Melody's triggers didn't fit his full fingers, so Davin went with his tips. Slower rate of fire, less accuracy.

Beat exploding into goo when the ship depressurized in a second.

Mox started off towards the cut line, explaining he'd punch them as soon as the hole broke free. Davin grabbed the man, Mox's ridged exoskeleton almost poking through his suit, and held him back.

"When they blow that doorway," Davin said, his voice carrying through the suit's comms, "everything in this bay's gonna rocket towards them. Maybe they'll be dumb enough to eat it."

With that hope in mind, the two took cover behind some

musty nutrient goop crates—no expiration date on those bad boys—and took aim at the glowing spot.

Watching the *Jumper* get its hull burned through felt a little like getting his eye gouged out, but Davin did what he could to focus anywhere else. He checked his breathing—slow, even—Melody's power pack—ready to go—and Mox's positioning—excellent—before starting a silent count in his head.

At five, a meter long and wide panel tore off the *Jumper*'s outer hull, the docking bay door, and disappeared into deep space. A rookie, someone not paying attention, might've shot just then and given away their position. Davin and Mox held their fire, waited to see what crawled through.

The first guy—or girl, hard to tell beneath the bulky suits, the helmets—climbed in first, leading the way with his wrist. As his arm made it inside the *Jumper*, a device on the wrist popped open, expanded into a long and flat rectangle, a blue-purple glow covering its surface.

Portable energy shields, gotta hate'em.

The man carried a standard shotgun on his waist, one he reached for without urgency. Behind him, another form filled the missing panel's gap.

Davin's eyes flicked to Mox, hoping the big man understood what Davin knew: the intruders didn't realize the Nines were here.

At Davin's look, Mox, by his legs and out of view, flashed fingers counting down from three. Davin refocused, not on the guy with the shield, but on the person coming in behind him. Why?

Because when Mox's fingers finished counting, the big man shoved his nutrient goop crate with an exoskeleton's strength. In zero-g, the crate launched like a bullet, Mox passing momentum by pressing his feet into the inner hull behind him.

The poor idiot had an energy shield, sure, but that shield wasn't made to catch hundred kilo cubes. The box bashed into the dude, pushing him back hard against the docking bay door and clearing Davin's firing line.

Melody's signature green lanced forward into the second comer, a devastating fireball making the small bay glow emerald for its second-long flight.

The orb broke against the space suit, shattering into a crawling flame. Both intruders caught the blast, a heatwave dying fast without oxygen, dying slow enough to melt both suits to slag.

Mox followed up.

The metal man kicked past Davin, heading like a missile for the second intruder, one now bearing a large hole in their suit. With a single fist, Mox punched the stunned, possibly dead person through the hole they'd created, launching them off into vacuum.

The shielded wonder, having been bashed with a crate and half fried by Melody's blast, tried to get his shattered self back together, an effort put to a sudden end when Mox grabbed the man's helmeted head and mashed it against the docking bay's outer door.

"Two down," Davin said, keeping Melody trained on the hole. "Zero to go?"

Mox ripped the shield off the man's wrist, jammed the rectangle through the cut hole. Not quite a perfect fit, but enough to block any casual entry. Davin helped push more crates in the way, pinning the stolen shield in place. The *Jumper* wouldn't be able to pressurize the docking bay any time soon, but they'd have time to react to any new intruders.

"What do we do with this one?" Mox asked after they'd assembled the junk.

Davin knelt, took a closer look, very conscious the other Nines might be fighting for the *Jumper*'s core right that second. All the same, a rapid rescue that left open a back-stab wouldn't be worth much.

The captain didn't need to worry: Melody's blast had burned a clear hole through to the man's skin. Any oxygen he'd had would've been sucked out. At least the death would've come quick.

"He's gone," Davin said, trying to ignore one more body added to his climbing count. "Let's go."

7

THE STORY OF A LIFETIME

Davin much preferred starting parties to ending them. Going up to a bar counter, making some grand pronounce-ment followed by shots soaring into the crowd, finding lush in liquor, stuck out as a singular joy. Same with waltzing into a tense standoff, delivering a line every one in the room would remember until they, often moments later, bit the big one.

So when Davin and Mox yanked the hard lever, exposing the Jumper to vacuum for a rip-roaring several seconds, he expected the sealed door on the other side—thanks to Mox and his monster muscles for that—to be an introduction. Specifically, introducing Melody to a second invader crop.

Instead the Jumper's core sat empty. Phyla's yelling came down from up top, of course, a cursing litany that seemed to cease only when the pilot found time for a breath. The yellow diodes gave little detail, but they highlighted blast scores on the walls, the floor. A spent power pack drifted in the air.

"What happened?" Davin said, popping his helmet. "Did we win?"

"Phyla is still alive," Mox joined Davin in ditching the suit. "So we didn't lose."

With Melody at the ready, Davin kicked into the Jumper's middle, wheeling to face the hatch. The circular door sat open, giving view into a blue-lit tunnel leading from the Jumper to the boarding ship.

Nobody there either.

"Phyla?" Davin shouted up, keeping his eyes on the tunnel. "You okay up there?"

"Does it sound like I'm okay?" Phyla called back down. "We're going to have to replace half these wires!"

"Uh, sure. I mean, are you alone up there?"

"Not the time to get jealous, Davin!"

Davin tossed a questioning look at Mox, who confirmed the Jumper's other rooms were clear. The man shrugged back.

"Know where Opal, Merc, and Vi might be?" Davin tried a different tactic.

"Puk's up here with me." Phyla's head popped over the railing, looking down. Puk hovered behind. "The bot said we had it under control."

"Then where'd everybody go?"

Through the damn hatch, that's where they went. Davin and Mox, through the scientific process of elimination, crossed off every option until they found themselves traipsing down a thin membrane connecting the Jumper to the ugly, too-modded cube ship.

Going through a docking membrane felt like, so Davin imagined, what all those characters in cartoons getting swallowed by monsters experienced. Close in, flexible tubes clinging in on all sides. The air, pumped in and recycled, had a stale edge. Plastic off-gasses. Davin's feet slipped on the thin filament, which in zero-g meant he was constantly falling forward, backward, and generally looking like a moron.

Not that Mox managed things much better. He used his superior reach to span the tube like some spider, one leg or arm moving forward at a time.

"This is why we never use these on raids," Mox muttered as they went on. "Too messy and slow."

Direct docks required getting up close and personal, though. Perhaps not the best thing if you thought your target might blow itself up, or you might do some exploding yourself.

The membrane had ribs running around its sides, ones charged to relative stability by electric energy. They ran the fifty meter connection, the maximum length for these kinda things, and one Davin had some choice opinions about.

"Why make it this long?" Davin asked nobody in partic-ular. "Just so the walk takes forever?"

"Buy time?" Mox offered. "Dudes might've thought their reinforcements would be coming from the other side."

"They could've stayed in their own ship then, waited for an all clear."

"Maybe you'll get to ask them yourself, Davin."

"Hope so. This is ludicrous."

Davin's grousing didn't get them to the end any faster, but when they arrived, another open hatch greeted them. With the hatch, thankfully, came friendlier sounds. Vi, Opal, and Merc tossing barbs back and forth.

"Space'em," Merc's voice came out, sounding way more bored than he should've been. "You play the game this bad, you ought to suck vacuum."

"I think they've learned their lesson," Vi came next. "Right guys? You won't do this again?"

Davin kicked harder, slung Melody over his shoulder and made a reckless dive for the hatch. The last thing he needed was Vi making some naive deal that let these bums off the hook for the damage they'd caused to Davin's ship.

The Wild Nines captain soared into the enemy craft, hands above his head in a pointed, slimming dive. For added effect, Davin leaned into his motion, flipping upright as he went into the new ship's common space.

Like the *Jumper*, this boat had its main square surrounded by offshoots. A design great for outer space and clunky for in-atmosphere work. Unlike the *Jumper*, which Davin kept relatively clean for cargo-hauling duty, this one looked ready to party.

Couches, some with locks to click potential prisoners into, formed a circle in the main space. Centering that circle was a throne, a thing Davin hadn't seen in a long time, and not outside of the worst sorts of prisons: a monitoring chair, where one person could spin themselves around and, with a button press on any of the consoles facing them, initiate pain and punishment to their prisoners.

Not only bounty hunters, then, but the kind who treated their targets like dirt.

Davin's first look took in all the bad implements, and his second saw how clean they all were. The couches looked spotless, the monitor gleaming as though it'd never been spat on or sprayed with worse bodily fluids. The carpet—carpet?—beneath him glittered a starry blue. A jazzy jingle played throughout.

"Hey cap," Merc said, holding up a new, seized rifle. "Welcome aboard the *Maisie's Revenge*."

Davin's trio stood on the monitor's far side, holding

court over a cuffed and disarmed quartet. Davin made his way over, using the monitor as a jumping off point to soar a couple meters over everyone else.

At first, from Merc's tone and Vi's words, Davin expected to see a bunch of kids. Maybe some rich parents indulging a child's fantasy, forgetting that such fantasies could get them killed.

Instead...

"What in the nine planets is this?" Davin asked, counting more gray hairs among the foursome than he'd ever seen in one place. "Are we getting attacked by the original Apollo crew?"

Science had its way with human lifespans, pushing them out a good bit, but Davin didn't see too many spacefarers hitting the century mark, and none taking an aggressive approach to the business.

These four, three men and a woman, looked up at him with disappointed disdain. Davin flashed back to Vagrant's Hollow, to the stern stare a merchant might give when five year-old him sticky-fingered a fruit or played with a spare part.

"Don't joke about your betters that way," said the leftmost man, a soft collection of wrinkles. "We've seen and done more than you ever will."

"Do you know who you're talking to?" Davin countered. "We're the Wild Nines. I'm the damn hero of Earth."

"Old news," said the woman, and Vi laughed. Even Opal tried, failed to hide a small smile. "We're what's new."

Shaking his head, Davin looked to Merc, "Nobody else on the ship?"

"Not a soul. Vi and I did a run through."

"What happened to the third hunter out there?"

"He ran when we caught you," the woman announced, apparently proud. "Saw we had the rights and left."

"Excuse me, the rights?" Davin asked. "What?"

"Bounty law," said the fourth man. "We're the ones who hooked you, so we're the ones who get the reward."

"And the ones trying to burn their way into my ship from the other side?"

"Contractors," Softy sniffed. "Not very good ones, apparently."

"Dead now," Mox said, coming around Davin's left.

"Good, one less bill to pay."

Davin ran his hand over his forehead, over his eyes. Every time he thought he had a bead on this life, someone came by and turned it all around.

DETAILS CAME QUICK ONCE Davin opened the door, after he sent Vi and Merc back to the *Jumper* to help Phyla with repairs. The quartet, who gave themselves a name Davin refused to remember, were locals to Jupiter space and had decided to spend their later years ditching day jobs for daring-do. All those blast scars in the *Jumper*'s cargo hold came from random firing, an overwhelm-and-win strategy advised by countless idiotic videos and books on how to be a bounty hunter.

Were they evil, these four goons with more cash than sense?

No.

Had they damaged the *Jumper* enough to render it dead in space? According to Phyla, the grapples had blown connections between batteries and the *Jumper*'s engines, rendering the Nines ship inert.

"So you're going to pay to fix this," Davin said to the

foursome, still locked on the couch. Mox stood with him, the others having gone back to the *Jumper*. "Then you're going to re-evaluate your life choices."

"We're not going to pay you anything," the grumpy would-be leader declared. "You're all wanted criminals."

"Did your little fairy tale include getting blown out into space?" Davin countered. "Because that's where you're headed, buddy. A long cold sleep."

Davin expected some blanching skin. Some sweat. Maybe a glance between them as they realized this wasn't some kid's game but one packing real consequences.

Instead, Davin earned a laugh.

"Sure, go ahead and try," the man said, "and by the time you're done, the frigate will be here and you'll be well and truly screwed."

"Frigate?"

"The one telling us we'd get the full bounty if we kept you here long enough for them to catch up." The man strained, couldn't turn far enough to read his wrist watch. "I can't see the time now, but if the Eden bird can fly, it should be here any minute."

Options fluttered through Davin's head. Barring a miracle, the *Jumper* wouldn't be escaping anything soon. The Nines could abandon ship, take this one and try to escape. Piloting someone else's ship wouldn't be easy, but better than falling into Eden's hands.

"Mox, get Phyla over here," Davin said. "We need to get supplies shifted and these grapples off."

The old man laughed again, "Can't take our ship. It won't fly without us telling you the codes. Fat chance we do that."

"Guessing threatening you with death won't change your mind?"

"Not even a little bit."

"You're getting real annoying, know that?" Davin looked at Mox. "Any ideas?"

"Don't think we can beat a frigate all by ourselves, Davin."

The captain rolled his eyes, "Thanks for the reality check."

But Mox's remark had some truth to it. An idea, even. The Nines couldn't escape the frigate in the *Jumper*, couldn't out-shoot a whole ship's worth of soldiers. Strip away those options and a couple new ones presented themselves.

"You've got this fancy ship," Davin said, leaning back against the monitor and staring down the quartet, "so are you really doing all this for the money, or for the adventure?"

Eyes flicked back and forth. Two shrugs.

Time to press a hunch.

"What if you helped us, instead of doing the dull thing and siding with Eden, the big nasty company?" Davin played the odds here, hoped people surfing this far out from Earth held less loyalty to the behemoth corporation. "I'll forgive the damage to my ship, I'll forgive all those pot shots you took in my living room, and I'll give you the story of your lives."

"What story?"

"You get to save the rebel's general, her love, and this guy right here." Davin tossed his head at Mox, who blinked.

"Who's that?" The lumpy leader asked, looking at Mox. "Some robot?"

"A Centurion," Davin replied, layering it on. "You get them away from Eden, you get your story, and you still get to collect the bounty on me."

"Davin, what the hell?" Mox asked.

"Think about it," Davin said to the captives before

pulling Mox aside, out of hearing. "Here's the deal, buddy. They're not taking the threats and we're running out of time. You three get away, Vi and Phyla work on the *Jumper* while I buy time with Eden. Then we rendezvous."

"You're skipping a lot of steps in there, Davin," Mox said. "Like how Eden might just shoot you."

"That's gonna happen anyway. You three getting away gives us a chance. You can still get to Alissa if Eden gets murdery."

"You're—"

A loud yell from the hatch, Opal calling Davin's name, cut Mox off. The Eden frigate had arrived.

"HEATH, pal, can I call you that?" Davin said from the *Jumper*'s cockpit, looking at the light blue version of the Eden captain.

Heath, whose close encounter with the exploding shuttle seemed to have left him twitchier than before, mustered up his bulging eyes and squeezed them into a glare.

"Call me what you like, Masters," Heath said. "I'm more interested in how you appear to be free, despite word saying otherwise."

Behind Davin, noises rang throughout the *Jumper* as Mox, Opal, and Merc scurried supplies through the membrane into their would-be rescue ship. The quartet had given into Davin's idea, with Davin figuring the cave was about half due to the adventure and half due to, well, not dying.

"Oh, they caught me," Davin said, holding up his palms. "We're stuck. Dead in the water. Now there's a phrase that doesn't make much sense these days, does it?"

Heath sighed, "If they caught you, then why aren't they responding to my hails?"

"They're busy popping bubbly, I expect." Davin put on a pout. "They hurt my ship, Heath. Would've torn her apart if I hadn't thrown up the white flag."

"Glad to hear it," Heath replied. "Then you're ready to surrender? And your crew along with you?"

"What crew?" Davin glanced over at Phyla. "Just me and my girl on board. We ditched everyone else on our way outta Saturn."

"Ditched?"

"Those rebels are sneaky, my friend. Little ships everywhere ready to scoot their own somewhere safe." Davin leaned forward. Time to close this deal before Swane dug too much further. "You want to come get me, now's your chance. Promise you won't scuff up my *Whiskey Jumper* anymore and I'll come quietly. Guaranteed."

"I'll take no more guarantees from you, Masters. The shuttle will be on its way in moments, and should a single thing go wrong, I swear I will blow you into atoms."

Heath blinked off, leaving Davin to shrug Phyla's way.

"At a certain point, the threats just stop meaning anything don't they?" Davin asked.

"I'd be fine with fewer of them."

"This from the bored racer."

"There's a difference between a thrill and a threat, Davin."

"It's all the same adrenaline to me, love."

The quartet blasted off with Davin's trio aboard, their grappling hooks tearing some more *Jumper* metal apart on their way out. Vi and Puk found their own hideaway in the *Jumper*'s hidden cargo compartments: cramped space that'd be enough to ride out cursory inspections. Then Vi and her bot could get to fixing up the ship, making the *Jumper* space-worthy for what was sure to be a daring escape.

Davin and Phyla waited for the docking shuttle at the hatch, clothes packed into bags like they were going on a vacation. Melody sat safe in her locker. Phyla's only weapon was her attitude, and that was more than enough.

When the hatch opened, a familiar Eden squad leader charged through, all armored and weaponed up for a fire-fight. She seemed almost disappointed when Davin's free-handed grin greeted her, the fingers slow to come off her rifle's trigger.

"I'm not a sore loser," Davin said by way of explanation.

Coming in peace didn't mean Davin and Phyla were treated, well, peacefully. The Eden soldiers slapped cuffs on the pair, forced them into restraining seats on the shuttle. Davin and Phyla waited while Eden did that sweep of the *Jumper*, confirmed it wasn't set up to blow like the last ship.

It wasn't until the whole shuttle crew came back on board, the Eden craft disengaging that Davin realized things might be going awry.

"Are you not taking her?" Davin asked the squad leader, who'd popped her helmet off, who stared at Davin like she was going to break his brain with her concentration. "You're leaving the *Jumper*?"

"Captain doesn't want it," the woman said. "Not hard to see why, that trick you pulled."

"What trick?"

The squad leader's hand shot out, put cold gloved fingers around Davin's throat. Not a tight grip, but a loose touch, the tips feeling around.

"The shuttle bomb," the squad leader said, tilting her head, more focused on her fingers than her words.

"The hell are you doing?" Phyla asked.

"Typical spacefarer sickness," the squad leader said, letting Davin's throat go, then doing the same to Phyla. The *Jumper* pilot tried to evade the grasp, but when your head was bordered by metal restraints, there wasn't much you could do. "So many years out here weakens the bones. I could snap them so easily."

"Let's hope it doesn't come to that," Davin offered.

The squad leader, her fellow members paying close attention stuffed in the shuttle behind her, slid her eyes back to Davin.

"Davin Masters. You mocked me on the cruiser. I won't forget it." Surfed those eyes back to Phyla. "Who are you?"

"Go suck a supernova," Phyla said.

The squad leader frowned, "I don't get it."

Phyla opened her mouth, readying another insult, but the squad leader covered it. "Not because I don't have a sense of humor, but because your humor is not mine. So if I do not laugh at your jokes, it's because they aren't funny. To me."

"Wasn't a joke," Davin said. "She's telling you to throw yourself into vacuum because you're helping an evil company be evil."

The squad leader didn't look away from Phyla. Instead, she studied the pilot with more intensity than before, as if memorizing every feature.

"I think I will keep you," the squad leader said. "You seem more interesting."

"Keep?" Phyla couldn't help but ask.

"You may call me Aya," the squad leader said. "Welcome to our world."

"That did not answer my question," Phyla replied.

Aya gave the faintest smile in reply, ran a gloved hand up along Phyla's face, measuring her jaw, her cheeks, until the shuttle's pilot said they were docking, the maneuvering forcing everyone to strap into their seats.

Captain Heath Swane met Davin and Phyla in the landing bay, wanting to get a good look at his new captives. Davin tried to live up to his reputation, offering a scoundrel's slouch, the easy-living vibe. He expected Heath to be a model Eden citizen, dolled up in a spotless forest green uniform, following every commandment to the letter.

Heath defied expectations.

Despite the clipped official tone on the transmission, Swane waited at the shuttle's off-ramp with a frumpy look. The man's uniform bore an Eden rank, sure, but it held splotches too. Wrinkles, a couple stains. The man stood tall, helped by what looked like two artificial feet, rigid and not disguised at all.

Beside him stood a doctor, a nurse bot, and the ensign, with her nose in her wristlet.

The surroundings captured the sterile banality of all docking bays: bright fluorescent white streaming down from above, smudged tiles on the floor. Stenciled lines on plain gray walls guiding crates, fuel, and everything else to their proper places. The Eden soldiers preceding Davin down the ramp went to their own square, forming up and looking real bored in the process.

Only Aya, airy, stayed near Heath after descending.

"Come on, you two," she said, calling up the ramp to Davin and Phyla like a tour guide welcoming the pair. "Time to come down."

"What is this?" Phyla whispered. "Did we get caught by the weirdest ship in Eden's fleet?"

Davin shrugged, accepted the oddities. They'd been all

over the solar system, seen plenty of people normal and not. No reason Eden would be different.

"Let's just hope they're not sadists," Davin muttered.

He led Phyla down the ramp, stuck out his hand towards Swane. The Eden captain reached out with both of his, gave Davin a vigorous shake. A slow, broad grin stretched Swane's wrinkled face.

"Davin Masters," Heath said. "Despite our earlier disagreements and our present situation, it truly is an honor to meet you."

"Uh, same?"

Heath nodded at his own feet, "I'll get this out of the way: you put a laser in the man who did this to me, and for that I will be forever grateful."

Davin ran through his all-too-long rolodex, trying to think of what victim might've been Heath's enemy.

"Bosser Oates," Heath answered, seeing Davin's thought. "A truly terrible person. So thank you."

"You're welcome." Davin rolled with it. Any plus was, well, a plus. "Always happy to meet my fans. Have a picture? I'll sign it. Then, if we could borrow a few parts and a ride back, we'll let you get on with it."

Heath laughed, a wet hack. "Masters, I'm so glad to see the rumors are true. You are a funny man." The grin faded to a simple smile. "Unfortunately, you are also a terrorist. You'll be staying with us until, I imagine, I am ordered to throw you out an airlock. Perhaps not the end you were hoping for yourself, but I assure you, I shall make it quick and painless."

Heath stepped back, glanced at Phyla. "And the racer! Excuse my rudeness, my dear, but I am prone to getting starstruck. Aya has already asked for permission to work with you, and I have granted it. She is, I think you'll find, a most fascinating creature."

PHYLA'S middle finger transcended the glass between their detention cells, beaming right to Davin's eyes across the narrow hall. She sat on her cot, really just a metal slab with the thinnest sheet over it, looking across at Davin, who returned the gesture with one of his own.

Their clothes had been taken, replaced with simple robes. They'd been subjected to showers, to probes for drugs and other tools, and had been dumped in these cells with nothing more than gray metal around them.

"You can't say this was my fault," Davin said, knowing Phyla wouldn't be able to hear the words. "I wasn't flying the ship when we were caught."

Phyla squinted at him. Trying to read his lips. Failing, hopefully.

Worse, Heath agreed with Aya's assessment, saying they would be leaving the *Jumper* to drift towards whatever fate awaited it. Vi and Puk would be on their own, left to fix a potentially too-damaged ship.

Then again, shouldn't Davin be worried about himself? With Heath, his number one fan, getting approval to shunt Davin to deep space, it seemed like his luck might've run out.

Up above, in the ceiling, a panel slid away. A small screen dropped down, Davin noting a similar one falling in Phyla's cell. The monitor hung a few centimeters below the ceiling, angled towards the cot, powering up with a spring-time chime.

"Welcome to detention," a calm robotic voice said as the Eden logo splashed on the screen. "We hope you enjoy the following presentations, meant to keep you peaceful until your fate is decided."

An awkward start. When the Eden logo disappeared, a baby deer replaced it, stumbling its way through a serene forest. Soft music began to play, the sort Davin might expect if he were getting a massage. Doing a meditation.

Just where the hell had Davin put himself, and how could he get out of here?

8

SHOE GAME

They took Phyla after an hour, sixty minutes into background footage of elk grazing mountainside slopes, butterflies flitting among flowers, and the occasional wave crashing onto serene beaches. All accompanied by loose flutes and guitar strings. Davin might've felt relaxed if not for, you know, the hard metal around him, the harsh lights, and the prospect of quick, quiet, elimination.

Because what else would Eden want with him? Vi had it right when she'd said Davin's reputation would make a public execution a difficult thing. Their announcement beamed through the solar system would only put a cherry on top of Davin's heroic sundae: Earth's hero returning to the spotlight to fight for peace?

Not even Eden could absorb a blow like that.

Right?

Phyla's abductors were two stiff, forest-green clad Eden grunts. Hired arms bearing the rigid requirements of a corporate master. No personality, all purpose. Gross. Davin managed to get their attention by pounding on his cell's window, and when they looked his way, Davin flicked up a double finger.

At least Phyla smiled at that. Then they led her away in stun cuffs.

She'd still be alive though. No reason the Eden squad leader would've been so weird only to throw Phyla out like yesterday's trash. Now, Davin mused, that didn't mean Phyla wouldn't *wish* she were dead. Humans could be all kinds of strange, terrible, and power tended to magnify those traits.

Which was why Davin regarded Captain Heath Swane with skepticism when the man showed up outside his cell door not ten minutes after Phyla vanished. Still in his rumpled uniform, Heath had what looked to be either coffee or hot chocolate in one hand, a stain on his upper lip that the man wiped off with his sleeve. The cell's glass barrier stood between them, not another soul in sight.

Heath studied Davin, the word springing into Davin's mind under the Eden captain's intense gaze. When you're a celebrity, you get used to people picking you over with your eyes, but Heath had a different flavor to his look. Less admiration, more analyzing. Not so much *who is this guy* but more *what's his muscle mass, heart beat, and how could I kill him quickly?*

"You keep staring and I'll charge a fee," Davin said.

"I'd gladly pay it," Heath answered, a response Davin didn't expect given the glass between them. At Davin's look, Heath pulled back a sleeve, tapped his wristlet. "Always listening."

"You mean *you're* always listening? You specifically? Not some Eden flunky, but you? At all hours?" Davin popped out a lip, nodded. "Interesting strategy, captain."

The slightest of smirks.

"You'll find interesting strategies everywhere aboard my ship, Captain Masters."

"It's Davin. Only my crew gets to call me captain."

"Is that what makes them love you so much? Your insistence on avoiding titles?"

"Natural charisma, Heath."

Davin, in the post-android apocalypse party on Earth, had found himself dancing through one interview after the next, building a reputation around thankful and fascinated fans. At the time, show hosts had given Davin tips on how to build an audience, how to warm a crowd. Manipulating them into love felt a little icky, but the end result cleared the Nines of any charges, let his crew dash off and follow their dreams.

Worth it.

Heath held up a finger. The glass cell door shunted aside. The Eden captain stood not two meters from Davin, evidently unarmed. Davin could rush, try to take the man hostage, negotiate a release.

A greener man might've. Better opportunities would come.

Heath frowned as Davin kept his distance. "Aren't you supposed to be impulsive?"

"But not stupid," Davin said. "What were you saying earlier?"

"Come with me," Heath replied, not at all answering the question. "I'd like to understand who you are."

The first steps out of his cell did not make Davin feel like a free man. Perhaps that was because several guards fell in behind him and Heath. Perhaps that was because the frigate's hallways had an eclectic personality, with various commandments ordering the crew to be at once 'in tune with themselves' and 'vigilant against outsiders'. Perhaps it was because the idle music piped in through the frigate's speakers blended a spastic jazz with the same soul massage sounds as Eden's videos.

So no, Davin didn't feel free, but he did feel in a free fall.

"I take it you haven't seen a ship like mine," Heath said as they stood at a lift pair. The captain put a spin on the words, as if Davin ought to take it as a joke, but the man's face kept a set look. Monologuing. "I'm sure you understand wanting to leave a mark."

What kind of mark did Heath want to leave?

Davin didn't ask the question. Better, here, to listen and see what details Heath might reveal. Better, too, to catch the frigate's layout, look for signs that'd show where Phyla wound up. Vi would get the *Jumper* running again eventually, and when the rescue came, Davin had to be ready to lead the breakout.

"Individuality's always been my hallmark," Heath continued as the lift arrived, the captain ushering Davin inside. The guards followed, crowding into the space. "Why bother doing anything if you're not going to do it in a new way?"

"You tell yourself that when you're making coffee? Taking a nap?"

Heath's narrowed eyes told Davin all he needed to know about the man's humor, his pride.

"Eden works with mercenaries all the time," Heath said as the lift sped—Davin thought it went down, but space always made it hard to tell. "They're useful tools, when they stay in their place. Collect their cash and move on." A hand on Davin's shoulder, more the pressure of a commander about to deliver unpleasant news than a friend offering comfort. "That's not you, though, is it?"

Angles. Whenever he was in a negotiation—and this

was most definitely a negotiation—Davin tried to figure out not just what his opponent wanted, but how they were going to get it. So far Heath had shown strength—the guards, getting Davin out personally—and a chilly camaraderie.

Why?

Was he *not* going to space Davin?

"I'm not an idiot," Davin shrugged as the lift settled into its destination. "I'm also not a machine, or evil. You hire me to kill kids, I'm not going to do it. You hire me to run cargo from Saturn to Mars, I'm in."

The lift opened. Lights flicked on. A fat cargo bay sat before them, loaded up with food, ammunition, and other necessities for a fighting vessel. Heath beckoned for Davin to step out, then the captain took over. A central aisle split the cargo bay into halves, and Heath kept to the middle.

"Eden didn't hire you to run cargo, though, did they?" Heath asked.

"You mean Europa? That was a security job."

Not to mention a trick being played on Eden by the very rebels Davin was trying to help now, but Davin kept quiet on that point.

"When you failed, what happened?"

"When we failed?"

"Inspectors landed, didn't they?" Heath kept walking as he spoke, letting zero emotion get into his voice. Around them the innocuous crates loomed. The guards, their steps echoing off the metal, trailed several meters. Not another soul, another bot joined them. "They died, yes?"

"Sounds like you know the story."

"The official record says they died in an unfortunate explosion. An accident." Heath took a left, a narrow branch between coffin-sized boxes with spare Viper fighter parts. "That record is a lie."

"Your words, not mine, boss."

If Davin's snark gave Heath any qualms, the captain didn't show it.

The captain did, however, finally stop wandering in the cargo maze. Heath nodded at a huge box, one disguised by ordinary nutrient goop crates around it. With silver edges, blank metal sides save for an Eden logo square in the center of each, the box seemed expensive. Not something Davin would find on the *Jumper*.

"Know what this is?" Heath asked.

"Looks like it's yours."

Heath shook his head. "Everything in here once belonged to one Bosser Oates."

"Man was a bastard. Sorry you wound up with his garbage."

"You're right about Bosser, but not about what he left behind." Heath put a hand on the crate, touch almost reverent. "The man lived quite a life."

"He ruined more."

"Including mine." For once, Heath's calmness quivered, and Davin caught anger in the man's tense jaw. "But Bosser was kind enough to give me a chance to get it back." Heath looked over his shoulder at Davin. "Do you know why I haven't killed you yet?"

"Was hoping you'd tell me. Still hung over from that cruise, you know."

"The stage isn't set quite yet," Heath said. "When it's finished, when everyone can see it just as I need them to, you will die. "

Androids. For all the work scientists did creating the humanoid robots, Eden and a few other ambitious companies ruined the experiment. Gave'em weapons, speed, and an unflinching legal line to deliver death to any criminal unlucky enough draw the wrong attention. Any cynic worth their salt—and Davin, here, had salt to spare—figured out quick enough the legal window dressing served only to give those pulling the strings a squad of pristine assassins. For a while the machines perused the galaxy, slinging kill shots and capturing poor souls with impunity.

Davin would've been one, except Fournine overplayed its hand. Brought itself into the wrong fight, odds even its incredible reflexes couldn't wring into a victory. Now that skill spliced the *Jumper*'s coordinates together. And Bosser, the man trying to stitch all those androids into his loyal army, met his end thanks to Davin and Vi. While Vi didn't want the celebrity status, Davin soaked up the cash that came with the fame, spilling Bosser's scheme around the 'net and the airwaves.

Androids were trashed, turned into fancy coffee makers and flight calculators. A big win for society.

A big loss for Captain Heath Swane.

DAVIN LEANED his head against his cell's wall. Watched Eden's meditative garbage on the screen. Still no Phyla. She might not come back at all. Even if she did, Davin might not be there to see her.

Heath hadn't outlined his plan, hadn't gone all villain and monologued the play in the cargo bay. Instead, Heath claimed the androids were misunderstood, that Bosser had ruined an awful lot of livelihoods. Davin's death, Heath claimed, had nothing to do with Eden, the rebels, or anything else. The mercenary would be giving his life to bring back a noble enterprise: the solar system's deadliest killing machines.

How, exactly, Davin dying would do that was anyone's guess.

The when and where, though, weren't mysteries. Heath had his frigate gliding towards Jupiter's foremost broadcasting point, a network buoy that'd catch the video of Davin's demise and spam it across the stars with minimal delay, no chance for interference, for sabotage.

"Everyone will witness you," Heath had said before turning Davin around and marching him from the cargo bay.

Davin drummed his fingers on the floor. Some small part of Heath's words appealed: in a grim way, it'd be neat to go out as a legend. Thing was, Davin hadn't yet hit fifty. Going out now just seemed like a waste, especially with Phyla's racing career on the upswing. He had so many bets to place, so many bar fights to start.

His eyes walked the cell. Toilet, cot, TV with its soothing sounds, and the door. Not a laser one like Eden Prime and newer prisons. Old school, thick. Davin stopped, squinted at the glass. Old cells meant a frigate some years past its prime. The etchings on the walls, the lackadaisical dress said Heath didn't run a tight ship either.

Davin popped up, went to stand beneath the monitor. He wasn't a giant, but with a solid jump, Davin could get his hands on the screen. That, too, showcased an old style: Davin would bet new Eden cells would have this stuff projected, maybe embedded in the walls. Everything to keep a prisoner from getting ideas, tools.

He went to his cot next, took off the mattress. Improvising. Propped the bed against the cell door lengthwise, the thin, stained mottled rectangle covering the door's width.

The toilet didn't offer any parts to play with, but that was fine.

Davin had what he needed.

Reaching down, Davin untied both his shoes. Eden had searched him, taken away his possessions, given him robes and shoes. He popped one off, then the other. Every move made slow, as if Davin was thinking the process through while doing it.

He lifted one shoe, tossed it up and caught it in his right hand. Angled the heel. Rubber, but thick enough. The Eden broadcast shifted to a sublime tropical beach. Sand that'd go just perfect with his soft-soled shoe.

"So much for peace," Davin muttered, cocked his arm back, and launched his footwear.

The shoe flipped once in the air, slammed into the screen and shattered it. Glass sprinkled, sparks followed. The audio, unfortunately, was unaffected: Eden still wanted Davin to relax, imagine the ocean, let the waves come over him.

Like the waves, two half-assed guards came running. Both had stun batons at the ready as they arrived at Davin's cell, one looking aside to slap his badge against the cell control panel. The glass door slid away, the mattress falling into the new space. The first guard, the one who hadn't scanned his ID, leapt in swinging. An all-out bash, one Davin figured would've left him dead if it connected.

But going all out was a predictable move. Davin went forward into the guard's range, swinging his other shoe up as the guard's overhead smash whiffed past Davin's head. Holding the shoe's top, Davin's makeshift weapon hit with whip-like momentum, rubber crashing into the guard's chin hard enough to knock the man aside.

And open a lane for the guard's buddy.

Number two came in with more savvy, stepping over the mattress with his baton held upright at waist level. Cautious eyes. A face weather-worn. A uniform crisper than any Davin had yet seen on the frigate. Experienced.

"Hey," Davin said, eyes flicking over the guard's shoulder, as if talking to a friend.

The guard twitched, looking over his back shoulder for a split second. This time Davin went with his left fist, a clock to the guard's gut. When the man bent over, Davin shoved with his right hand—dropping the good shoe to the ground—and pushed the guard into his face-smacked buddy, just now getting off the cell wall for another heavy strike.

Thing was, stun batons didn't need to be swung to deliver the goods. A touch sent the spine-stinging shock all through, and the two guards tangoed enough to take themselves out. Twitching, the pair collapsed at Davin's sock-covered feet.

"Heath, buddy, you gotta get better help," Davin said, freeing the stun batons from their owners.

He put on his shoes too, taking his time to get it right: no grand escape deserved to be brought down thanks to a slip. When Davin finished lacing up, he heard the sound he'd been waiting for: some guard at the controls realizing the thugs hadn't made good on their harassment attempt.

The cell's glass door shot out, trying to seal itself, and punched right into the mattress. A modern laser gate would've burned right through the rugged cotton, but the glass only mashed it to one side. A solid half-meter gap remained, with the mattress pushed into a U.

"Best bed I've ever had," Davin said to the thing as he stepped over it into the prison hall.

Now, where was his pilot?

Davin's mental map of the frigate had some major holes.

He remembered the route from the docking bay to the cells, from the cells to the cargo hold, and that was it. Some off-shoots suggesting cafeterias, lavatories, barracks. None likely candidates, but staying in this hallway would only get Davin killed before Heath's curtain call.

The lift it was.

Breaking into a sprint, Davin left the cells behind for a flat run at the frigate's elevators. Eight cells meant a small prison, meant the guard at the controls stood between Davin and the lifts, nestled behind monitors. As Davin hoofed it, the guard peaked out, pulling an actual rifle and drawing a bead.

Davin threw a baton. The thing, glowing blue with nerve-burning energy, spun end-over-end towards the guard. But not quite at her: Davin trusted in his accuracy, but he trusted more in the odds.

As the guard raised her rifle, the baton smashed into the nearby monitors. Electrical energy poured forth into the poor screens, overloading their processors and blowing them out in a cascading collective. Smoke and white-hot embers enveloped the guard as she squeezed her trigger, a shot soaring over Davin's shoulder to leave a mark on the ceiling behind his back.

The Nines' captain pitched right, opposite the guard's chosen shooting side, to buy himself a half-second to get around the smoking monitors. His opponent opted for panic instead of predation, spraying fire in Davin's direction. Ducking behind the console station, a semi-circle facing the cells, with the lifts behind, Davin glanced at the crimson laser sky overhead.

Good way to waste a power pack right there.

Rolling to his right, Davin kept to a calf-burning squat and made his way around to the guard's location. She called out for his surrender a couple times, punctuated each request with a laser burst. Monitors continued to throw fits, each one crackling up more sparks, more white smoke. No alarms yet. Must be a manual trigger, and Davin had seen far too many guards hesitate to flip it when the poor performance might come back on their heads.

Easier to ask forgiveness when the prisoner was already in hand.

Davin sprang up, using his left hand to grip the console as he rose. The handhold let Davin pulled himself over, sliding onto a desk as the guard whirled, trying to get her rifle on point. She had speed, spinning fast with lasers blitzing the whole way.

If Davin had kept his feet, made the fancy landing like he'd been planning, he would've caught a shot to the chest. Instead, Davin hit a desk coated with slippery glass, with spilled coffee and random, laminated guidelines. His ass skidded like a sled, shooting him off the desk to the floor as the guard's snapshot singed Davin's highest hairs.

Davin might've lost his cool moment, but he rolled with the move, jabbing upwards with his second stun baton, stinging the guard in her gut and sending her forest green self reeling over. With a finger's flick, a hand's grab, Davin had turned off and holstered the stun baton, replacing it with the guard's half-empty rifle.

Stacked behind the console, unwashed and unceremonious, waited Davin and Phyla's clothes. A quick change to get off the obvious prisoner garb, and Davin had himself feeling close to normal.

The lifts, and Phyla, waited just ahead.

9

———

FRIGATE TOUR

The lift, as lifts tended to do, presented options. A simple screen, not much larger than Davin's hand, listed off the frigate's ten floors. As the levels stretched from bow to aft, though, each one couldn't be labeled simply as the cafeteria, the gym, the barracks. Instead Eden deployed a dictionary's worth of icons, the illustrated circles filling in after every level number. To someone with knowledge, it made for a snappy way to pick a destination.

To Davin, it made a mess.

He hit a floor at random, not wanting to waste time parsing icons with Eden reinforcements presumably en route. The lift chimed at his choice, but the doors stayed open. Davin waited, but nothing happened. Then realization struck.

"First time, you know?" Davin said to nobody as his hand went back to the console. This time he dinged the floor one up from his first choice, his own damn floor.

The lift took this request with more aplomb, doors shutting and whisking Davin away. The trip to the next level passed in the time it took for Davin to confirm his stolen rifle's power pack energy: too low to take on the entire frigate, enough to make an entrance.

A semicircle awaited him, one frothing over with junk loaded onto carts. Bright lights. Spotless, save for stripes running along the walls guiding transporters to such nebulous destinations as 'materials mineralization' and 'polymer processing'. Several Eden rubes glanced Davin's way as the lift doors opened, all in various cart pushing contortions.

No way Phyla would be here, and a glance at the small screen confirmed this level's sole icon.

"Wrong floor, have a nice day," Davin waved, tapped the next level up.

Two mistakes meant the third had to be right, right?

Davin spent the few seconds idle time between floors trying to remember if he'd ever seen a frigate devote so much space to construction work. The ships were meant for war, meant for speed compared to the bigger hulks. Freighters or gangly space bases had shapes better put together for manufacturing.

So what was Heath up to?

"Focus, buddy," Davin muttered as the doors opened.

Another semicircle, this one bearing Heath's trademark slapdash standards. Stained signs marking cafeterias, the barracks, and a training center gave Davin his three options. Three possibilities: He'd bet they hadn't taken Phyla to give her lunch—though Davin, with his rumbling stomach, wouldn't mind some—nor brought her to help make some beds in the barracks. But what squad leader wouldn't want to throw a prisoner to the wolves to help teach their troops a thing or two?

Like the manufacturing level, this one had people on it aplenty. Most sported Eden's forest green, but in Davin's first few steps he saw a couple in civilian clothes too. Visitors? Heath's friends or government inspectors?

"Hey!"

Davin turned at the call, one coming from a stern-looking fellow in Eden fatigues. The man pointed at Davin's rifle.

"You don't look like you're from here, but all rifles have to be holstered outside the range."

"Got it," Davin said, then hesitated. He hadn't stolen a holster from the guard, figuring the fights would be straight on to the end. "Actually, tell you what, I'm heading to the range. Mind pointing me in the right direction?"

Davin hoped the guy would just point him towards the training center, but Davin's ask only earned a harder stare. Without speaking, the Eden man, carrying what must've been lunch in one hand, walked right up to Davin. Half a meter apart. Davin had the rifle pointing away and to the ground, had a sloppy grin up on his face, but knew he could jack the man in a microsecond with the rifle's stock.

"Hold this," the man said, handing out his lunch, a square container filled with various nutrient goop flavors.

Davin eyed the sludge, his stomach agreeing with his eyes to postpone mealtime. More importantly, was the ask a trick? Did the guy plan on taking Davin's rifle as soon as the meal occupied a hand? How deep did the man's deception go?

You don't get to be a noted gambler by failing to read people. Davin looked up from the food, took in the man's face, his bearing, and made the call: this dude had all the guile of a rock. Letting his right hand off the rifle's stock, the gun swinging down in his left, Davin took hold of the food.

"Here," the man said, easing the rifle from Davin's grip and slipping it into a shoulder holster, which the man promptly slid off his back and handed to Davin. "We've got extras back at the 'racks. Don't know who let you off your ship like that, but we don't go weapons free here."

"Thanks." Davin handed back the lunch.

The guy nodded, dipped his finger in some blueberry goop and marched off. Davin stared after him for a long moment, wondering whether everyone on this ship was as weird as its captain. Speaking of, what was Heath doing? Someone had to have checked the prison feeds and seen the guards by now. How was the ship not flush with idiots tripping over themselves to collect Davin's head?

His parents, back on Minor Prime, used to tell Davin not to question good fortune when it came. The solar system didn't have much of it, so enjoy when a little went your way.

As a mercenary, Davin found that outlook to be the worst kind of bullshit. Something good happened without a reason? Best find one, and find one quick before you wound up paying a high price.

The training center, at least, proved to be close. The cafeteria sat at the frigate's bow while the barracks took up the aft, plopping the training center in the, well, center. Getting there meant putting on a scoundrel's shuffle and heading down a hall lined with class schedules, extra courses, and the occasional flyer for a hobby club on the frigate. One enthusiastic guy strung up a sheet advertising his cooking courses every meter, a heaping plate of meatballs on every one.

Davin's stomach did not appreciate it.

The training center itself wasn't a single square room but, rather, a whole set ranging from weight training to zero-g treadmills meant to combat gravity's ill-effects on a person —from his floaty step, Davin guessed the frigate's centrifuge and rotation generated a half g—to basketball and tennis courts. Davin's hallway split into a T, with the cross-wise walk replacing wall panels with windows. Flipping a mental coin, Davin went left.

The basketball looked fun: everybody able to dunk, make long floating passes across the court.

What Davin didn't see across the whole range? Aya and Phyla.

"Can I help you?" A woman coming up from behind, Eden fatigues, a badge putting her on training center duty. She flicked her eyes from Davin's face to his rifle. "The range is the other way."

"Ah, right," Davin said. "First time."

"You'll have to check in," the woman turned with Davin, leading him back to the T and the sole desk waiting there. "Nobody's allowed to live fire on the frigate without registering."

"Not looking to shoot, just store it."

A raised eyebrow, "I'll need your name for that too."

Davin didn't get a chance to give it. As they reached the desk, Davin's struggle to decide on his real name or a lie met its end on the lips of another Eden cadet, some flustered man running up to the desk. That he had a pistol drawn threw up Davin's warning signals, that he started his announcement by declaring the rogue rebel had escaped confirmed the intuition.

"Word of mouth only," the man followed, his eyes flicking to Davin then back to the woman. "Captain wants us to monitor the guy but not engage. Captain thinks he might come here, so . . ."

The man's eyes went again to Davin, seemed to take him in for the first time.

Ah, the slow, delicious moment when a mistake is realized. Davin could all but see the checklist rolling through the man's mind: scruffy middle-aged man? Check. Long black coat? Check. Twinkle in the eye? Absolutely.

"Why's the captain think he might come here?" Davin asked as the man took a step back.

Being deep in enemy territory meant keeping tabs on your surroundings, and Davin counted at least ten Eden employees wandering the halls before, behind, and to his right. While none held rifles—range only!—their sheer numbers would've put Davin at a disadvantage. He needed to get somewhere with a tighter corridor, an escape route.

"Captain didn't say," the man stammered. "He, uh."

Davin felt the woman looking at him. Her curiosity said she'd pegged Davin just like the man, but she'd seen what the man hadn't: a shootout here would end in Davin's decisive immolation. She'd also noticed another Eden pair heading towards them, oblivious so far, down the hall. Another twenty paces would make the count an unstable four on one.

"Here's the game, kids," Davin said, both because he liked the sound of the phrase and because both these Eden cadets appeared green around the space-faring gills. "I need to find my pilot, and she's been taken by your resident squad leader. A lady by the name of Aya. Point me her way and I'll let you get back to your date."

The man blushed. The woman folded her arms, frowning. Fifteen paces. Davin moved his left hand up to his shoulder.

"Aya's always around," the woman said. "You want to find her, go straight this way. Door at the end." A glance towards the guy. "And he's not my type, so watch your mouth."

"Done and done," Davin tipped an invisible hat at the woman, strode off in the direction she noted. As he passed by the cadet, the one holding onto a wavering pistol, Davin whipped out his right hand, grabbed the pistol by the barrel and yanked it free. Flipped it into the air and caught it on the handle. "Thanks for this, bud."

Orders or no, Davin wouldn't be letting some kid keep a pistol aimed at his back. Behind him, the two approaching crew reached the woman, one's question reaching Davin's ears: "Who's that guy?"

"He's got business with Aya," the woman answered. "I'd leave him alone."

Smart cookie, that one.

The hallway's end made it clear this wasn't simply a corridor quitting on itself. Instead, the walls and ceiling seemed like they'd had a crisis and come back with a new lease on life: simple, dirty grey had been mottled with color, as if someone had stitched rainbow lasers into the walls. The ceiling panels sported phrases, insipid ones like *What makes you happy? How can you fight your fears?*

For a moment Davin wondered if he was still on an Eden frigate or if he'd tripped off into a psychedelic dream. Would Heath flood his ship with hallucinogenic gas just to mess with Davin?

Probably not.

The door at the hallway's end had a green-lit scanner. No lock, then. Just come right in and join the party. Davin considered: go in guns out, or keep playing the confused visitor, see how far that would get him?

Well, not very, seeing as Aya would know exactly who he was, why he was there. Guns out, then.

Davin dropped the pistol into a coat pocket, flipped the rifle into his hands, put a finger on the trigger, swung his right elbow to tap the door entry panel. Without complaint, the barrier slid aside, opening into another wide training room. The frigate's other workout areas matched their labels: big spaces, lines for games or exercises, weight machines and treadmills scattered throughout.

Aya had other ideas.

Ten stations—Davin couldn't think of what else to call them—spread evenly throughout the room, colored tape on the floor marking the breaks. Each station held a chair or bench, and not the friendly kinds Davin might see at a park or cafe: cuffs and straps littered the things, gleaming in the scattershot light from above. The fluorescent lines elsewhere were patched here, blackout curtains stretched across sections to create a shadowed checkerboard glow on the floor. As weird as all that was, though, Davin's main focus snapped to the helmets hanging above every chair and bench.

The *Jumper* had several simulators packed into a secondary cargo bay. Looking like big pill capsules, the simulators could put you just about anywhere you wanted to go. The surrounding oval held your body in place, let the simulator keep you immersed. These would be different, would give you a half-assed version for your eyes and ears while the restraints ensured you wouldn't charge off into a wall and hurt yourself. Nobody would use these for training, nobody would use this setup for fun when the full-body variety existed.

Thankfully, Davin could get his questions answered.

Aya, together with three other Eden goobers, stood near the last station on the right. There, buckled on her back to a wide bench, with a helmet on her head, was Phyla. A portable monitor, wheeled over, took up the Eden attention. Davin was too far away to get a good look, but he'd bet it showed a feed of whatever Phyla was seeing, maybe some bonus numbers like her vitals, brain activity. Erick, the Nines' old doctor, would've been able to parse those things.

Not that it mattered: this wasn't an experiment that'd be continuing.

Aya didn't play her cohorts's games. She bypassed the monitor, leaning over Phyla with one hand wrapped around Phyla's wrist. Like in the shuttle, Aya's inspecting look, her leaned-over stance suggested an observation, an experiment.

On Phyla.

"Hey," Davin announced, aiming the rifle at the Eden group, "party's over, people. Get her out or the lasers start flying."

The Eden staffers matched Aya's incredulous look before their leader sighed. Shaking her head, Aya waved a cutting motion to the Eden trio as she stepped back from Phyla, dropping the pilot's wrist.

"Heath didn't tell me he would be starting so early," Aya said as Davin came further into the room.

Davin took several leftward steps for every one forward, letting him turn and cover the door he'd just come through as well as the Eden group. There didn't seem to be another exit. Not great, as that meant Davin would have to plow his way back out through the lone hallway, but you didn't always get to choose your battleground.

"Guess you and Heath oughta work on your relationship," Davin said. "Is she off?"

Phyla still had the helmet on, but Davin referred to the simulation. Hard cutting someone free from a virtual world could be all kinds of problematic, so most systems wouldn't allow it unless in an emergency. Instead, you'd get a ten-second wind down, with a calm voice telling you the experience was ending as the universe faded to a pleasant white or black.

"She's off," said one of the Eden jokers.

The three huddled, with their monitor, back against the room's far wall. Aya remained within a couple meters of Phyla. The squad leader's hands kept twitching Phyla's way.

"You're interrupting important work, you know," Aya said as Davin approached, slow.

"It's a habit of mine." Davin snapped the rifle towards the cuffs. "Unlock her."

Aya reached into a pocket—she wore combat fatigues, all in Eden forest green—and produced a little keycard. Running it along the cuffs, Aya opened Phyla's restraints. The pilot's hands went to her head fast, pulled off the VR helmet. And there she was, Phyla, looking a little stunned but otherwise no worse for wear.

"Hey there," Davin said, waving Aya back with the rifle. "Welcome to your prison break."

Phyla blinked, saw Davin, caught the pistol he tossed her. "A little late."

"Had trouble getting directions."

The pilot rolled off the bench away from Aya, turned and leveled the pistol at the squad leader. Hesitated as Aya spread her hands, showed she didn't have a weapon on her.

"We're on a clock, love," Davin said. "Going to waste her, do it and let's go."

Instead, Phyla aimed left, fired, and burned a hole through the monitor. The Eden group scattered, one swearing the whole way like he'd been shot instead. Aya looked nonplussed, but, as Phyla aimed and fired again and again, the squad leader found her anger. Every shot Phyla squeezed off went right into a VR helmet, burning each one to bits.

A crippling move this far away from Earth, where new sets would be hard to find.

"Very satisfying," Phyla said, destruction done.

"Leaving her alive, but destroying the helmets?" Davin asked.

"She didn't try to kill me," Phyla replied. "If she does, she's dead."

"Cool. If you're done zapping hardware, you ready to go?"

"Very much."

With Phyla covering his back, Davin went for the door. All along the way ideas bumbled around Davin's head about how they'd actually get off the ship. Without the *Jumper*, there were two options: hijack another ship, or get to an evac shuttle and blast off. The latter definitely had the edge for viability, but then, Heath would know that too. Every one ought to have guards lingering outside it waiting to light Davin up.

Better to keep it unpredictable.

Davin hit the door, beeped open the scanner, and saw a hallway stretching straight towards an armed squad. The quick look confirmed body armor, confirmed rifles raised. Confirmed they were trapped. And yet, the Eden defenders didn't shoot before Davin ducked back into the room.

Not quick on the trigger, these people.

"No way out?" Aya asked from the far side as Davin relayed the not-so-great update to Phyla.

"Don't suppose there's a secret door from here," Davin asked Phyla. "You see any?"

"They brought me in through that door," Phyla checked her pistols power. "Davin, don't tell me you went through all the trouble get here just to get us captured again."

"I'm trying all right?"

"Did Heath outsmart you two?" Aya asked.

Davin brushed her off, glanced back towards the door. "Okay, new plan. We bundle up your rifle's power pack, throw it down the hall like it's a grenade. When they scatter, we charge."

"All the way to the lift?" Phyla asked.

"You have a better idea?"

"I might," Aya said, coming closer, still keeping her hands wide to show she hadn't picked up a murder weapon somewhere. "If you're willing to listen."

Ulterior motives. The damn things infested Davin's life. Nobody played it simple anymore, sticking to the good guys and bad guys. People always had to have another agenda. When Davin looked at Aya now, he didn't just see an Eden squad leader with a weird hobby, but someone more driven, or more desperate. Willing to risk it all on a play.

Either that, or Aya was about to offer up a heaping plate of crap in hopes Davin and Phyla would take a bite. Worse, Davin wasn't sure they had a choice.

"Talk," Phyla said, tuning her voice to ice in that way she had.

"Take me hostage," Aya said.

Silence. The Eden trio in the back had their eyes bugging out at the suggestion.

"Heath won't shoot me," Aya replied. "We can walk right out."

Davin looked to Phyla, "Guess that means if things go south, you can get revenge before we bite it."

"That is a positive," Phyla said. "Fine. Stand still." The pilot, handing her pistol to Davin, gave Aya a pat-down. Found no weapons, no dangerous tools. "She's clean."

During Phyla's search, Davin listened, tried to hear if the people outside the door were on an approach. Thus far, nothing. As if Heath had his fighters waiting Davin and Phyla out, despite, well, Aya and her researcher buddies in here. The stance went against just about every conflict directive Davin knew. Eden had numbers, had firepower, had their targets trapped, but did nothing.

So when Aya put herself at the door, hands held high, and said she was ready, Davin felt a cold chill. This escape wasn't going well, and if Davin was a betting man—and he definitely was—he'd put all his cash on it getting worse.

10

AN ESCAPE

How to fight your way free on a hostile ship, lesson one: bring a valuable hostage. Davin couldn't, didn't trust Aya at all, but when the alternative meant getting gunned down in a creepy gym, well, you made your peace with it.

"Lead on," Davin said to Aya, letting Phyla keep eyes on the back.

Not that she needed to: Aya's researcher trio looked queasy at the idea of combat. Sometimes Davin forgot there were professions, whole lives out there that didn't revolve around finding clever ways to kill other people. Like finding a rare rock, seeing those three.

"Where do you want to go?" Aya asked as they approached the exit and the phalanx waiting on the other side.

"Nearest shuttle, if you would," Davin said.

"That'll be quite a walk," Aya replied. "Sure I can't convince you to take something closer?"

With Davin standing behind Aya's back and Phyla in Davin's shadow, the three formed a single file line as they left the gym. The psychedelic hallway made Davin feel like he was leaving a dream, one crashing into a terrible reality: eight stacked soldiers with firearms up and pointed dead at them.

"Just get us out of this hall for starters," Davin said.

"Of course." Aya waved her arms. "Don't shoot. They have me captive."

For a hostage, her tone sounded sedated, like an actor going through the fiftieth take of a dull scene.

But hey, the soldiers didn't fire. They didn't back off either, yet as Aya kept going, with Davin and Phyla hugging her every step, no lasers gunned the pair down. A few half-hearted orders to let Aya go echoed their way, shouted by some commander behind the group. When Davin made no move to obey, the soldiers didn't attempt anything new.

"These gotta be Eden's worst," Davin said as the trio made their slow way towards the soldiers and the intersection. "They're not even trying?"

"We don't train for this," Aya replied, keeping her face forward. "How many battlefields require hostage negotiation?"

"Just keep moving," Phyla cut in. "This isn't coffee."

Aya led them to within a few meters, to the point where Davin figured even a questionable shot might risk taking him and Phyla out. Still, the soldiers held their fire. They backstepped, even, retreating from the intersection like some scared crab.

Contributing to the surreal moment, the frigate's overhead announcer began reading off the dinner menu: lobster nutrient goop with a multivitamin smoothie. No alarms, no calls to arms.

Heath was officially the weirdest captain Davin had met, and that was quite a list to top.

"Stop," Davin said as they reached the intersection, rifle

nuzzled right into Aya's back. "Check your left. Anything in the hallway?"

"Nothing at all. Clear right to the lifts," Aya said. "Aren't you lucky?"

When he looked back, Phyla met his confusion with a head shake. Things weren't adding up. Davin could buy a stroke or two of good fortune, like the dude who'd fixed him up with a rifle holster on this level, but now?

"We don't have a choice," Phyla said.

Agreed.

"Keep moving," Davin said. "You lie to us, you lead us to the wrong place, you're the first to die."

"I would expect nothing less from hardened killers like yourselves."

Davin winced: hardened killer wasn't exactly his favorite adjective. You could make the argument—some had—but Davin had yet to agree to an assassination mission. Until that day, any deaths were an accessory, not the point.

At least, that's what he told himself.

Davin confirmed Aya's clear path assessment, then rotated the hostage to keep her in the soldiers' aim while the three went down the hallway. Again the soldiers held their fire, again certain death stayed its hand.

Reaching the lifts and the semicircle crossing around it, Davin and Phyla—Aya had herself parked behind them now, interrupting sight lines—found the area deserted. Not a soul wandered from the cafeteria, no armed guards charged from the barracks.

"Level two," Aya said, "is where you'll find the docking bays."

Phyla called the lift while Davin covered, though he was starting to feel the whole thing unnecessary. Would the soldiers have shot if he and Phyla had skipped out, whistling a tune?

Level two housed the frigate's shuttles. It wasn't deserted, but nobody seemed to be paying attention to them. To try and keep it that way, Davin holstered the rifle and let Phyla, with her more innocuous pistol, direct Aya along.

Compared with the earlier sections, the docking bay hallways were larger, were often packed with materials and bots shuffling through. More crates coming in than going out, with cargo drones blasting on and off the ship.

"What's all this?" Davin couldn't help but ask.

"We're restocking," Aya replied. "Io is close, and we're due for another Uranus swing."

Restocking with high-end circuit boards and carbon fiber? Not just power packs but long use kinetic batteries? Not the usual provisions, but when Davin pressed Aya on it, she replied that Eden had strict requirements on what to carry.

"Heath, of course, exercises some discretion." Aya laughed, an airy thing. "Who's going to stop him, way out here?"

The fifth docking bay held the same shuttle Aya and her squad had used to board the *Jumper*. It sat, charged up and resting, waiting for someone to give it a fly.

"You want us to escape in this thing?" Phyla asked. "They'll blow us apart."

"Not if we take her with us," Davin said. "They haven't fired a shot, made a single threat since we took her hostage. Figure we let that ride."

Aya laughed again, looked to face Davin as they stood inside the docking bay's entrance. Like the other bays, this one had its crate share, had various maintenance bots and tools strung up along the sides beneath a black-stenciled 04 on the walls.

"I'm not going with you," Aya said.

"Good to know," Davin replied, "but the thing about hostages is that I don't need to give a crap about your opinion."

Aya moved fast. A coiled spring unleashing. Her left hand snapped out, smashing Phyla's pistol free from the pilot's grip. Before Davin could flip his rifle over, Aya jabbed his neck with her right hand, sending Davin back, coughing, towards the docking bay door.

On cue, someone finally sounded an alarm, the lights flaring red and the overhead calling—still in a polite after-noon tea tone—for help with a prison break.

Davin tried to find a way to breathe while Phyla dove for her pistol. Aya ignored the pilot, instead kicking into a run at Davin. The captain had a hot moment to get his hands up, throwing a beleaguered block to catch Aya's snapping kick. The force behind the blow pushed Davin the rest of the way into the metal wall, the doorway's left side.

Turned out, steel didn't make a comfy landing.

Davin, though, hadn't been socked a hundred times without learning to turn momentum into a counter. He came off the wall into a right haymaker, cocking his shoulder and leaning in with a fist forward face wrecker.

Aya, of course, dodged. She ducked to her right, angling to get Davin between her and Phyla. Smart move, predictable move. Davin kept stepping through his wild swing, using the momentum to reverse places with Aya, get a meter between them.

Time enough to flip the rifle down, time enough to draw a bead.

And find four more guns aiming at him. Eden soldiers,

dockhands, whomever: they'd come fast, real fast at the alarm. They had Davin caught without cover, Phyla not much better as she snagged her pistol deeper in the bay.

Aya's smile turned so smug Davin wanted to shoot anyway, just to wipe it away. A good last act.

But not fair to Phyla, his crew.

"Guess you got us," Davin said, only for Aya to ignore him, look over at Phyla.

"Get on the ship and take off, now," Aya said.

Phyla, pistol in hand, blinked, "What?"

"You heard me. The shuttle is ready to fly. Get in there and go."

"Don't give'em a chance to change their mind," Davin jumped into the silence. "Let's get outta here."

A laser blitzed by Davin before he took a step, crossing between him and the shuttle.

"She can leave," Aya said. "Not you."

"No deal," Phyla snapped. "Davin's with me."

"If you leave now, he has a chance," Aya replied, Davin glancing between the two, at the guns stuck to him. "If you persist, neither of you have one at all."

"Why?" Davin shouted, the damn strangeness of it all conquering any sly influence. "What the hell are you all doing? You want to kill us? Then kill us. You don't? Then let us go!"

Aya ignored him. Kept looking at Phyla.

"Well?" Aya asked.

"Davin?" Phyla said. "I don't want to leave you."

"Well, that's a relief," Davin replied. "Awkward timing, but I'll take it."

Phyla laughed, cried, waited. Aya kept saying it like they had a choice, but there wasn't one here. Whether Davin's whole prison break had been a show or if his luck had finally failed, the only option now was to grasp at straws. See what they could scavenge.

"Go," Davin said, his mouth drying out as he said the words. "Get out of here. I'll meet up with you later."

Phyla met his eyes, Davin summoning up enough courage to throw up a smile. A grin, really. The lip curl saying everything would be fine. It always had been, always would be.

The pilot shook her head, but when Aya changed her aim, held the pistol to Davin's skull, she made the choice that had to be made.

"Don't be late," Phyla said, then ran up the ramp.

The hissing chunk started, the ramp retracting after Phyla. Engine whines filled the bay, the shuttle powering up. The whole time Aya kept the pistol on Davin's forehead, the whole time Davin kept his eyes on the shuttle, at the red hair just shining through the thing's windshield.

His own hair whipped as the shuttle's microjets kicked it off the docking bay, the engine noise washing out every other sound. Phyla turned the craft around, a slow swing. No hurried escape here, just a gradual play.

Davin grinned a little wider. Phyla would be milking seconds, learning the ins and outs of the shuttle, its every secret. When Eden came after her, as it had to, as they would every member of the Nines, Phyla would make that shuttle do things nobody would expect.

Aya pushed Davin into the bay after Phyla's departing shuttle roared out. They walked right up to the magnetic shield, a near-invisible wall holding back vacuum at a huge energy cost. The frigate should've been shutting heavy doors, but instead the stars beckoned, Jupiter's giant bulk visible off to the left.

"Watch," Aya said.

"You shoot at her, I'm going to shove you through this shield," Davin said, only for the soldiers behind him to grab his arms, hold him back.

"Just watch."

As Phyla's shuttle streaked off, heading towards Jupiter and, hopefully, the *Jumper*, another bright streak flashed by overhead. A small craft—the engine wash was too large for a missile—blazing after her. Far faster than the shuttle, the fighter caught up quick. Without scanners, Davin couldn't see anything more than dots dancing, but tiny flashes went from one dot to another. Red bolts.

Davin's expletive library ran long, his insult dictionary a thousand pages thick, and he burned through them all in that docking bay, watching those tiny darts, knowing Phyla had no escape.

Knowing he was useless as the dot holding his love vanished into a bright ball, and then nothing.

Davin had been here once before. On Miner Prime, in a posh suite where Bosser gunned down Lina, leaving her to die in Davin's arms. A static, hollow shock. A thousand memories buzzed by, each one replayed in full yet not seen at all, a fervent cascade, as if by glimpsing each moment Davin could preserve them forever right now. His veins went to ice. His heart beat raced, his pulse blotting out any other sound. His knees went shaky, but only for the time it took the orange glow to fade.

See, the enemy stood right there. Waiting.

Without really realizing it, in a black-and-red way, Davin lunged at Aya. The squad leader held her fire, let Davin close before flipping him past her, a kick to Davin's ankles sending him sprawling to the docking bay's floor.

Not the best start, but anger overrode any sensible strategy. The only thing to do was act, and act now.

Aya's trip sent Davin beyond the docking bay's door, into the bay and out of sight lines from Aya's reinforcing troops. As he hit the ground, Davin noticed coolant canisters, meter-long steel cylinders, stacked against the wall. Aya reset her pistol aim as Davin yanked a cylinder out, held it towards the woman while still on the ground.

"Don't make me kill you," Aya said. "It would be such a waste."

Davin snarled, pushed the canister's emptying button. The nozzle at the cylinder's far end, pointing towards Aya's ankles, slid open. Chalk white liquid sprayed out, frozen vapor climbing out around the explosion. Aya skipped to her right, catching the coolant on her feet. The pistol shot never came.

She'd had time, but Aya didn't deliver the kill. Davin couldn't figure why, didn't much care now either. He hefted the coolant canister, resisted its push-back as the liquid kept shooting out, and lurched around the doorway.

The coolant canister offensive only had a few seconds to play out, but the Eden squad decided not to take it, abandoning their line-up to back down the bay-crossing hallway. Two carried Aya, who seemed utterly calm despite her feet, boots and all frozen to a pale blue.

The other three? They had rifles beaded on Davin, but they didn't fire. Kept up the retreat, swiping docking bays closed on the way. Limiting Davin's options.

Fine. Davin would go where they wanted, and he'd destroy whatever waited for him at the end. Tossing the spent canister aside, Davin walked after his enemies.

Aya and her carriers raced ahead, vanishing into a lift. The others bustling about the docking bays had disappeared, leaving Davin with his trio and their directions. Crates stacked around Davin offered no weapons, no options. Just ship parts, provisions for the frigate's personnel.

The rifles waved Davin towards the stairs.

When Davin tried to refuse, tried to take a step towards the lift the three protected, one actually shot. The orange-red bolt skipped off the floor at Davin's feet. Again, the rifles pointed towards the stairs.

"Why?" Davin asked, still playing in shock, in a life that didn't feel real. "What's the point?"

The three didn't reply, set faces flicking towards the stairs.

"Is this some sick game Heath has you playing?" Davin folded his arms. "Tell him to come down here so I can kill him, if that's what he wants."

When the trio didn't respond, Davin tried turning around. Go back towards the docking bays, test the limits. He didn't even take a step before another bolt flared past him, scoring into the hallway wall.

No way back, only one way forward.

At once, the shock drained away to exhaustion. The anger stayed there, bubbling away, but Davin didn't have anywhere to spend it. Charging headlong at the three would mean instant death. Going up the stairs offered a route, but without a target. He'd been caught in a net ever since Davin broke from his cell, a stupid plan that'd cost Phyla her life.

"Can you just shoot me and get it over with?" Davin asked.

The trio held their fire.

"Of course not. Because your boss is an ass."

Not a single emotion. Well-trained, these Eden bums.

"Fine, I'll walk your dumb stairs. How many levels?"

"Four," said the trio's middle man, the one who'd fired both warning shots.

Davin gave him a particular finger in return, then went through the flat door to the tight metal steps. Relegated to afterthought status, the stairs on this and most ships saw compact steps, tight quarters, and claustrophobic design.

At least the low gravity meant Davin could hop from one small landing to the next, scaling the four levels in a few seconds. At the designated door, Davin hesitated. He could go higher, try to throw a wrench in Heath's plan.

"Too bad," Davin said to the door, skipped up one level higher and tried the fifth level's exit.

The door opened to show two more Eden guards waiting there, rifles drawn and aimed right at Davin's heart.

"One level too many," said the guard on the left, the same woman who'd been helping Davin at the gym not thirty minutes ago. "Down one, please."

"Does this make you feel powerful or something?" Davin asked her. "Is this what you signed up for with Eden? Terrorizing people?"

"You're the terrorist," the woman countered. "Go down or we'll shoot."

"He killed my wife a second ago, you know that, right?"

"How many of us have your rebels killed?"

Davin found his fists clenching, opening. He took a long breath, turned and shut the door behind him. Everyone was human, everyone had their beliefs, chose their sides.

He wouldn't get their sympathy, but Davin could earn their respect, their fear.

Back at the fourth level, Davin checked himself. No coat anymore, just an old shirt, pants, and those nice boots. No weapons, just stubble and hair that could use a trim. A lavatory would've been nice, along with a meal. Otherwise, though, he was healthy. Ready.

"Please oh please, let Heath be on the other side," Davin muttered, then flung open the door.

Heath wasn't waiting on the other side. Nothing was, beyond a thin hallway's opposite wall. Davin tried to place where he was on the ship, a process made easier by the directory sign to the right, across from the lift banks. As Davin read it, the lifts opened and his escorting trio fanned out, blocking Davin from continuing down the hallway aftward.

The wall map made it pretty obvious where Heath had Davin going.

"He wants me on the bridge?" Davin asked the trio. "Good. I can blow you all to hell from there."

The threat didn't phase the guards. Made of stern stuff, these guys.

The walk to the bridge brought Davin past rooms of all kinds, and all were sealed to his entry. Red-glowing locks and occasional speakers telling Davin his credentials—or lack thereof—were no good here. Usually, Davin would've been one to hate the cramped lines, the lack of options.

Now focus was his friend. Davin went straight for the bridge, boiling anger, despair, and who-the-hell cares frustration fueling every step.

Heath let him come. The hallway expanded to another lift set at the bridge's entry, thick blast doors withdrawn to give Davin easy access. The trio kept pace with Davin too, always several meters back, never saying a word. Nobody else waited, so Davin went right on in.

The frigate wasn't some giant battleship like the one Opal commanded. This wasn't a cruiser like the *Galaxy's Song* or a big freighter, so the bridge here looked like a small restaurant. Tables, each lined with consoles, sat in a loose U shape around the room's center. There, on a raised platform so he could look over his subordinates, stood the man Davin needed to hit with a severe sucker punch.

The silence cut Davin's march. Davin found bridges always busy. People, communications, calls, chatter should've been everywhere. Instead, all the tables were deserted. A few consoles blinked alerts, but nothing pinged for urgent attention. Heath truly was alone. The trio didn't even follow Davin in.

Heath himself looked more tired than the cargo bay chat. Like he'd pulled an all-nighter, though Heath had a dry vigor to his stance that said he'd done what he'd stayed up to do.

"Why'd you have to hurt Aya like that?" Heath said to start things off, leaning on a rail around his central platform and looking at Davin like they were buddies catching up. "She might lose both feet."

"I lost Phyla."

Heath shrugged, a motion that almost had Davin running up the steps right then. The only thing holding Davin back was the certainty that this was, in some way, a trap. Blind fury played itself out back in the docking bay, now cold vengeance held Davin's strings.

"We all lose people," Heath said. "It's how life works. Most of us move on. You won't have to."

"Because you're going to kill me?"

"Not quite," Heath replied, then glanced at his wristlet. "Ten more seconds, my friend, and then your pain can be put to rest."

Davin took a step towards the center platform, then two. Heath folded his arms, looked down the ramp at Davin.

"Ten seconds and then what?" Davin said, gauging the distance. "Unless you're a better draw than you look, a pistol won't save you."

Heath shook his head, "I'd never waste you on something so petty as revenge."

"I'd waste you for it," Davin said. He'd moved to put a straight line between him and Heath, unobstructed. Easy. "Think I'll do that now, actually."

Davin dashed forward, pumping his arms, heading right for Heath. The older captain started to reach for something, but it wouldn't be fast enough. Davin would mash the man to bits, bash Heath against the console and get in a fatal blow or two before that trio took Davin out.

As the meters between them dwindled, Davin held back his right arm, ready to drive it forward. The timing had to be perfect, right into Heath's smug face.

And it would've been too, if a body hadn't dropped between them. If a face, framed with long red hair, hadn't blocked out Heath. If Phyla, green eyes blazing, hadn't caught Davin's punch and held his hand firm.

A split second's confusion drowned in cynicism, in experience, in the imperfections Davin instantly noticed. Not enough freckles, no scars. Life hadn't been lived by the Phyla standing in front of him, a fact so obvious hope never had a chance to rise.

Instead, as the android whipped Davin up and over the railing, as the Nines captain flew and crashed into some painfully sturdy consoles, all Davin could think about was how his damn life just couldn't get any worse.

11

SHOWTIME

Among the many miseries Davin had dealt with, having broken glass and shattered shelving digging into his back while the mechanized copy of his love tried to murder him . . . well, Davin would figure out where that ranked once he escaped.

First order: getting off the busted table. Davin rolled, feeling something crunch in his shoulder, the tiny shards poking his back, but he left the busted furniture behind. Hitting smooth tile was cold comfort, because Mecha-Phyla jumped down to meet him there. The name came instinctively, a merging of movies and the current moment.

He wouldn't, couldn't just call this monster Phyla.

"This man, Earth's hero," Heath shouted, and while Davin couldn't see the man's face, he had the distinct impression the words weren't meant for him, "is trying to escape his punishment. He would have murdered my crew, shot me to death, except for this android."

'This android' picked Davin up by his collar, lifted Davin up off the floor, and would've likely flung Davin into the wall if Davin's shirt, too beat up and run down, hadn't torn. The android found itself holding a ragged collar while Davin hit the tile.

Fighting an android amounted to folly most times, and with only his bare fists, for Davin to attempt straight up combat would mean a quick shuffling off of the ol' mortal coil. Instead, Davin ran left, towards the bridge's entrance and more options.

"Safe, reliable, and obedient," Heath continued ranting, "my androids are the saviors we need to stop these pointless wars, these rampant killings."

Davin reached the next table, heard the press on the tile behind as Mecha-Phyla jumped his way. Grabbing a chair, Davin pulled and swung the thing, a heavy wheeled monstrosity. Something pulled in Davin's back with the move, a new ache to add to his collection, but the pain was worth it: the chair hit the android as it landed, getting its awkward bulk all in Mecha-Phyla's limbs. As the jangle hit the floor, Davin pressed off the table with his hand and made for the exit.

Five meters never felt so long. A flat run along the tile right to the bridge's double-wide doors should've been doable, and, in his prime, Davin might've made it. Davin cut the distance in half before something huge crashed into him from behind, drove him to the floor again. A wheel hanging near his face told Davin the chair he'd used had come back around for a second appearance.

"Able to handle even the most skilled adversary, my next generation androids are ready," Heath crowed as Davin pushed the chair off him, saw Mecha-Phyla looming. She raised a foot, perhaps intending to squash Davin's head like a grape. "Put them into action, and watch our enemies crumble!"

Davin reached with his right hand, pulled the chair back over him as Mecha-Phyla's foot came down. The plastic-and-cloth chair took the hit, mashed into Davin's face. The tile pressed in from the back, and Davin felt like he might explode, a thousand-star headache kicking up.

With his hands, Davin pushed up and forward on the chair's back, giving his head a micrometer of space and, more importantly, using Mecha-Phyla's planted foot against it. The android's balance shook as its right foot slid aside, while Davin used his own legs to push against the tile, squeeze out from beneath the trap.

The chair banged, cracked as Davin escaped, letting Mecha-Phyla press the furniture to the bridge floor. The Nines captain pushed himself back on his butt, trying to get distance, knowing he wouldn't be able to get away.

But Phyla wouldn't be avenged if Davin bit it here.

"You win!" Davin shouted as the android kicked away the chair, resumed its stalk. Heath shut up his incessant sales pitch, blinked at Davin from his platform. "Your android's got me."

Mecha-Phyla didn't accept the surrender, again looming over Davin. This time it cocked back a fist, ready to deliver a mortal mashing.

"I'll help you sell it," Davin kept going, raising his hands to cover his face. "I'll admit how strong it is. Eden'll have to listen."

Heath whistled and the android froze. Literally. No getting back to its resting position, just standing there, a bizarro version of Phyla ready to swat Davin into the stars.

So Davin took a breath. A deep one. Tried to unscramble a plan from what his mouth had just blurted out.

"An interesting offer," Heath mused, and Davin saw the frigate captain tapping his chin there in the bridge's middle.

"But I don't believe you'll help me alive any more than dead."

"You don't know how charming I can be," Davin said, getting his feet set right, ignoring the thudding pain from his back.

"I know how dangerous you are," Heath replied. "No, I think I'd prefer you eliminated now."

The captain whistled again. The android punched, its fist screaming towards Davin. Towards a Davin no longer set in place, but one already breaking into a roll as Heath's whistle started. With its punch partway through, the android couldn't adjust: its fist blew into the tile, cracking the floor.

Davin kicked himself up, ran the last couple meters to the door as the android reset itself, began its pursuit. Heath's manic commands rang out.

Davin hit the bridge doors, but they didn't open. Locked in. Mecha-Phyla charging his way. Nowhere left to turn.

If you don't have a weapon, best make the enemy shoot themselves.

Davin whipped off his coat as the android closed, Mecha-Phyla's hyper-aggression driving the android into a flying punch. Davin threw the coat up, putting its black curtain between him and the android. Keeping his feet planted, Davin leaned left, giving the android no visible signal his position had changed. Mecha-Phyla did what she was programmed to do, punched right through the coat to where Davin's head had been a split second before.

At least three hairs tore off Davin's head.

The bridge's blast doors weren't closed, the android instead punching into tinted heavy glass. Stuff meant to block sound, provide separation without too much security.

It took the hit in much the same way a nice window might, cracking and shattering with the force.

Davin pivoted, burst through the opening. Heath swore. The android recalibrated, followed Davin into the bridge lobby. The soldier trio backed off, the android's door-busting appearance clearly not expected. With their rifles high, Davin had his clear moment, assessed his options.

Right ahead sat the trio and the hallway. Locked doors everywhere, no easy escape. To the right were the lifts, and fat chance Davin would be able to call one, get inside, and pick a floor without the android smearing him across the walls. Which left option three: a small hatch to the left.

Davin broke towards the life boat, the escape pod mandated near the bridge just in case. The hatch sat closed, but the panel beside it glowed green, ready for use. Davin slapped at it, saw the spiral hatch open, started to dive inside when his momentum stopped, shredded shirt pressed tight against his back. This time, the cheap fabric held and the android threw Davin back across the lobby.

After the table, the floor, hitting the wall next to the lifts just felt like more awful. Stars swam. His lip and nose bled. Davin groped for something to help him up, hit the lift panel, which dinged a cheery chime. Not exactly great music to die to.

Mecha-Phyla stomped across the lobby towards him. No flying punch this time. Maybe the machine learned faster than the earlier versions, adapted to Davin's combat techniques.

Or maybe Heath had made the things sadistic, the android enjoying the moments leading up to Davin's demise.

"Know what?" Davin said to the machine as he stood up,

put his fists forward as if he were going to box the thing. "You're ugly."

Not his best insult, and Davin wasn't a huge fan of how the beatings made his voice slur, but beggars couldn't be choosers.

The android went for a kick this time, one Davin tried to block, turning into it and using his arm as a shield. His left wrist went numb and Davin stumbled right, his back against a lift door.

The android came on again, going for a second kick. Davin ducked this time, catching the blow on his shoulder, a hit that spun him back, back into the opening lift.

A chance!

Davin tried to reach for the lift's panel, to hit any floor, but the panel sat on the lift's left side and Davin's arm wasn't working real well over there. So he turned, reached with his right hand and slapped at the thing. Hit the buttons, heard the cheery acceptance, and felt the android slug him in the ribs as it followed him into the lift.

The blow pressed him into the lift's side as the android took the center. It busted something inside his chest, brought Davin into a perfect clarity. Everything fell away except immediate survival, there in that moment. Animal rage, a desperation against death.

Davin snarled, spat, spun and swung his right hand at Mecha-Phyla's vaguely wrong face. The android didn't give Davin the satisfaction, smashing him and his hit aside with its right arm. The blow sent Davin sprawling, flying from the lift to crash into the lobby's middle.

Nose bloody, tongue bitten, eyes bleary from the several concussions, Davin twisted, looked towards what should've been his death, and saw a closing lift door lock the android behind it. A loud thud, an outward dent appeared, but the lift went on its way.

And so did Davin.

All that pain, all that terror pushed Davin's right arm, his legs into a swimming, scrambling escape. Heath's guard trio, too far back to give the android space and left without a plan, hesitated too long. Heath himself, his shadowed figure still on the bridge, managed a feeble curse as Davin crawled into the lifeboat and jammed the eject.

The little things were made to cram ten people apiece, more if everyone was willing to snuggle real close. Davin had the whole craft to himself, and he drifted as the engines punched him away from the frigate. Zero-g, actually, had never felt so good: less pressure on his busted bones, his bruised lungs.

Simple necessity took over after the first few minutes, Davin reaching for the boat's first aid kit and patching himself up. He expected the frigate, or maybe an Eden fighter to come along and blow him up any second now, but the fatal shot never came.

Heath being weird again?

Pain pills popped, some nutrient goop gulped down, Davin looked out the viewport. Somewhere not too far away, Phyla's burned body would be drifting just like him, out here among Jupiter's moons. He could join her now, pull the manual release lever and kick himself into space.

"But that's not my style," Davin muttered, floating back against the bulkhead.

When Bosser killed Lina, Davin had vowed revenge. It'd taken time, twists and turns, but he'd helped put the man down. He'd done it once, and he could do it again.

Heath Swane. Next up on the hit list.

Davin looked at the boat's small monitor, the little thing telling him the oxygen percentage, fuel amounts, and the destination. Most lifeboats updated their targets based on their position, and this one had found the closest inhabited moon. A big one, a place Davin knew well.

He'd need to get his crew back, and Ganymede wouldn't be a bad place to start.

You'd think the hours burned on the escape pod would've been ripe for reflection, that Davin would've stared out at the stars and thought about Phyla, about how he'd nearly died for Heath's ludicrous whims. Instead, thanks to a particular drug in the boat's kit, Davin slept the whole damn way.

"Hey, you awake?" Asked a curious voice, and Davin opened bleary eyes to see a green-garbed nurse standing over him.

A patient's room, with cream walls and optimistic slogan art pasted around, served as a startling contrast to the spare lifeboat.

"Uh," Davin said, coming to realize he was in a bed, an IV attached to one arm. More surprising, he didn't feel any restraints on his hands, legs. "Where am I?"

The nurse nodded at Davin's question, as if it was a reasonable ask.

"You overdosed yourself," the nurse said. "A mining crew found your ship heading for entry and brought you in. You're banged up, so here you are, Mr. John Doe."

Davin had overdosed himself? He remembered taking the syringe, filling it up to the right amount. The details, though, seemed hazy. Had it been a six or a nine? One dose every hour or two every day?

Concussions did that to a person.

Wait, did she say John Doe?

"You don't know who I am?" Davin asked.

"What, are you some hot shot?"

Davin was about to reply that maybe he was, but the more surprising thing was that Heath hadn't broadcast his escape. Eden should've blown him from the sky, not brought him back to life in what looked to be their hospital.

"Guess not," Davin said.

The nurse veered back to the routine in a hurry. Davin's treatments, his schedule outlined, followed by a particularly critical question: how did Davin expect to pay for all these nice things?

"You have Eden insurance?" The nurse asked, her face indicating exactly how likely she thought that was.

"Sure do," Davin said. "Name's Heath Swane. I'm sure you'll find me."

As soon as the nurse stepped from the room Davin reached over, pulled out his IV. Yanked off the sensors on his chest. The ragged clothes he'd been wearing were piled up on a chair in the corner, and the captain slid himself to the bed's edge, stepped off in their direction.

Nausea struck hard. A dull ache in his back rose up too, though the painkillers Davin must've been swamped with kept the worst away. Holding onto the bed frame, Davin steadied himself, pictured Phyla, how he had a job to do. One he'd never complete if Eden's thugs caught him in here.

Stumbling over to his room's door came next, a lurching, grasping walk made easier by Ganymede's light gravity. Davin fumbled, sure, but he fell so slow he had time to catch himself, adjust. Shutting the door gave him enough privacy to ditch the gown, throw on the clothes. They were filthy, but someone, at least, had given Davin a light bath and swapped in some new underwear.

All on Eden's dime, too. Nice.

One problem: the torn t-shirt didn't hide the IV, the obvious 'I'm a patient on the run' look Davin had. Short of trying to knock someone out, steal their clothes, an action Davin wasn't up to at this particular moment, he'd have to use something different: moxie.

Pulling open his door, Davin peeked out into the unit. The sensors that'd been attached to him had been dinging a confused alarm from the moment Davin took'em off, and now Davin understood why nobody responded: the unit was slammed.

Nurses and doctors and their supporting bots ran this way and that, patients filling the gaps. Injuries, illnesses abounded out here, on moons where the slightest mistakes could cause grievous disasters. Davin's nurse probably figured she could leave him and his stable vitals for a while, tend to some sucker who'd been depressurized or had a limb sliced up building some new ship at Galaxy Forge.

That name brought the first grin to Davin's face as he joined the press, shutting his door behind him and limping into the crowd. His left arm still felt cold: moving it felt like trying to lift some wayward weights. His legs, though, seemed up to the task, and Davin shuffled towards some lifts, ignored and unpressed by a too-busy staff.

Galaxy Forge. The biggest shipyard in the solar system, one now controlled by Eden. Its former masters, though, happened to be Vi's parents. If Davin wasn't totally luckless, they'd still be on Ganymede, with a house Davin knew how to find. They'd have resources, a way to contact the *Jumper* and the other Nines.

Having a plan put some pep in Davin's step, suppressed the headache, the gonna-hurl twinges. As the elevator took Davin to the ground level, squashed in with other patients in various stages of disarray, the Nines captain played out his revenge scenarios.

He'd take the *Jumper* and do a drive-by on Heath's frigate, have Vi pack a digital bomb and dump Fournine on it. Let the former android infect Heath's ship and turn it into a disaster, drain the oxygen, turn the lights off and on, play a recorded message from Davin on loop.

Or they could go the slow burn route, figure where Heath was going to be, wait for him, and ambush the bastard. Then Davin could deliver the end personally. More satisfying.

Either way, the frigate had to go. Mecha-Phyla was an abomination, as were the rest of the androids Heath must be building. Going by that captain's cracks during Davin's life-and-death battle, Heath wanted to bring back the bots.

No thanks.

Not a soul bothered Davin as he left the hospital, standing beneath a thick glass dome on Ganymede's arid surface. Primary transport on the moon meant scooting through tunnels, underground havens serving as radiation-shielded homes for most of the populace. The shuttles were cheap enough, but as Davin watched them pass by, he hesitated.

The Nines had funds, but using his wristlet to buy a ticket would scream a signal out that Davin was here. Even if Heath didn't feel like chasing Davin with his frigate, the Eden authorities standing all of a few meters away directing traffic would be happy to make the arrest.

Instead, Davin pulled up his wristlet. The small text

blurred here and there, and the screen did nothing good for his headache, but Davin managed to put in a query. Found Vi's parent's house, and plotted a course. A long, long walk, but then, Davin had spent a long time in a tiny capsule.

He could use the exercise.

12

SNEEZY SABOTAGE

The *Red Rocket* wasn't red, had zero rockets Davin could find, but it had an owner who wasn't a bot, an owner Davin knew from deliveries another lifetime ago. With his body aching, his clothes looking like they'd been stolen from the trash, Davin left the underground urban center and stepped, floated, bounced into the *Red Rocket*'s mirror-lit interior.

Glitzed up to look like you were drinking inside a rocket engine during launch, the bar and gastropub—according to the sign out front, anyway—had faux flames lining every wall. They played out an animated sequence, one repeating every thirty minutes simulating an old Earth countdown. Pick the right seat and you'd even get a vibration at the end, enough to get unsuspecting idiots to spill sips.

Davin didn't choose the place by accident: the walk from the hospital, spent half falling while Davin grew used to Ganymede's Moon-like gravity, worked as a nostalgia drip, replaying his time with Phyla. One rosy scene after another ran out behind his eyes, the occasional curse from someone he'd bumped knocking Davin back into reality.

The goal had been to get to Vi's parent's place, leverage

that connection into something more fruitful, but as Davin had gone bouncing down from the hospital along Ganymede's wide tunnels, he'd realized showing up in these rags, with this crap hanging over his head, wouldn't work for anyone. Wouldn't work for himself.

He might not be his cocky smuggler self for a little while, perhaps not ever again, but if Davin was going to go all in on vengeance, he'd need a refresh.

Not that Sandeer would give him one for free.

"Don't care," Sandeer said, arms folded behind the *Red Rocket*'s substantial bar counter. "You get one beer. A light one. And that's because Phyla was a damn good woman."

"Then you're kicking me out?" Davin said, on a stool. One that would, most definitely, rattle his ass in twelve minutes when the next rocket launched. "Thought we were friends."

"Friendship goes both ways. You drinking away all my profits? How's that friendship?"

Davin looked around the bar, crowded for a mid-afternoon. Sandeer had outfitted the tables with screens, so patrons could just tap their next order for a bot to provision. Sandeer himself seemed about the only employee in the place, surveying his kingdom from behind the counter.

"Doesn't look like you're hurting too bad," Davin countered.

Sandeer shrugged, "Because I don't let all my friends drink for free."

"You say that like you have friends."

"I'm a bartender. I have plenty of friends."

Davin proposed a toast to Phyla, one Sandeer joined in with a small glass of his own. The prickly man, like so many others, had a heart beneath the shell. A heart that, upon hearing Davin's story, offered up hard information.

"Ganymede used to be its own show," Sandeer said, Davin nursing his sole free beer. "Now Eden's all over it. They've annexed Galaxy Forge and anything here they want. Try to resist and they buy you out with their guns in your face."

"It's how they operate."

"I'm telling you that so you understand your situation. I've seen your face plastered on so many screens around here I was sick of you before you walked in."

"Gee, thanks."

"I'm saying you're going to get yourself cuffed you go walking around lookin' like you."

Davin glanced at himself, made a show of tugging at his ragged shirt. Put his finger through a hole in his shredded coat and wiggled it around.

"You're saying this is what I look like?"

Sandeer rolled his eyes, "I'm saying I don't want to see you get caught."

"So nice of you."

"Because if they catch you, they'll trace you back here, and I don't want Eden knowing I exist."

"Taking back that thanks."

"You can have it," Sandeer said. The barkeep let his eyes go for a run around the space. "Look, as long as you're here, might be something you could help me with. I'll give you some cash to get yourself made over if you do."

"Sandeer, Phyla's dead. Getting back at the people who killed her is all I'm after."

"Of course. Know what I think she'd say to that, though? You're an idiot, Davin. That's what she'd say."

Davin had a good grip on the glass. The counter offered zero protection. With a quick wrist flick he could send the thing smashing into Sandeer's face. He'd get kicked out, arrested, probably shot by some Eden flunky, but it'd feel good.

"Look," Sandeer said, perhaps noticing Davin's ugly expression, "this would hit Eden too. You're helping yourself, hurting your enemies, all in one shot."

"It's nothing you can do?"

"I've got a bar to run, Davin. Can't be missing shifts for this."

As Davin eyed Sandeer, the man's grin only grew. Whatever Sandeer wanted, it would be a crap gig, but then, what choice did Davin have?

If Eden had Vi's family under their thumb, Davin couldn't show up with nothing and expect guest of honor treatment. No, better to go in prepared, armed and ready.

"Tell me," Davin said, pushing his glass forward. "And I'll be needing a refill."

This time, Sandeer didn't object.

DAVIN PULLED THE CAP LOWER, the bill almost covering his eyes as he waited on the bench. Around him, a town square spread beneath a red-rock ceiling. The stone garden park, sporting a few imported trees fed with UV lights around their base, hosted crossing sidewalks leading to the park's corners. Various higher end shops and restaurants surrounded the space, with one side dominated by the city's administrative building.

Unlike the older places on Ganymede, this town had a newer, fresher look. The buildings weren't just stacked blocks and sheet metal, but had been carved right from Ganymede's rock. They didn't have roofs, just continuous columns crawling from top to bottom. Concave windows laced with lights added to the mirrored glow from shafts drilled through from the surface. Even though, by Davin's reckoning, the time was nearly midnight, reflected glows from Jupiter meant it looked like a hazy twilight down here.

The hour, at least, did mean fewer people hopped around. A skiff or a speeder zipping by here and there. Prime delivery time, in other words.

Davin felt the pistol Sandeer had given him, the snub-nosed piece barely fit for a lover's quarrel, much less a mission on this order. Nevertheless, holding the weapon gave Davin a certain grounding, a feeling he had some power again after all the beatings.

At least with this, he could blow off Mecha-Phyla's face if the machine ever showed up again. Sure, it'd have to be a perfect shot, but for that one, Davin figured he could make it happen.

Before that, he'd have to meet his end of Sandeer's little bargain. Still in his rags—Sandeer promised a nicer outfit, but better to commit the crime in old clothes—Davin swept his low look around the square. Still no sign.

Ten minutes left, then the window would be closed.

To keep from drifting into Phyla-induced despair, Davin ventured into other questions: had VI managed to get the *Jumper* fixed? Where'd she gone once she had? Jupiter had plenty of moons, some with the barest amenities. Eden wouldn't be on them all yet. Vi would probably land, make more complete repairs, then reunite with Merc, Opal, and Mox.

His crew would make a cursory pass through Jupiter's space, see if they could pick up any sign Davin and Phyla survived, then, as agreed, they'd jet on to Earth. Find Alissa, stop the war. Something like that.

Davin scratched at his nose, swept his eyes around

again. Caught something more interesting across the way this time.

Pulled by a tug bot before and behind, the speeder-length box trundled into the square, angling for an Eden-branded bar on the far corner. The place had a big 'coming soon' banner hanging over the entry, promising cheap drinks, good food, and discounts for every Eden employee.

"Impossible to compete with a place that has Eden's backing," Sandeer had said. "So I need you to tilt the odds in my favor."

The bartender wanted some sabotage, but Davin balked at the simple plan. Sure, disabling the big machine here might buy Sandeer some time, but Eden could replace the thing without a care.

No, you want to hurt the competition, you ruin the trust. Damage the reputation.

Davin rose from the bench, struck an intercept course across the park. Across the way, on the Eden machine's far side, a group left a restaurant, talking loud. A more fun night than Davin was having.

In the pocket opposite Davin's pistol, the man had a bag filled with Ganymede rock dust. The fine-grained stuff would be packed with radiation, would spoil anything it touched. Slip some into the thing rolling by, which was, by Sandeer's reckoning, a vast beer-and-coffee maker, and people would get sick one by one till Eden had to shut it all down.

A little vicious for Davin's taste, even though he'd suggested the move, but he found a hollow gap where his morality used to live. He'd become more flexible after Lina, more willing to play without the rules in a solar system that didn't care about anybody. Without Phyla, Davin found himself sharing the solar system's view: screw-em all.

Other than his crew, anyway.

He picked up the pace, matching the tugs. Hopefully bots would be handling the installation. Hopefully they'd be cheap ones, not able to handle security at the same time.

The bar's front doors sat wide open, giving Davin a clear trajectory. The tugs were closing in on the corner, they'd have to turn left to get around the intersection, and then a hard right, up over the sidewalk and in. Davin had already cased the area for cameras: the best blind spot to get beneath the box, get into the bar unseen would be during that hard right turn. He'd slip by on the right, bend down as if to tie a shoe, and then—

"Hey, hey you," the call, slurred and washed, came from Davin's right, but aimed at him. "I know you."

Davin glanced that way, saw a young man, younger than him anyway, splitting away from his restaurant pack to stumble towards him. The dude's friends laughed, watched. Davin put together a quick assessment, tried to slot the dude into a known acquaintance: clothes nice enough to go out, but barely. Rough hands, stubbled face, a slight burn scar visible in the soft orange-white light. The man walked like he'd lifted heavy loads for a long time.

Davin didn't know who the hell this was. And the tugs were moving.

"Sorry, wrong guy," Davin deflected, turned back to his walk.

Someone else in the guy's group called out a name, Riley. It rung the dimmest bell. Not one Davin could afford to investigate at this particular moment in time.

One he had to when Riley's hand landed on Davin's shoulder, a couple meters away from the street as the tugs made their left turn. Riley put on enough pressure to force Davin around, and the sorta-familiar face glaring at the

Nines captain this time wasn't that of a jolly drunk, but a look Davin knew well.

He'd been making it a lot himself lately.

"What'd you do with her, you bastard?" Riley asked, then swung his right hand in a clumsy punch.

Davin swept the blow aside, backed out of Riley's reach. He held his own hands up, calling for peace. Last thing Davin wanted now was some dumb Eden police bot, or human, to come give him a once-over.

"Like I said, you've got the wrong guy." Davin looked over Riley's shoulder to the man's buddies, but the restaurant crew seemed as tied off as their friend, watching and laughing from a distance.

"No way I do." Riley jabbed a finger at him. "Your face is everywhere."

Damn Eden and their propaganda. Guess there were downsides to being a celebrity.

Behind him, the tugs stopped, started to shift the container right. The blind spot would be opening up in a couple seconds.

"Don't know what you're talking about," Davin said, back-stepping the right way.

He couldn't turn his back on Riley, though, not with the murderous glint in the man's eyes.

"Yeah you do," Riley said. "She went with you, again, and now she's gone. Again. How many times are you gonna make her throw her life away?"

Time was, Davin might've turned those words into a self-indictment, followed them into a spiral about Phyla, Lina. Right this very moment, though, there was too much going on. His senses were too tied in, adrenaline rushing too fast.

This was Ganymede, home to Galaxy Forge and Viola's

parents. She'd made a life here well before Vi had ever come to the Nines. A life that might've had time for old boyfriends, or friends who wished they were something more.

"Hold on, bud," Davin said. "Tell you what, I'm busy right now, but if you want, we can continue this conversation tomorrow. Say, noon? *Red Rocket*?"

"Screw you," Riley replied, again stepping forward into an obvious punch.

Some men were fighters. Some men were, well, not.

Davin side-stepped the strike, watched as Riley's red-rimmed eyes tried to follow, winced as Davin's own counter socked Riley up and over, putting the man hard on the gravel rock garden. Lights out.

"He'll need help getting home," Davin called to Riley's friends, most of whom were laughing, jeering at Riley's fate. Not a one ran at Davin looking for blood. Davin frowned down at the glassy-eyed guy. "You need better buddies, my friend."

The sound of tugs on tiled floor spun Davin around. The front tug, treads grinding away, had entered the bar. The rear tug was about off the street, meaning Davin's narrow window was just about closed.

Spitting a quick curse, Davin broke into a run, dashing past the rear tug on its right side, crouching and slipping into the half-meter high gap between container and ground. Davin's back protested as he scrambled on elbows and knees, trying to match the tug's pace. His frayed jacket lost more fabric, his shredded shirt disappeared, leaving Davin's skin bearing the burden. His boots, the best things he still owned, weren't good for crawling, and Davin felt the rear tug's treads nipping at his heels.

The bar door passed by on his right, a steel flash, and

Davin rolled at the sight, getting free from the container as it passed into the bar.

Sitting up, pulling on his hat after the roll knocked it free, Davin watched the tugs bring the container into place against the bar's back wall. The big box settled to the ground, taking up two-thirds of the place's rear, leaving the remainder for doors to back rooms, bathrooms. The bar's interior decorating looked half-done, with scattered Eden decals pasted up on green-painted rock walls. A few bulbs hung down from the ceiling, giving a shadowed cast to the whole place.

The whole *empty* place, Davin noted, taking his right hand off the pistol. Despite Sandeer saying nobody would bother being here, Davin's recent experiences had him expecting a fight at any turn. Besides, who would trust two tugs to deliver something this complex alone?

The answer came after the gentle thud, the tugs setting the container down and rolling away. The two machines didn't open the box, just trundled on past Davin and out. At some signal—from the tugs? On a timer? Someone watching?—the bar doors closed and the lights snapped off.

Great. Davin stood in a low-lit, thanks to glows coming from outside, bar with his goal still locked away. To get the poison in its place, Davin would have to open the container.

Worse, for Eden to suspect nothing, he'd have to close it up again.

"Sandeer's going to owe me more beer for this," Davin muttered, feeling his way through the thankfully empty bar to the big box.

For all the griping they'd done about hauling cargo, the experience proved its worth here. The box itself was a standard high value protective container, a stuffed rectangle with opening circles on the corners of each side. Turn'em and the box would fold open like a flower, with a skeletal frame that could be broken down after. Smart people could then take the container, now flat and easy to carry, back to their local shipyard and sell it to someone else.

"Let's see if you'll open for me," Davin said, finding the first two dials along the nearest long side.

A first twist went nowhere, a stiff block that earned a sigh. Of course they'd bothered to lock the container. Davin confirmed his suspicions on the box's left side, where a small pad, hidden before by the tug, asked for a code to unlock the box.

Davin stared at the pad, for a long second thinking it might be better just to screw the whole thing. Disappear, pawn Sandeer's pistol for some cash and make it work.

Because that's what Davin, famed mercenary captain and Earth hero, would do. Skulk away into the dark, failing once again.

"Oh, get over yourself," Davin said, aware how much he was talking to himself, but a bar without conversation felt weird. "There's gotta be a better way."

Ditching the container, Davin circled the box and went towards that back hallway. With the bar itself empty, maybe a possibility waited in its storerooms.

At first, the hallway gave Davin nothing more than the ordinary: some restrooms on the right, a path to a small kitchen and prep area on the left. An office, empty, as the last option. Davin wheeled back, headed to the kitchen.

This seemed like the only finished place in the bar, sporting a large grill top, freezers, and a central island for food prep. Davin's stomach asked him to check the freezers, see if there was a snack maybe not made from nutrient goop waiting inside.

But it wasn't the freezers that held possibility. The

refrigerator offered more hope, a floor-to-ceiling two meter wide behemoth. Davin hadn't heard a sweeter sound than its steady whirr as he moved closer, embracing the potential. And, unlike the container, these doors weren't locked.

With a soft thunk, the fridge unveiled its glory, bathing Davin in a white-blue light.

He'd never seen anything so wonderful.

For a drifter, bar snacks had long been a Davin Masters mainstay. Here, they sat waiting for their chance to shine: cheese curds, stuffed pretzel bites, jalapeno poppers and so much more.

Davin stopped himself as he laid a hand on a pretzel bag. Eden was Eden, meaning they'd be keeping tight tabs on the inventory. They'd probably notice if something went missing.

"But only one bag?" Davin said. "What place wouldn't chalk that up to an error?"

His rational, resistant mind didn't put up a fight, leaving Davin to yank down the food. A quick tear and he had chilly pretzel in his mouth for the first time in days, since the cruise ship. Admittedly, not the longest drought—Davin tried not to remember the dark times, those long journeys across the solar system with nothing but nutrient goop for weeks.

As he munched, musing how much better these would be if Davin took the time to microwave them, the captain looked into his other venture.

With the container unusable, Davin needed to find another option. Thankfully the fridge, that amazing appliance, delivered again. All along its bottom row were jar after jar of coffee and tea mixes, stuff that'd fuel the big machine out there. Dumping the dust into these wouldn't hit all the areas Sandeer wanted—beer, for one, would stay pure—but better a little than nothing at all.

The jars were low tech, nothing more than lids on liquid here. Kneeling, in between pretzel bites, Davin delivered the dust. Eden's shiny new investment would find its customers sick, its reputation shot, and the *Red Rocket* would keep its position as this town's premiere pub.

Mission accomplished.

Davin started out the same way he went in, heading to the bar's main entry only to stop. Outside, in the park, blinking red and blue lights indicated police. They weren't close to the bar, so Davin, still snarfing pretzels—so salty, so delicious—crept up to the front windows, looked out.

Riley. The guy Davin had knocked out, stood with a friend holding him up, delivering an account to a couple cops.

"Bet he's not mentioning how he swung first," Davin muttered. Not that it mattered: Davin was a man wanted by the only power Ganymede respected: Eden. The cops would take him in for that and nothing more.

Guess he'd use an alternate exit.

Through the hallway again, this time to the rear door, Davin slipped out into a back alley. Built for trash collection and late deliveries, the alley was empty. Davin chose left, a longer route, one that'd take him behind the city's main government building, but he'd be farther away from the police before catching open air again.

Phyla would be proud, Davin mused as he hopped, glided, bounced down the alley. Here he was, hitting back at Eden, taking care of himself, and somehow he'd managed not to kill a soul. Phyla hadn't cared so much about that last part—scum was scum, and everyone fighting the Nines happened to be scum—but corpses tended to draw attention, tended to make careers as a racer hard. For some reason, sponsors frowned on body counts.

Not that Phyla would need sponsors anymore, not—

Nope, not doing that, not now.

Davin pulled his bill down, swung a left as he reached the alley's end. Went back into the square, needing to cross it to the other side, head down a few blocks to the *Red Rocket*, where Sandeer said he could hook Davin up with a place to crash for the night. Provided, of course, Davin had done the deed.

Riley and the cops were still chatting. Another one had shown up too, likely meaning Riley had given away Davin's game.

Cool.

Davin took a hop, staying quiet, staying low as he left the alley and began the cross-park trek. The orange-yellow lighting kept things at twilight levels, a musty rust-glow over everything. Speeder engines echoed throughout, a soft thrush soundscape. After his first jump, Davin hesitated, but nobody seemed to notice him. He bounded again, another few meters. Not a soul looked his way.

His throat tickled. Dry from all the pretzels, the salt begging for water to wash it down. He'd get a beer at Sandeer's, just had to make it there before—

The cough came up fast, the chalky salty breading making its demands known. Davin hacked up half a lung, steadying himself on a bench.

When he looked up, a spotlight shone in his eyes. One of the cop speeders drifting his way. Riley, the man's crew, hustling over too, shouting *there Davin was, there he was.*

You wanted to be a captain, sometimes you had to know when you could run, when you needed to hide, when you needed to give up. Davin lurched over to a community trash bin, pretended to cough again and fished out the pistol, dropped it inside.

Better to be unarmed.

The cop speeders veered around from both directions as Davin took a seat back on the bench, put on a smuggler's grin. Panic, fear, neither seemed to touch him. After Heath and his androids, Ganymede's local cops weren't worth it. If they handed Davin off to Eden? Well, Davin had escaped that before, plenty of times.

Besides, as the cops lifted Davin off the bench, as Riley approached and pointed a bleary finger Davin's way, the captain had a new idea.

"Vi's all alone out there," Davin said to Riley's face, the man's bluster dying at her name. "I was the only one that could help her, and now she's going to die. All because of you."

One of the cops told him to shut up, slapped some stun cuffs around his wrist, but Davin didn't break his stare with Riley, not till the speeders jetted off into Ganymede's night.

13

EXTRACTION

Getting stuck in cells felt real old. At least this one didn't have Eden's meditative crap playing on a TV. In fact, the cell didn't have a TV at all. Just blank walls. A metal bench. A more modern laser gate cutting off the outside. Davin didn't get a phone call, didn't get an explanation of his rights, and he didn't have to ask why that was.

The cops told him straight out: they didn't care about him punching Riley. Eden wanted Davin's guts, and they were going to get'em.

Look on the bright side, the officer said as they brought Davin into the station: Davin wouldn't get booked here. He'd have no criminal record on Ganymede. Then the cop laughed, saying if Eden did what everyone expected, Davin wouldn't have to worry about a criminal record anywhere.

Real jokers, these guys.

So Davin sat, laid down, twiddled his thumbs. Stared at the slate wall across the way and tried to imagine replays of his favorite movies. Listened to the occasional chatter from elsewhere in the station, though the late night kept things quiet. Eventually, curling up on the bench, Davin tried to sleep.

More hours shot passed, Davin only waking up in full when a new trio, all done up in Eden-green garb, appeared before his cell. He recognized the one in the middle, wearing a thick boot over her left foot.

"Didn't make it very far, did you?" Aya asked.

"Good morning to you too," Davin replied. "How's that foot?"

Aya's eyes flashed ice, but her surreal demeanor remained. She looked to her left, told the cops to open the cell. The lock clicked off, the Eden guy to Aya's right slid the door open.

And Davin went for it.

They'd left the cuffs off him in the cell, necessary freedom for things like food and using the toilet, so Davin leveraged his fists. First, he caught the cell door, swung it back across his body and into the second Eden guard stepping in. The iron bars mashed the man into Aya, leaving Davin with a one-on-one with the last Eden goon.

The man pulled a stun baton, came at Davin swinging. Backing up a step to buy him a second, Davin threw off his grungy coat, wrapped it around his right hand. When the guard swung the baton again, Davin caught it. All those electric nerve numbers faded out against the leather, letting Davin pull the guard close for a gut punch from Davin's eager left.

The goon gave a good gasp and Davin threw him aside, ripping the stun baton free in the process. A flip from his left, dropping the jacket, and Davin had the baton in his right hand ready for use.

The cell door clanged, locked. On the other side, Aya leveled a laser at him.

"You're always so much fun," Aya said, then fired.

Once, twice, three times.

Davin hit the ground, his body a rattling mess. His vision went black, blurred, snapped into focus even as his head exploded in a migraine's shattering pain. He bit his lip, his left hamstring snarled in a legendary cramp.

One bolt would numb a man. Two would knock him out. Three overloaded everything, wild spasms everywhere, and Davin writhed as his muscles lost control.

"That's better," Aya said, and while he couldn't do anything, couldn't really comprehend what was happening, Davin heard the cell door open again.

Sensations made sense several hours later, when, stuck in an Eden speeder, Davin stopped thrashing. Aya and her goons tied him up, strapping his arms and legs together like some flimsy cargo. They had Davin pressed up against the side window in the bubble speeder, a long and narrow craft built for swiftness.

The ship's microjets operated in concert with the thruster pair at the speeder's back, propelling the cone-like craft with its domed roof along Ganymede's highways. Those highways operated underground, so Davin's twitching eyes caught smoothed rock walls, orange and brown and beige, and little else.

"Awake?" Aya asked. She sat next to Davin in the speeder's two-by-two setup, with the guard pair up front. "I always find three shots so much more fun than one or two, don't you?"

Davin couldn't muster the control to turn his head around. He could breathe though, so he tried an angry sigh. Mostly failed.

"You can learn a lot more from someone when they're out of control," Aya said. "The expressions are really so unique. Perfect for modeling."

Modeling? What? Davin closed his eyes for a second, tried to concentrate. Even shut his eyelids splayed rainbow bolts, synapses going crazy.

"You didn't seem as terrified by the android as we expected," Aya continued musing. "Captain Swane wasn't so happy with that, but we did have to work fast. You interrupted our process, you little meddler you."

Mecha-Phyla? Is that what Aya was talking about? Davin managed a shudder at the machine's distorted face. Close, but with too many imperfections. Eyes stretched a little too far, the nose at too sharp an angle. Teeth too perfect for any human.

"And then you go and land way out here. No spots for our frigate to dock, and with your lady having taken our only shuttle, we had to make quite a trip." Aya clicked her tongue. "Next time, if you would please do as we ask, it will be so much easier."

"Die?" Davin wheezed. His tongue flopped fat in his mouth. "You want that?"

"Exactly, but in a particular way, or you will be of no use," Aya continued. "Captain says we have enough footage now from your earlier fight to make the message work, though. So congratulations, your job is almost done. Now all we need is the finale."

Davin tried isolating his muscles. One by one he wiggled his toes as Aya talked, then his calves and his hamstrings, climbing up his body. With effort, he could shove aside the spasms, quiet the tremors.

It'd be a bit yet before he could elbow Aya in the face and get her to shut up, but there was hope.

Outside, the walls opened into another town. More buildings cropped up, closer together and populated than the place Davin had been. Ganymede had a few cities scattered across its surface, most serving various Galaxy Forge shipyards. The smaller outposts, like where Sandeer's *Red Rocket* held serve, hosted the nuts and bolts people keeping Ganymede running: farmers, mechanics, brewers.

Especially the brewers.

This place hummed with activity, enough to force the Eden speeder to slow down as it entered traffic. Other speeders, trundling bots, and humans on various single-person craft clogged the roadways. Aya, mercifully, killed her monologuing and turned to her wristlet.

Which meant she didn't see the rumbling skiff coming up from behind. Davin caught the craft from its reflection in the window, the skiff swerving around traffic in a dead heat towards them. A barreling bruiser craft, one meant for heavy duty work, the skiff didn't match the svelte Eden speeder on a straightaway, but it had momentum and surprise.

One of the Eden goons up front noticed, started to ask what the hell was going on. Aya glanced up, turned, shouted —still without the real panic Davin would've expected—to move. The Eden speeder lurched forward, crunched against a tug waiting for a hovering traffic light to change. The Eden guard cursed. Davin flexed his hands, found them ready to work.

The skiff swung out right, scraping against a building and scattering people, trash bins, a poor plant from the sidewalk. It swerved back towards the Eden speeder and slammed its back right corner.

The skiff's sloping front sent the Eden speeder up and over, into a low-gravity tumble. The glass bubble roof shattered, shards falling away from Davin as the speeder turned over and over in the air. Someone screamed.

Davin focused. They'd tied his hands together, yes. Dropped them in his chest, down near his waist. Right where the clasp for the seatbelt sat. As the speeder tumbled, its underside smashing into a building's roof and bounding higher, Davin found the clasp's release. Pressed it.

And fell.

Low gravity collected its fee as the speeder turned faster than Davin dropped, whacking Davin in the back as it spun. The hit gave Davin extra speed as he slammed into the building's roof, striking gravel, spraying rock everywhere.

Not a perfect ten landing, but Davin could live with it.

Lunging to his left, Davin rolled onto his back. With his hands and legs still tied together, he wouldn't be going anywhere. Stun cuffs couldn't exactly get removed by rubbing them against sharp rocks either.

So what next?

Davin stared upward, Ganymede's rock ceiling splaying across his vision. Sirens and shouting carried through the air, expected after a skiff crash like that. Aya and the Eden boys would've had the worst of it, rolling along the rooftops. Davin tried to look right, brushing his cheek against gravel, and saw only a battered break in the roof's lip where the skiff had gone over.

What a fun ride that would've been.

The rescue's stall didn't last long: Davin's mental timer, a skill honed from too many precision tasks, put the gap between his falling from the skiff and the team rushing onto the roof at six minutes and thirty three seconds.

Just enough time to ditch a vehicle, scale a building, and find Davin lying there like a perfect package for the picking up.

The four folks rushing him looked, well, looked like home. They wore more wraps than actual clothes, stitched outfits showcasing colored patches, fabrics, leathers. Goggles abounded, scarfs fluttered in the air-purifying breeze.

"Stay still," said the first one to reach him, voice gravelly and modulated. These folks really did not want anyone finding their identities. "It'll go faster that way."

"You see me moving?" Davin replied. His commitment to corpse-like rigidity increased as a sharp whine struck up, a laser saw getting ready for business. "Be careful with that, okay?"

The person didn't reply. The other three fanned out around Davin, all carrying Eden-grade rifles. Pistols. Grenades. The Eden branding threw Davin—did the big company have factions so at odds with one another to get this aggressive?

He felt the vibration as the saw bit into the cuffs around his wrists. Felt the stinging sparks bite into his skin as metal melted. Davin cursed, then closed his mouth. He didn't know these people, couldn't show weakness.

Soon enough, the cocky scoundrel would have to make an appearance, and they'd have to believe him.

As Davin's rescuer popped his wrists free, one of the other trio shouted, raised their weapon and pulled the trigger. A lime green bolt flew out, Davin following the aim to see its target: an Eden drone, a squat cylinder coated in cameras and weapons. The machine took the hit, spun to hide the damaged section, and fired back.

The wrapped person took the hit on the shoulder, grunted, and returned fire. The other two joined him, the laser trio laying into the drone too fast for it to compensate.

With a pop, the bot dropped from the sky, clattering to the roof.

The fighter who'd taken the hit started towards the drone, stopped by a whistle from the one cutting Davin's leg's free.

"No time for salvage," Davin's cutter said. "Did the shot get through?"

"It's not serious," the wounded one replied, holstering his rifle, apparently quick to change priorities. They bent over Davin. "Can you walk?"

With a snap, the cuffs on Davin's legs broke apart. Sure, he still had the metal bands on his ankles and wrists, but now they were fashion accessories. Curling up, Davin took the offered hand to get to his feet.

"I can hop," Davin replied. "Where to?"

Davin's cutter, who Davin took to be the leader of this particular squad, looked towards the rooftop door they'd used to get up here. Started in that direction, until a resounding boom shook their building, smoke rising up.

"That's the skiff," said the wounded one beside Davin.

"Not good," Davin said. "Tell me you have a backup?"

"Several," replied the leader, spinning on their heel in the gravel. "Let's get to the extraction."

Deciding to play the follower, Davin kept in line as the foursome turned southward, back towards the highway everyone had come in on. Acting a bit like superheroes, the whole bunch took running leaps off the building's roof, soaring into the air. With Davin in the middle, the group hit the next building before jumping off again, bounding along.

"So, thanks and all, but who are you guys?" Davin asked the wounded one, who's breathing crackled but otherwise seemed okay. "Want to know if I'm getting rescued, or just swapping torture chambers."

"Worry about that after we get away," the person huffed, voice sounding the same garbled gravel as the leader.

Getting away initially looked like a good bet: besides that one Eden drone, probably already assigned to monitor Aya's speeder, no other souls tried to intercept. Drones didn't fill Ganymede's underground air, nor did shock troops jet up to their faces and demand surrender.

No, for the first few jumps, the only problem seemed to be sticking their landings. Davin, least experienced at the low gravity hops, tended to travel a few extra steps every jump. The others found difficulties in their outfits, rogue wraps tripping them up, ill-fitting boots not catching the right grip.

Davin's professional eye said the group had guts, had good ideas, but weren't exactly pros.

A judgment that would've been fine if Aya had been a stock-standard Eden pencil-pusher.

Davin and the other four bent their legs, cleared the last building for a drop to the ground. The city's edge lay before them, the development petering out into ramshackle storage sheds and sedate construction equipment. Stuff that would spring to life once more investment capital came in.

For now, Davin landed next to a hulking digger, using the thing's giant shovel to balance his descent.

"C'mon, hurry," the leader said, pointing towards a particularly battered shed.

Isolated towards the construction yard's back, getting to the shed required a fifty meter straight sprint or a jump through the same, a trek started by the leader and finished, for them, not five meters later.

Soaring through the air, the one who cut Davin free took three red bolts in succession, all to the side. Lasers didn't kill momentum, so even as the wrapped figure slumped, his body continued through the air only to land in a crumple near the shed.

"Dammit," cursed the wounded one, drawing the rifle again. "Move and shoot, don't stand still."

Good advice, better if Davin had a weapon. He said as much as the now-four of them broke for cover. The wounded fighter tossed Davin a pistol as they hunched behind the digger's shovel, looking for enemies.

And seeing none. The yard was quiet. No drones. No approaching squads. Flashing police lights echoed over the rooftops, blocks away.

"Where are they?" called one of the others, crouched behind the digger's big treads to Davin's left.

"Obey your own words," Davin said. "We can't sit here."

"But we don't know where they are," the wounded one replied.

"They know where we are, and that's bad. Get going."

When the other three hesitated—the third with their back to the digger halfway down its bulk—Davin realized he really was dealing with rookies. Brave ones, but not people ready for a serious fight.

"You and you," Davin said, changing his tone from helpful buddy to the commander these folks needed, "break back towards the dump sled. You and me," Davin nodded to the wounded one, "get to watch, see if we get any looks."

"We doing what this guy says now?" Asked the figure by the treads. "Isn't he—"

Two more red shots lanced out from behind them, striking the speaker in the chest and sending them down to the dirt.

Davin wheeled, raising the pistol and aiming, catching only a blur shifting behind some stacked sewer line piping.

"New plan," Davin said. "You two, break for the shed now. I'll cover you."

This time, neither one questioned Davin's orders, jumping right to it. The two bouncing towards the shed did exactly what Ganymede begged them to: using the big digger, both jumped and bounded off its upper cabin, getting height to cross the distance in a single leap.

Sure, they might've been able to creep past vehicles to keep themselves better defended, but who needed that with Davin and his wounded pal providing cover fire?

With the pistol raised, Davin held down the trigger, sending shot after shot towards the sewer cylinders. His buddy did the same, the man's rifle burning energy to fill the air with crisp green death.

The attacker didn't show. The two bounders hit the shed, slipped through the doors. Davin let up the lasers, registered the slim remaining power in his pack.

"Tell me there's a way out in there," Davin said, slow-hopping around the digger, looking everywhere at once.

"Should be," the wounded one said, tailing Davin close with the rifle raised. "Where is this guy?"

"Scared'em away, maybe?"

Not that Davin believed it. Since the start, the odds had only gone in the enemy's favor. Retreating now wouldn't make sense. Not unless . . .

"Get to the shed," Davin said. "Now."

"But—"

"I'll cover you."

The person didn't argue. They did, though, toss Davin their rifle before making a lurching, half-hearted hop towards the shed. Slipping the pistol into a pocket—hardly a good holster, but Davin lacked options—the captain raise the rifle and went deeper into the construction site.

Stacked blocks, carved Ganymede stone lay about ready to be hauled. Heavy duty speeders sat near other diggers, closed down cranes. Ganymede's constant yellowed light slanted in from drilled mirrors above. Dust clogged the air, as it always did underground.

Davin kept tight to cover, stepping around one crate to another bulldozer, to a third collection of steel beams. He checked the ground, saw no footprints. Checked the air, saw no drones.

And yet, all his experience screamed ambush. The rescue attempt started strong, but they'd been slow crossing the rooftops in the open. Eden could be caught flat-footed, but their sheer power meant any advantage disappeared before too long.

"Davin Masters," Aya's voice called out, rising over the distant sirens, the whirrs of technology at work. "You are a hard man to catch, you know that?"

Davin said nothing. Kept low, tried to trace the sound.

"I don't find these games fun," Aya continued. "I am not a hunter. I am a scientist, like Captain Swane, and I hope you understand why we need you."

Not really, but chalk that up to things Davin didn't give a damn about.

"So if you would be kind as to come out, then we can all get on with our lives?"

Davin stopped, held his breath. The big barrels stood on his right, a broad nothing on his left as Davin worked the site's outer edge.

Aya wouldn't be talking unless she'd readied up the next part. Wouldn't be chancing a discovery if she wasn't planning on it.

Okay, hotshot. What's the play?

Davin fished the pistol from his pocket, threw the

weapon in a spinning arc over the barrels. It flew high, almost floating in the light gravity.

And there it was, the slightest shift off to his left, nestled near a monstrous backhoe. The light changed, a shadow moved to track the pistol.

Time to stop playing quiet.

Davin took one, two steps to round the barrels and kicked off with the third, bringing up the rifle as he left the ground behind. Again the shadows shifted, their splay out beyond the backhoe's block cabin giving Aya away.

She pivoted around the corner, her own rifle ready, right into Davin's drawn bead.

Davin pushed the trigger, sent the bolts crashing towards Aya. They struck home as she flung herself behind the backhoe. Davin couldn't tell how many hit—two, three? —before he landed, falling forward enough to catch himself with his left hand. Pushed off to keep up the run.

But when he rounded the backhoe, Aya wasn't there. Just a blood slick, warm and on the rock.

Davin whirled around, wondering where the ambush was. No way Aya called him out just to fight one on one.

The backhoe shuddered, causing Davin to spin around. The cockpit was empty, the source not level with him but above. Tilting up, Davin groaned.

"You again?" He said, Mecha-Phyla looking down at him.

She'd been dressed up in an Eden uniform, had a stacked belt and several holsters with weapons of all kinds. If she'd outmatched Davin on the frigate's bridge, here she outclassed him and all his rescuers put together.

As Davin saw her, Mecha-Phyla drew a pistol, aimed a shot. One Davin couldn't hope to dodge.

So he fired instead, his arms not yet making the same trek as his eyes. The rifle lanced into the backhoe, lasers burning deep into electronic equipment, into the batteries. Davin let the machine do his dirty work.

The backhoe exploded, launched Davin backward, the heat washing over him as Davin blew through stacked pallets. His hands went numb, his face took a hundred cuts, splinters made their marks everywhere, and Davin landed on his back in the dirt. The rifle long gone. His vision swam. He coughed up something that might've been blood, might've been Ganymede rock dust.

And while his ears rang, while his nose smelled his own blood, Davin nonetheless heard a vibration he recognized: the low, constant hum of a speeder's microjets.

The janky craft, as covered with dust and neglect as Davin himself, pulled up next to him. Arms reached down, picked Davin up from the dirt and dropped him in the speeder's back seat. The open-topped craft shot forward, veering away from the construction site and into an open, underground plain.

"Sit tight, Davin," said the wounded one, sitting up front. When Davin failed to reply—his lungs couldn't seem to fill with air—the man looked back, frowned. "You okay, captain?"

You okay?

You okay?

14

BOUNTY BROADCAST

The water had a weird smell. Davin noticed, seeing as it went up his nose on the second splash. He blinked his eyes open, expecting a headache, expecting aches and pains and feeling none.

Even though the sight of Sandeer, of a motley bunch looking him over in the *Red Rocket*'s bowels should've inspired plenty.

Then Davin noticed what Sandeer was throwing at him.

"Beer?" Davin coughed, and Sandeer grinned. Heads nodded, the crowd started to disperse. Show's over, captain was awake. "You're throwing beer at me?"

"Keg was old anyway," Sandeer said. "You're always asking me for free drinks."

"Not exactly what I meant."

"Be more specific next time." Sandeer put the glass down. "Welcome back, Davin."

As to where he was being welcomed back to, Davin wasn't sure. He guessed the *Red Rocket*'s basement only because stacked cases and kegs to his right bore the bar's decal. Davin himself felt a loose tablecloth beneath him, protecting what appeared to be a standard metal work-bench. Hardly a hospital. While he wasn't hurting, Davin did feel itches here and there, and a crawling exploration with his fingertips confirmed stitches and long thick lines still moist with healing jelly.

"Now I wasn't there, so I'm not going to criticize, but next time maybe you try to get some distance between you and the thing you're blowing up," Sandeer said, grimacing at Davin's injury exploration. "You're lucky Eden's pissed off everyone on this planet, including the doctors."

The remark prompted questions, and Sandeer, for once forthcoming, gave answers. When Eden decided on their takeover-by-force of Ganymede, streaming in with their ships and soldiers and sweet nothings about working together, those who knew better banded up, started operations to make Eden's life hellish.

Odd, how that seemed to happen with the places Eden trampled on.

"Don't get any grand ideas," Sandeer said. "Nobody here thinks we're gonna kick Eden off our rock. You're not getting an armed uprising from me."

Davin, still laying on the bench, laughed.

"Do I look like I'm ready for that?"

"You look like shit, but you always did."

"Cuts deep, Sandeer." Davin slid his elbows, sat up. Felt something lurch in his guts at the move. "Why'd you bother coming after me?"

"I didn't want to," Sandeer said. "Apparently you said something that has Riley all—"

"Riley? That kid's in your band?"

"Sometimes I wonder if every 'kid' on Ganymede's in our band," Sandeer shook his head. "He's got a good mechanical head on his shoulders. A bit hot, likes the pints too much, but he'll fight for what he believes in." Sandeer pointed at Davin. "Which is, for reasons unknown to me, you."

"Not me," Davin replied. "Viola, the girl he grew up with. She jumped back in with us. I told him that before the cops grabbed me."

"Young love?"

"Don't know about her," Davin said. "So Riley has enough pull to get you guys to throw a team together?" As he spoke, Davin remembered the casualties. "Ah, damn. Sorry."

Sandeer's eyes flashed, a bartender's mask keeping the sentiment suppressed. "It's getting worse, and it's going to get worse still unless we do something bigger. Riley says you're the key to the plan."

"What plan?"

"Shutting down Galaxy Forge."

The solar system's biggest shipyard didn't exactly operate on a switch. Davin couldn't wander into the right room, tug a cord from an outlet, wipe his hands and watch as a thousand ships ceased construction in an instant. Riley, though, insisted something close to that really existed, the switch just looked a little different.

"Every shipyard runs on a single connected software platform," Riley said, this time up in the *Red Rocket*. Five of them, Sandeer not included, huddled over pints in the early evening—Davin had burned the day in recovery. "All the steps to get a fighter out looking perfect, get a frigate made to spec, they all come through the computers."

Riley burned through the explanation with an idealist's energy, giving most of his glances to Davin. Whatever heated hate Riley had from the previous night seemed gone, despite the bruise on the man's jaw where Davin had walloped him. Riley hadn't yet revealed the why for the change.

Maybe it was pity, as Davin had to be helped up and into the bar booth by a couple others sitting with them. His pint glass held water, not beer. Nutrient goop smoothies had been his sole food all day. A nightmare.

"So we kink the software," said a man to the right, another youngster. His eyes twinkled with artificial enhancements, jagged lines on his arms said he embraced a cybernetic life. "Can't be that hard."

"It is," Riley said, again looking at Davin. "Why do you think Eden's kept Galaxy Forge's founder alive? He's got the key, the only universal backdoor that could bring down every project at once."

"Why?" Cyborg dude asked. "What's the point in making something like that?"

"Life insurance," Davin answered, drawing eyes as he nodded to the cyborg man. "You get where he's at, you attract bad motives. I'd bet he has Galaxy Forge tied in to his heartbeat. Someone offs him without the right code at the ready and it's over."

A risky move if you had competition wanting you knocked out, but Galaxy Forge had none. Not on their scale. Humanity's space-ward expansion wouldn't grind, but collapse if all these shipyards shut down.

Back to Riley, Davin continued, "Question. Why would he want to shut down Galaxy Forge? Eden's not going to go away if he does."

"He won't," Riley said. "No chance. But he's not the only one with the code."

Sometimes, running a process of elimination takes time. Others, it's a finger-snap and done.

"He gets it," Riley continued, watching Davin. The man

had a limp smile, as if he was ashamed about what he was going to say. "Viola will know what it is. If we can get her here, I bet she'd be able to shut the whole thing down."

Davin relayed her last known circumstances: adrift, alone, possibly dead.

"Not what you believe though," Riley countered, the others at the table picking up this had become a two-man game. "You wouldn't have said her name if you didn't think she was alive."

Davin wasn't so sure about that: manipulation was manipulation, but crossing this guy on his crush while in recovery seemed like the wrong move to make. Davin's stomach recoiled at the idea of taking another punch.

"Then we need a way to get a message out," Davin said. "Don't suppose any of you jokers have a comm handy?"

The group looked among themselves, sharing in some stupid secret Davin didn't know. Finally the woman spoke up, leading in with a self-incriminating sigh.

"Nobody's got long-range comms anymore. Started with the rebels," the woman shot a glare Riley's way. "Don't give me that look, Riley. Alissa's bunch weren't all saints either. Didn't want anyone getting Eden cash for selling secrets. Took all they could find, and then Eden comes here and does the same thing, same reason but opposite sides if you get what I'm saying."

"Bunch of paranoids," another man said. "Now we gotta reserve time at the central comm center to send a message. It all gets reviewed too, so don't get your hopes up."

Davin drummed his fingers on the table. Felt the sticky aftermath of a thousand beers between each touch. Ganymede's time had come a while ago. Most of its infrastructure, by space standards, was old. Which meant opportunities.

"Riley," Davin said, "think you could get me in that comm center? Right into its beating heart?"

"Beating heart?"

"The middle. Where the messages go through."

Confusion reigned, and Davin had to remind himself he was working with bartenders, with shopkeepers and teachers. Not soldiers, splicers, spies.

By the time he'd put together a plan, Davin had swallowed a second round of pills, Riley had switched to beers, and the *Red Rocket*'s regulars had arrived for another night in Jupiter's shadow.

DAVIN SPENT three days lingering in the *Red Rocket*'s basement, getting a poor man's spa treatment. Ointments, dressing changes, even a half-hearted massage by someone Sandeer knew. When he wasn't sleeping, Davin lounged with other incoming and outgoing members of the upstart faction. They had a nasty enthusiasm, if not the guerrilla skills to go with it.

Eden drones were everywhere, their soldiers in the streets supplanting local cops. Captain Heath Swane cut radio and television announcements calling for Davin, a reward on the offer. The man didn't have much dramatic flare, only his talking mug facing the camera with an end-cut to Davin's old mercenary head shot.

"Gave you about ten years there," Sandeer said, showing Davin the video on the basement's sole frizzy screen. Sandeer may have been reluctant to give free beer, but water flowed readily, the glasses coming one after another. All recycled, of course. A mental leap anyone living in space had to take.

"Feel I'm more refined now," Davin said, stretching a leg as he stood. "Wisdom and all that."

"That so?"

Davin saw Phyla there, off to the side rolling her eyes. She'd be telling him to move his ass. Stop lazing around. Sure, his muscles, his busted up body could use the time, but the drugs were doing the work. Davin could make it.

"Yeah," Davin replied to Sandeer, keeping his eyes on the screen. Sports updates now, teams Davin used to follow back in the days he wasn't getting shot at. "When Phyla and I ran cargo the last few years, we had the chance to take a good look at what, at who we were."

"Found much there to your liking?"

Davin was about to answer when he stopped himself, looked at Sandeer, the man sitting, relaxing off shift and yet projecting that bartender aura so strong. An ear ready to listen, advice set to deliver.

"What do you care?" Davin asked. "We're all just here to use each other, get what we can till someone blows us apart."

"Nihilist now?"

"That'll happen when . . . " Davin shrugged.

"Best way to break out of funks like what you're in is to get something to do," Sandeer said. "Thankfully, that job's waiting, ready to go tonight."

"Is it? Me, half-crippled, and what team?"

"No team. You and Riley. The kid's good with computers, he'll get you the connection. We've got a diversion ready, should draw all the attention away." Sandeer put his hands on his knees, gripped them tight enough to press seams into his stained jeans. "Nobody wanted to go with you, Davin. Not after what happened to Callie and Aiguo."

The two who'd died saving Davin's ass.

"So you're cowards then. Not ready to give it all up."

"We're business owners. Civilians. The ones who used to pay your Nines to keep us safe," Sandeer said. "We want all this to end, just like what you've been saying, because it's damn bad for business. But I'd rather take some rough years on the balance sheet than lose my life."

"Good to know how committed you are."

"Wars are fought by the soldiers, Davin. Get to it."

GANYMEDE'S NIGHT didn't look all that different from its day, especially outside the comm center. Built on the surface under a radiation-blocking dome, the comm center resembled a sea urchin, albeit one whose spines made you tingle with all their transmissions. Davin couldn't see the wires spreading out into the ground from the building, veins leading all over the moon to deliver Internet connections, streaming data, but all the signs made it clear: stick a shovel in the ground out here and you'd split a settlement from the system.

He and Riley had themselves shrouded in coffee and stale snacks, ensconced in a booth at an all-hours restaurant meant to serve those hungry talkers coming and going from the comm relay. If you had your own ship, happened to have enough money to buy your own long-distance comm, you could beam a message right from Ganymede to Mars. Otherwise you could package up your message, drop it into the long traffic stream shot out from here to satellites. Would take a while, would need compression.

Wanted a live chat? You came here, synced up with your counterpart, enjoyed the few minutes time delay between sides.

Davin confirmed his count: two people had gone in the

comm relay since he and Riley arrived. None had left. Late enough to slow down visitors, but time differences ensured places like this would be open at all hours.

"No collateral damage," Riley repeated between coffee sips. "I know how you do things, but we're not that way."

"How I do things?" Davin asked, swirling cream around his own mug. The beige ceramic thing had a shadowed Jupiter with a smiley face on it. "And just how is that?"

"There's a reason Eden wants you."

"Yeah, because I'm real good at beating them." Davin glanced over Riley's shoulder, saw Phyla shaking her head at him in the diner's buzzing platinum lights. "Real talk, Riley. You ever done anything like this before?"

"I helped Vi steal her father's ship," Riley replied. Davin wasn't sure whether the man's confidence was an asset or a trap. "I've gone along on other jobs. Bar fights."

Davin nodded, swirled his cream again. No answers arose from the steam or the white-brown mix.

"Then you're going to let me lead, okay?" Davin asked. "If I need you to do something, I'll give you the cue."

The captain expected some pushback. Riley declaring this was his idea or some other crap. Instead, the young man accepted the terms. No resistance while they waited for Sandeer's diversion.

Davin found the reason for Riley's playing nice without much trouble.

"You want to get off this rock," Davin said.

"Hells yes," Riley replied, shoulders going slack, as if Davin punctured some tense mystique. "Please, if we get your crew and ship back, let me go with you."

"Every member on the Nines has a point. What's yours?"

"Need a fixer?"

The diversion crackled. Popped. Smiled. Sang. A bulky

speeder, a yellow-blasted box about the length of the diner, pulled up in front. Its microjets burned to keep it steady till the landing struts came down, settled the speeder on the flattened rock. Amid all the pastel yellow were pink words, ones advertising cheap, delicious tacos. Jaunty music popped out as the speeder settled, imploring anyone listening that their day was about to be made better.

"This is what Sandeer's talking about?" Davin said, doing his best to remain credulous.

Riley nodded, grinning, "It's owned by one of us. You're not from around here, so you won't understand."

But Davin could see, and what he saw was astounding. The diner's own meager guests, and all the human employees he could see, hustled from their booths outside. The couple-dozen strong crowd swarmed the truck. Seconds later, the comm relay's doors opened and more streamed forth from there too.

Five, in fact. The two visitors and what looked like three Eden employees. Everyone all about the tacos.

"What is this?" Davin asked, finally giving in and downing his coffee.

"Stardust Salsa," Riley said, and Davin could've sworn the man licked his lips as he spoke. "Best tacos in the solar system right there."

"Sure, but now?"

"Doesn't matter, Davin. Stardust shows up somewhere, you drop what you're doing and get it. Never know when or where it'll appear again."

Davin stood, the opening was there, even if he was more fascinated with this mysterious taco truck. "Tell me as we walk."

Riley did: Stardust Salsa had a few speeders like this cruising Ganymede. They kept their hours unpredictable, offering only cryptic hints about where they might appear next, and when. Among the moon's populace, Riley figured there wasn't a game more played than puzzling out Stardust's schedule.

"The ones who do it best get so many followers. I know one, he's got sponsors of his own now, makes a solid living just telling people where to get their tacos," Riley said as they hop-walked towards the comm relay.

"If it clicks for you, I suppose."

The diversion also worked its own wonders. Nobody accosted Davin and Riley as they step-bounced towards the entry, a single-wide sliding door pressed into the rust-red comm relay building. Various decals sat around the entry, each one calling out a company sponsoring this or that satellite, this or that network. A separate standing screen alongside the door posted by-minute prices for outgoing chat, video, and file packages.

Back on Miner Prime, sending a message off-station meant a journey to the higher levels. Meant getting sideways looks from wealthier folks wondering what someone dusted up might possibly have to say to the universe at large.

Getting the long-range comm on the *Jumper* had been more than a necessity, it'd been a thumbing of the nose at all those who'd given Davin all that silent judgment.

And now he'd get one more chance to deliver some payback against the haughtiest, nastiest company out there.

Davin led, and the inside lobby made good on its promise, setting newcomers into a square space with a broad screen on a back wall. The several-meter-wide monitor showcased options, and a taped up sign beneath held a black arrow pointing left, to a second door that, another sign declared, would only unlock once payment had been accepted.

Not the way Davin and Riley cared about.

Staff came and went through the right side, a standard rectangle with a standard ID scanner lock.

Riley fished a card from his pocket, lifted from a comm relay staffer after a few free drinks from Sandeer and a subsequent dance party.

Apparently that was the preferred method here: all subterfuge, all subtlety.

Davin dinged the card against the scanner, the door clicked open, and the pair went right on in.

You think you know computers, how complex things can get once you'd seen the cockpit of a ship like the *Jumper*, with its myriad systems and analog back-ups to every digital operation. The comm relay's central room dwarfed the *Jumper*'s arrays, spreading them out in a circular circuit forest that had Davin whistling as he and Riley made their entrance.

Soft red lights embedded in the floor gave off just enough glow to keep toes from stubbing on the rolling chairs scattered throughout, but otherwise dimness seemed to be the day's order: dark-mode monitors arrayed through the space detailed incoming, outgoing, and scheduled transmissions from everywhere.

"Busy busy," Davin said, angling for the override console on the right. "This place is the catch-all for the moon?"

"This half of it," Riley answered.

Conversations between ships, between spaceports and their visitors, between land-based travelers . . . it all routed through here. At a tap, if Davin wanted to, he could listen in to any frequency, rebroadcast it as needed to other bands. He could, say, blurt out a litany of Eden's crimes and send them on every wave.

Hmm.

But business first.

The override console required another ID tap, but then Davin and Riley were in. Fournine and the *Jumper* always listened to a specific frequency, one the Nines had decided on years ago, so that made a destination for the message. But what about Mox and the others? What would their bounty-chasing party bus be using?

"Spray and pray?" Riley offered.

"We send it everywhere, Eden's going to be on us quick," Davin replied. "I've got a better idea."

Eden's bounty list went out on a specific frequency, a call out for those who wanted to know who could be rounded up for cash. The party bus would be listening to that, or at least they had been, and Eden itself might not pay too much attention to a frequency they probably automated. A weekly blast dictating whose heads should be collected didn't need constant review.

"Makes sense to me," Riley said, then he glanced back towards the staff door. "Make it quick?"

"Can't rush genius, Riley."

"This is genius?"

"You're lookin' at it."

Davin tapped up the frequencies, opened the mic, and said what they'd composed earlier. A spaceport to dock at and nothing more. Sandeer had people watching, and any other details would chance Eden coming out in force.

"Done and done," Davin said. Not a soul had come through the door. "Now, for something a little extra."

"Extra?"

Davin swiped away the two frequencies, tapped the emergency override to send this next burst on all available bands.

"What're you doing?" Riley asked, and Davin held up a single finger.

The captain pressed the broadcast button.

"This is Davin Masters, captain of the Wild Nines, Hero of Earth, and general badass. Calling in here to say Captain Heath Swane's a traitor to all that's good and right, and if Eden had any honor left, they'd kick him out the nearest airlock. Until that happens, I'm calling on every Eden employee to ask themselves why they're on the wrong side. There's always room on mine." Davin took a breath. Grinned. "And to the best pilot I ever knew, love you Phy."

Davin released the broadcast button, spun himself around in the chair and shrugged. "Sorry, had to be done."

"So much for Eden not knowing we were here."

A click came from the only door in, signaling a scanned ID badge. Davin kept up his grin.

"That's the thing, Riley," Davin said, lurching up from the seat, pulling out the trust pistol he'd secreted inside his banged up black jacket. "I want them to know I'm coming."

15

PRESSURE POP

Riley did not take the change in plan particularly well. The man's eyes bugged out, which made a great first impression for the comm center workers, a panicked duo, as they came rushing through the staff entrance.

"Hey there," Davin said, ignoring Riley and beckoning the pair inside with his pistol. "Take a seat, chaps. We're going to be here for a while."

Hostage A, whose convenient name tag labeled Cal, didn't object. The guy threw up his hands, blubbered out something apologetic and heaved himself to a seat without further complaint. A paler man Davin had never seen.

Hostage B, name tag Lonnie, had herself an attitude. She gave Davin's pistol the same look Davin tended to give his nutrient goop breakfast every morning. She didn't move from the door's shadow, but folded her arms and announced, disappointment dripping, "You have any idea what the hell you're doing in here?"

Spicy.

"He doesn't," Riley said, head shaking as he backed up. "This wasn't the plan."

"You had a plan?" Lonnie asked, and Davin whistled, sucking all eyes back to him.

"Lonnie, you seem like you have a good head on your shoulders, a stiff spine too," Davin said. Always important to soften up the subject before a request. "How about you show me how we can lock this place down?"

Lonnie snorted, a real solid crackle.

"There's no locking this place down. You think this is a bomb shelter or something? We're sending out everyone's love letters, nobody's going to care if we get hit."

"What about all those spaceships up there depending on your relays?"

Lonnie rolled her eyes, "They have their own comms. All you're doing holing up in here is pissing off the locals."

Davin puffed out his lower lip, nodded. Okay, so there wouldn't be a huge immediate response. At least, not without a little nudging.

"Riley," Davin said, and when the guy took his hands off his head, Davin tossed the pistol his way. "Keep an eye on these two. And see if you can't find a way to lock the doors."

"What're you gonna do?"

"Tell the truth."

As it happened, the truth Davin told was a subjective one. Namely, broadcasting over all bands, The Wild Nines captain channeled a latent who-gives-a-damn fury, lambasting Eden, Heath Swane, androids, and the relentless assault of money-grubbing corporations on people just trying to make their living in the hardscrabble solar system.

As he spoke—Cal, at Riley's gunpoint urging, snagged Davin some rehydrating water so his voice stayed limber—Davin kept his eyes on the clock, counting down the minutes until Eden would show up and in force. The company, though, wasn't the first one on the scene: that honor belonged to the local cops. Riley, sweating now and likely far further into this than he'd ever expected, turned another shade paler when Davin interrupted his insults to claim they had two hostages inside.

"Two innocents caught up in this power struggle," Davin said into the microphone. He tossed a wink at the utterly unamused Lonnie. "They won't be harmed unless you all out there make the wrong move, unless anything happens other than my one to one meeting with the hideous malcontent captain Heath Swane." A deep breath. It'd been a minute, so time to once again mention it. "This scum, this worthless pile, sent Phyla out to die for nothing other than his own amusement. That's who Eden hires, folks. That's who, if you call Eden your employer, you're working for. Consider that."

Another halt, another drink.

"You know every second you're on those waves, nobody can land on Ganymede," Lonnie said. "Nobody can call for help if they need it. You're not some saint, you're a jerk."

Davin scrolled, found the emergency response band. A frequency he'd left clear. "I am a jerk, Lonnie, but I'm not a monster."

Lonnie just sighed. She did that a lot and was welcome to it.

Eden took three hours to roll up a response. The local police—who knew how many were on Sandeer's side—were content to leave the situation to the big company and made zero entrance attempts on the comm center. They even facilitated the delivery of some Stardust tacos upon Davin's request.

They were, as Riley had advertised, exquisite.

The Eden response team arrived in four hulking armored speeders, ones likely rolling off Heath's frigate and made for ground assaults. Looking like curled up caterpillars resting on knife blades, the speeders offered a bulky, turreted solution.

Davin watched them ride up, watched them disgorge forty-odd troopers and special forces soldiers. The groups ran down exit ramps, assembled in squads before the comm tower. Eden drones joined them, a hovering swarm coating the relay's outside.

"C'mon, big guy," Davin muttered. "No way you miss this one."

Behind the caterpillar trio another speeder pulled up, a sleeker Eden-branded cone craft. Forest green all over, this one settled on the ground, had a glass roof swinging up to give, at last, Captain Heath Swane, Aya, and a particular android an exit.

Mecha-Phyla looked worse for wear after Davin's blow-em up play back at the construction site. While the red hair had been re-wigged, jagged black lines ran up and down the machine's body, accompanied by blast patches. Heath evidently hadn't wanted to go for a repainting, instead leaving the android scarred.

"What is that thing?" Riley asked, he and the hostages joining Davin to watch the arrivals.

"That is an abomination," Davin replied. "If I had to guess, that's what Heath wants to ruin our little escapade."

It stood to reason Eden wouldn't want to lay waste to the entire comm relay. Blowing out half of Ganymede's communications would endear the company to precisely no-one, and while Eden had a nasty way of dealing with rebels and small outposts, Ganymede had a populace. Public relations were a factor.

So when Captain Heath Swane, man of theater, strode with his android to the head of his forces, Davin wasn't surprised to see the Eden officer command them to lay in wait. To wave his android in.

"Here we go," Davin said, scooting back from the command console. He stood up, stretched out his arms, legs. Sandeer's pain meds were starting to wear off, niggling aches making advances up his nerves. "When she comes through, you all can go."

"Go?" Riley asked.

"Yup," Davin replied. "Just give me that first."

Like a kid throwing away a hot potato, Riley tossed the pistol back. Davin looped it around his finger, settled in to a straight aim at the staff door, and hoped he'd bought enough time.

Mecha-Phyla had no difficulties with the doors, namely because Davin told Lonnie to unlock them all. The android strode towards, through the outer entrance. Davin heard her feet, saw the android approach the staff door on a monitor to his left. Up close, the android's ragged appearance came into clearer relief: this was a machine due for some time in a repair bay, time Heath must've thought he didn't have.

Or maybe Heath just had that much faith in his creations.

Davin ordered Cal and Lonnie to come closer, told Riley to hide in the room's back. The hostages nudged up near Davin's shoulders, forming a three across as the android reached, opened the staff entry door with a tap.

Davin, pistol raised, fired as the door slid aside. Scored a burning hole right in Mecha-Phyla's shoulder. The android didn't show any pain, but darted in at Davin with a blank rage on her face.

So Davin hid. Pulled Cal in front of him. With a shrieking skid of boots on metal, the android adjusted her approach, breaking left to avoid Cal. The halt gave Davin time for another shot, another hit to the android's side. Something inside the monster sparked.

But she kept coming.

Davin went left, pushing the sobbing, panicked Cal towards the android. Mecha-Phyla dodged the human bullet, kicking past Cal in a swipe at Davin. Its fingers caught Davin's jacket as he went back, forcing Davin to drop the pistol and slide his arms free from its sleeves. The android tossed the garment away as Davin kicked the pistol.

The little gun whacked off the android's shin, bounced high enough for Davin to scoop it from the air, fire low as the android swung a punch at his chest.

A fiery gout came from the android's right leg, while Davin felt the air leave his lungs as he skidded back, struck the room-ringing console.

Those things could hit.

Limping, the android continued its advance. Davin, gasping, raised the pistol and fired again. Another hit, this time to the android's gut. Not that it stopped the machine. The hits just blended in with the other scars, made Mecha-Phyla look less and less human.

Before Davin could pull the trigger again, the android yanked the pistol away and flung it aside. Up close, the machine smelled acrid, heat boiling off as components struggled to deal with the damage. Its face, burned, smudged, broken, had the same set look as ever. A few red curls still dangled, the rest charred black.

Davin tried to find an appropriate insult, just coughed instead.

The android picked him up, held Davin by his throat. Spots came quick, dancing in Davin's vision. His lungs burned. His legs and arms felt numb, even as the Wild Nines captain grabbed at the android's arms, tried to force them apart.

And yet, inside, Davin held to the plan.

The pressure grew on his neck, a realization that the android planned on something more decisive than a choke job. The old neck snap, an android classic.

"Goodbye, Davin Masters," the android said, a hollow voice talking in Heath's words.

The red flash had a surreal cast, Davin's low oxygen level turning everything blurry and slow. He didn't feel the drop, the return slap to the floor. The smack as his head cracked against the console, more aches added to his collection.

Davin did, though, have a perfect view of the android collapsing to the floor before him. Mecha-Phyla's head now a smoking ruin. Several more red flashes turned the android's body into char.

And who was the hero?

Riley bent over Davin, snapping his fingers beneath the captain's nose. In the man's left hand, the pistol wiggled, Riley's nerves making it evident the dude lacked experience in android murder.

To be fair, so did virtually everyone alive.

"Davin, hey," Riley said, glancing between the captain and the android, as if he thought the latter might rise back up zombie style, "you gotta get back with it. Don't think they'll give us time."

Davin gulped in the air. The stale, smokey stuff in the comm center nonetheless delicious swooping through his bruised throat. His mind snapped back, woozy, but adrenaline worked its sharp magic.

"They're coming in," Lonnie, the hostage who'd escaped her role as android deflector, said. "You're both screwed now."

"Seal the door," Davin rasped. "Hard. Air tight."

When Lonnie hesitated, Riley changed the pistol's target. Cal kept up his crying in the corner. Davin felt bad for the guy: some people really did want to punch the clock, not deal with stuff like this. He'd just drawn the wrong shift on the schedule.

Lonnie, though, Lonnie was an all-star. She checked Riley's intimidation tactic, shook her head and did as the man asked. The comm center's outer door locked hard, all the windows around the place slamming shut as metal seals raced to cover them.

Standard construction regs for anything on a moon's surface: dome or no dome, rapid de-pressurization was a risk and had to be covered.

And in this case, Davin hoped to hell the risk was very real.

With Riley helping him stand, Davin looked at the feed. Eden's several squads decided to surround the building first, looking to lock down other exits now that the android's straight-on assault had failed. Take the outnumbered Davin and his buddy by storm.

"Don't think that will hold them for long," Lonnie said. "All this is meant to keep air in, not fight fire."

"That's all we need," Davin replied. He glanced at Riley. "Good shooting there. Thanks."

"How'd you know?" Riley asked. "How'd you know I'd do it?"

"Easy," Davin replied, "I figured you were smart enough to see the android would kill you next."

"What?" Riley blanched.

Davin shrugged, raised an eyebrow, "Guess I was lucky you had some courage."

"I just didn't want you, or anyone, to die."

"That's quaint." Davin patted Riley on the shoulder, turned his attention back to the monitor.

Eden's encirclement was nearly done. The time was now.

Please let his luck continue just a little bit longer.

The siren sounded out, clear and alive. It rang through the comm center's dome, delivering a warning anyone who'd ever left Earth understood well: the oxygen, atmosphere, humans needed to live was in danger.

A beautiful sound.

Lonnie didn't seem to think so, rolling her eyes and collapsing into a chair, muttering about the worst of days. Cal, remaining on his butt in a dark nook to the exit's right burst into a new round of sobbing pleas for his life to be spared.

Riley cursed.

Davin laughed.

On the monitors, the feed showed the Eden forces running back towards their skiffs. Armed and ready to fight, the troopers hadn't come equipped with exo-suits. No vacuum battles for this crew.

At least, that's what Davin thought.

Heath, though, planned ahead. Davin adjusted the feed to follow the retreat, saw the people inside the skiffs dumping out those very same exo-suits. Now it became a race, how fast could Eden swap out before disaster struck?

The comm chirped, the relay's many bands signaling, for once, a targeted reply to this very center. Davin waved for Lonnie to answer it, and a sparkling voice, a stunning voice, a miraculous voice came over.

"This is the *Jumper*, and I hope your butts are covered, because we're about to blast a hole in your dome."

Phyla. Davin had been hearing that voice in his imagination, his memories every minute since her shuttle had gone up in a fireball, but that was her. Iron determination mingled with flat competence. How she could be talking right now, Davin didn't know, didn't care.

She lived, and that was so much more than enough.

"Who's that?" Riley asked.

"Our way out," Davin replied, the moment sapping away the melodrama. "Lonnie, does this place have any suits?"

Lonnie gulped. "Five, for emergencies. They're in storage."

"Riley, take our friend here and get those. Cal and I will hold down the fort."

As the pair left, Davin turned his attention back to the monitor. Thanking Galaxy Forge and its attention to cameras, Davin tapped between feeds, giving himself a great view as disaster struck the moon.

The big domes dumped over buildings were meant to block micro-meteors, the occasional falling space debris. They were not designed to hold back hammering laser fire. The siren pulled all the curious peoples, including Stardust Tacos, back under ground, where a safety door sealed off any potential leaks. From Davin's eye, the only people still outside were Eden's scrambling forces.

Those troops looked up as a bright light flooded the feed's edges. The *Jumper's* two turrets laying into the dome, melting through. The Eden skiffs didn't plan on taking the assault lying down, their own turrets angling up towards the attack in a nicely coordinated swing. Six guns against the *Jumper's* pair.

But the *Jumper* had an x-factor: vacuum.

When the dome blew, the comm consoles died for a long second. When the feed returned—emergency backup power—the Eden forces were scattered, the propulsive sucking from the blown hole overturning the skiffs and sending the suited-up personnel flying.

Safe inside the sealed comm center, Davin felt a rumble, saw some new warning lights flash on saying to step outside would mean instant death, but otherwise he took a seat in a chair, wished he had some popcorn.

The *Jumper*, the most beautiful damn spacecraft Davin had ever seen, adopted a hovering stance, holding above the hole in the dome and lacing the Eden speeders with hot fire. Davin took a quick count, noticed that one speeder seemed to be missing.

So Heath was a coward.

Eden's forces found shelter where they could, some breaking for the diner where Davin and Riley had snagged coffee just a few hours earlier.

A couple tried spitting shots the *Jumper*'s way, rifles doing nothing against the ship's shields. The speeders found their guns the first targets, turrets reduced to ruins under precise, withering fire.

A few more minutes passed, Lonnie and Riley returned with suits, and Davin prepared to take a victory lap.

"Hey you," Davin said into the comm, beaming the message right to the *Jumper*. "Never thought I'd hear your voice again."

"Sorry to ruin your dreams," Phyla snapped back. "You ready to go?"

"Love you too," Davin blinked. "We'll be suited up in a minute."

"Make it faster. Eden's sending fighters this way."

"Don't want to get shot down again, huh?"

"Not the time, Davin."

Phyla, always the warm and cuddly sort. The four of

them threw on their suits, then, with pistol in hand, Davin gave the comm center back to Lonnie and Cal.

"Been a pleasure," Davin said.

"Screw off," Lonnie replied. Cal recoiled. "Hope you get a laser to the face."

Riley gaped. Davin chuckled.

"Can't please'em all," the Nines captain said as the two left the comm center's staff room. "Now we wait for our exit."

That exit opened by way of fire, the comm center's main door glowing orange before blowing away, a similar, shorter vacuum suck pulling Riley and Davin towards the new exit.

Seeing the devastation from the monitor feed was one thing, but up close, the carnage killed Davin's grin. Eden's forces lay scattered around the rocky plain, ruined by the *Jumper*'s assault. The vacuum killed fires quick, and no sound pierced the missing air, giving the whole thing a dream-like feel. Only the *Jumper* itself, its relatively massive bulk hovering inside the blown dome, kept Davin tethered to reality. Especially when Mox dropped the ladder from the airlock's hatch.

Davin tapped Riley's shoulder, focused the man away from the ruin and towards their escape. The mechanic caught on, hop-jumped towards the ladder, Ganymede's gravity just enough to keep it pulling down.

As Davin took one last survey, he frowned. All these people didn't have to perish, didn't have to get hurt. Eden could've kept to its own, but greed, anger, pride all pushed these paycheck poppers into do-or-die scenarios.

One more reason things had to change.

As Riley neared the ladder's top, Davin leapt for the bottom rung. Put a boot on, lifted himself up to the next. Went to go make another leap when a flash caught his eye, bright green-white. A laser slamming into the *Jumper*'s shields.

Up above, dark specks against Ganymede's Jupiter-dominated sky spat more fire, lasers crashing into the dome, the Jumper. And when Phyla kicked on the thrusters, the ladder jerked.

The suit, hardly made for skilled climbs, couldn't keep Davin's grip on the ladder, and he tumbled, a slow free fall towards the surface, enemy fire raining down around him.

A good plan, a bad ending.

16

CATCH AND SHOOT

Davin's slipped grip started a long, slow tumble to the ground, where he'd get picked off like a mouse in a hawk-swarmed field.

At least, that's what Davin figured until a far-too-strong hand snagged his wrist. Looking towards the contact, Davin found Mox, the giant man holding the ladder's bottom rung with one hand, Davin with the other.

"Even with the gravity, my friend, you've put on a few pounds," Mox grumbled, the voice coming through the near field comm in Davin's suit. "All that cocktail shrimp."

"All muscle, baby," Davin quipped back.

Phyla destroyed any further dialogue by kicking the *Jumper* forward, its engines lighting up as the ship's front-facing laser spewed death at the broken dome's remaining glass. Davin and Mox dangled while Riley, climbing the ladder with alacrity for a mechanic, scrambled inside the *Jumper*.

"How's that grip?" Davin asked, the dome crumbling before Phyla's assault.

"It'll hold another minute," Mox replied.

Going fast in Ganymede's vacuum felt strange: there wasn't any air resistance, but gravity still pulled. They were only a couple dozen meters over the surface, too, those craggy rocks streaking by fast enough to throw Davin's stomach into a tumble.

"Phyla, you gotta slow down or we're going to die," Davin tried.

"She can't," Opal cut in. "We've got three killers on our tail."

The Eden fighters swooped in from above in a spear-like formation. As they closed, with Mox starting to scale the ladder one slow rung at a time, Davin tried to fit the fighter class into one he knew.

Humanity's creative genius expressed itself best in its killing instruments, and fighters were no exception. Companies manufactured them in a dozen different ways and modders stamped on their own imprints. Eden, Davin figured, would fill its ranks with dependable craft like the Vipers Merc favored. They were fast, aerodynamic slashers good in and out of vacuum. Other pirating bands, devoted to asteroid belt ambushes, might favor three-sixty saucers for their all-around power at the cost of in-atmosphere viability.

But these goons?

Each one looked like a spoon's scalloped end turned upside down, a sloping ridge with engines on the backside. Sticking out from the carved-in middle appeared to be a heavy turret, a weapon that should've required a gunner.

"There's no way they can fit two in there," Davin said.

"That's what I thought in Heath's shuttle," Phyla replied. "Either Eden's got the best damn pilots that ever lived in those things, or they've figured out a firing program better than any I've found."

Phyla's words reminded Davin he'd have to ask how she

made it out of that one alive. Now that she spoke, though, Davin did see these were the same craft that'd blown her up outside Heath's frigate.

All the more reason to torch'em.

"What're you waiting for?" Davin asked as the fighters kept up their steadily shorter-range bombardment. "Don't think they're looking to parley."

Phyla set the *Jumper* on an upward hurtle, giving Opal or Merc a clean line from the top turret. Merc's cackle put the fighter pilot there, and he let loose with hot orange laserfire towards the fighters.

At exactly the same moment, the trio broke in different directions, rotating their curvy craft to keep their turrets firing the *Jumper*'s way. Merc's assault burned where they'd been, the pilot struggling to find which one to track.

"Impossible," Davin said.

"Don't say that," Mox replied. "We'll get'em, and we'll get'em faster if you take a rung."

Davin hadn't even noticed, but Mox had climbed up far enough, clipping Davin's suit into his own, to get Davin back to the ladder's space.

Getting a grip on something had never felt so good, a grip almost lost as Phyla bent the *Jumper* back around on itself, spinning the craft into a dive after one of the fighters.

"Need a call, Davin," Opal said. "We keep after these bastards till they're gone, or do we run?"

Take too long and Eden would find reinforcements, would lock down all the possible landing spots on the moon. Flee, though, and these buggers would probably follow. Would pester Davin and the Nines to hell and back.

"We kill them quick," Davin replied.

"Easier said than—" Merc started, his turret spouting orange, still yet to get a hit.

"Don't you dare finish that sentence," Davin cut him off. "We fight smart, remember? Think!"

An onslaught from the third fighter, one that'd snuck behind the *Jumper*'s engines, punctuated the words with a flashing hammerblow at the ship's shields. Lightning crackled as the *Jumper*'s generators struggled to redirect laser-licking energy. Phyla abandoned her pursuit, swung the *Jumper* wide left to clear the fire.

"Please don't let that happen again," Vi's voice, another back from the dead, swore over the comm. "I didn't fix her just to get her blown up."

"You try telling them that," Merc cracked. "Maybe they'll take some pity on us."

But pity didn't seem to be Eden's game plan. While Davin didn't relish his ladder-hooked viewing box, getting yanked around as Phyla put the *Jumper* through its paces, Ganymede's loose gravity meant less whiplash and more floating.

Meant he could see the trap closing.

The three fighters didn't rejoin their formation, instead using their turrets to take firing lines Merc and Opal couldn't match. Every time Phyla twisted the *Jumper* to bring a gun to bear, the smaller craft would twitch to one side or another, dodging a meter or two out of aim.

They needed another option.

"If I may," Fournine, the *Jumper*'s AI computer, ripped from an android's guts, jumped onto the channel, "I've been analyzing the techniques we are seeing, and I'm certain these aren't meatbags."

"'Scuse me?" Viola asked.

"Humans. Their reaction times are far better than any of you, and they seem able to handle maneuvers beyond your skills."

"Keep going, Fournine," Phyla muttered, "and I'll delete you."

"My point, friends, is that you are facing machines. With all their strengths, and all their weaknesses."

Davin and Phyla had fought androids flying fighters before, but Fournine seemed to be saying these ships, so svelte, didn't have anything inside them at the controls. In effect, they were wholly drones, and far better than the flimsy versions cheap security firms threw at penny-pinching customers.

Dammit, Heath. Figures he wouldn't stop his android rehabilitation tour with the humanoid version.

"Mox," Davin called up the ladder, the metal man closing in on the *Jumper*'s hatch. "Get your cannon."

"The hell you want that for?"

"Trust me," Davin said. "Phyla, just buy us a little more time."

All he heard in reply was another curse. More lasers blitzed the *Jumper*, her shields vanishing and popping back as Vi played the best power management game of her life. The android fighters weren't reckless either, content to give up attack runs as soon as Phyla moved to counter rather than striving for every possible hit.

When you knew you had your enemy dead, why risk anything?

Davin used the time between maneuvers, those short blips, to attach every possible hook, strap, belt his suit had to the ladder. He'd need both hands to handle Mox's cannon.

"What're you planning?" Opal asked.

"Keep'em off us till I'm ready," Davin replied. "Focus."

Opal and Merc didn't have to focus long. Mox went in

and out of the *Jumper*'s airlock in record time, returning with the big cannon.

Designed to lock into Mox's exoskeleton, the meter-long monster could spew heavy bolts at a rapid rate. On a normal world, Davin wouldn't have been able to hold it.

Here?

"Throw it!" Davin called up, an idea made ludicrous as Phyla threw the *Jumper* into a dive, putting Mox and the weapon below Davin rather than above.

Instead, Mox handed the cannon to another body behind him. Davin did a double take seeing Riley there, the mechanic holding onto the cannon, face pallid but firm. Somehow the kid had found his courage.

Davin regretted hitting Riley so hard the other night. A little.

Mox jumped up the rungs, and when Phyla pulled out of her dive for a surface-skimming straight shot, the metal man reached and pulled his way along the rungs. Halfway between Davin and Riley, Mox stopped, looked back towards the ship.

"Now you throw it," Mox said.

"Phyla, hold this course another ten seconds," Davin added, a tough ask with laser fire slashing all around.

Riley squatted, straightened and tossed the cannon. Their momentum, Ganymede's low gravity gave Mox a good shot, one he scored with a single hand snagging the cannon's left grip. The big weapon angled down, but Mox didn't look troubled as he straightened, brought the cannon back up.

"Ready?" Mox asked.

Davin hoped the comm relay kept their suits and all their pieces up to standards. Adding the cannon's weight to the g-forces Phyla pulled during her flips and turns ought to stress his snag job, and if a fall to Ganymede's surface would be rough, doing it with a heavy cannon would be way worse.

Vi swore. Smoke and shrapnel flew off the *Jumper*'s right wing. The ship's shields were at their breaking point.

"Now or never!" Davin shouted, held out both hands. "Give it!"

Mox scrunched up his face, doubt pasted everywhere on his mug, but the man knew enough to follow the captain's orders. With a single, exoskeleton-boosted arm, Mox heaved the cannon along the ladder.

It smacked Davin in the chest, turning end-over-end in the air so the barrel smashed Davin's helmet, etched a single perilous crack along the visor.

But his hands caught the grips, the padded handles way too big for Davin's regular human mitts. Using his wrists, Davin righted the cannon, pressing it back against his chest as his thumbs found the triggers.

"Ready," Davin said. "Now give me a shot."

"What're you talking about?" Phyla asked.

"Get up close, then we'll see how adaptable these things are. Trust me, Phyla."

The *Jumper* broke off from its surface run, Mox scrambling along the ladder back towards the hatch. The straight up rise left Davin trailing the craft, Ganymede below.

His first target right in front.

The android fighter swept their way, swinging skyward as its dive wrapped up. The attack angle was perfect, catching the dead spot in the *Jumper*'s engines where Merc's turret couldn't hit.

Where Davin's newfound cannon could deliver.

"Ready, Merc," Davin said. "It's about to come your way."

He held down the triggers, the cannon spinning up its power packs. Davin felt the thrum, the heat. The extreme heat. Mox hadn't mentioned this part, but Davin felt his chest getting real hot as the cannon started spewing light.

The nova blue bolts streamed towards the drone, the fighter reacting just as it would've to one of the *Jumper*'s turrets. It banked hard up and away, speeding out of Davin's firing line.

And right into Merc's. The gunner pierced the fighter with golden glory, his fire knifing the small ship's meager shields. The little craft's turret went hot, its power links boiling up and consuming the ship in a short-lived fireball.

"Hell yeah!" Merc cried. "That's what I'm looking for! Line up the next one, Phyla. We got this now."

Davin would've cheered too, except the heat had him gasping. Had the suit sticky, its fabric not built to handle this sort of contact. If the seal broke, if Ganymede's cold vacuum took him, Davin would only have seconds to live.

If the fighters shot down his ship, he'd have zero.

"C'mon, Phyla," Davin coughed. "Next one."

Trick an android once and it won't fall for it twice. The two remaining fighters blasted away, setting up a long range pursuit. In sight but beyond a laser's useful range. Phyla kept the *Jumper* coasting in Ganymede's atmosphere, low enough to dodge radar, straight enough for Davin, Mox, and Riley to snake in the big cannon.

"Won't they attack again as soon as you're inside?" Merc asked during the surgical procedure, which gave Davin's suit some much needed breathing room.

"Not how androids work," Fournine said. "I suspect these were given specific parameters for their attack. Very risk-averse. Once a clear threat exists, their goal changed to observe and report."

"So they're dumb then."

"They're limited," Davin said. "Heath's whole game is

getting androids back on Eden's good side. That doesn't happen if they're all blown up before they get to demonstrate their awesomeness."

The conversation continued, banter sliding into Davin's ears as he slipped off every hook. The suit's torched chest hadn't melted all the way, but Davin's oxygen, displayed in tiny blue-white numbers on his visor plate, dipped faster than he liked.

If those androids had stayed aggressive, Davin would've burned, suffocated, and died on that ladder. Phyla would've been left towing a corpse.

Yuck.

Instead, over fifteen careful minutes, the ladder trio clambered into the airlock. Mox held his cannon as the oxygen and pressure equalized.

And then Davin was home, yanking off his helmet and striding, hopping into the *Jumper's* central cargo chamber. It looked exactly as he remembered it, a bit greasy and wanting for some love. It looked marvelous.

More marvelous and deserving of the lip-pressing kiss was the *Jumper's* pilot, who broke off Davin's over-the-shoulder embrace quick, claiming they were still in a fight.

"Death hasn't changed you at all," Davin said, settling into the co-pilot's chair.

"Living's only made you worse," Phyla said. "When's the last time you had a shower?"

Admittedly, getting shot at, charring himself with a cannon, and holding hostages for hours had slathered Davin in sweat and grime.

"Thought you liked me more this way," Davin said. "Action packed."

"From a distance, maybe." Phyla lifted a hand from the flight stick, pointed to a screen showing two red triangles gliding behind the *Jumper*'s big green circle. "What're we doing about those?"

"They're small," Davin said. "Outrun them?"

"Might work," Phyla mused. "Want to hot foot it to Earth?"

"Our friend Heath's going to follow," Davin replied. "Better if we take him out here."

"He's got a frigate, Davin, in case you forgot."

Davin hadn't. But a frigate wasn't a capital cruiser, and Heath's wasn't the pinnacle of Eden capabilities. The man himself seemed to say he'd been tossed in the corporate backwater, left to founder unloved and ignored. He had his androids, but the man had just lost several squads at the comm relay.

"He might not have the strength to come after us," Davin said. "Not right away."

"So we're breaking?"

Davin was about to say yes when the comm beeped. An incoming call, short-range, on the Nines own frequency. Only a few people would have that data, and Davin owed one of'em.

"Sandeer," Davin said, hitting the button. "Thanks for everything, buddy."

"Shut up, Davin." Sandeer had, for once, ditched the barkeep's serenity. "You've royally screwed up our side of the moon. Thank you for that. But I'm going to give you a chance to make up for it."

Davin glanced at Phyla, who leveled out the *Jumper*, swung the ship in a slow circle to keep it within Sandeer's comm range. Outside, Ganymede's mountains and domed settlements sparkled beneath Jupiter's reflected light.

"You've pissed Eden off. They're all over us. Mind drawing their attention away?"

"How're you suggesting we do that?" Davin replied.

"You go for the king," Sandeer said. "Get Galaxy Forge offline and you'll take all their attention. You've already scrambled Eden enough, maybe you can get through to him."

"Until they get more reinforcements here," Phyla added, "Then they swarm us and we die real quick."

"But if we shut down Galaxy Forge, we slow the war. Maybe even stop it," Davin said. "Eden will have to come to the table then, even if we never find Alissa."

Speculating was all well and good, but stopping an enterprise as huge as Galaxy Forge needed more than ideas. It needed a person.

"Don't know what you're talking about," Vi said, meeting Davin outside the cockpit on the *Jumper*'s upper level. "If there's actually a way to do this, my dad never told me."

Phyla kept running rings around Ganymede, the android fighters keeping their distance. Eden hadn't responded in force yet, no doubt consolidating their efforts and deciding just how much Davin and crew were worth.

Of course, the body count back at the comm center would necessitate a hard response. Davin would have to talk with Phyla about that later, gauge the impact. Killing another person, even from a distance . . . you learned to live with it, but Davin found it came with an immediate cost. A graying of life, a dulling of its joys.

Until you forced yourself to move on.

"Riley thought you'd have an answer," Davin said.

"Riley thinks a lot of things." Vi rolled her eyes. She'd been giving the man a crash course in the *Jumper*'s engines, trying to make him a solid substitute so she could venture back to the workbench and her experiments. "My dad liked to mess with him too."

"You think it's possible? A backdoor like this?"

With Puk hovering behind her, Vi shrugged.

"Galaxy Forge is our company. Always has been. My dad's not the bomber type, but as security?" Vi flicked a glance towards the cockpit. "Besides, what other options do we have? Just run for it? Alissa's not going to give us a chance if we don't do something."

"Alissa's what you're worried about? Not your dad?"

Vi frowned, her hands feeling for the tools along her belt. Comfort. Davin did the same with his pistols, with Melody.

"Dad's going to be fine. Eden won't hurt him."

"Second question. Say we go and get your dad. Will he shut down his baby for us?"

"For you? Definitely not," Vi said, her grip on those tools getting harder. "For me? Maybe."

How to make a plan with the enemy on your ass? Davin had to keep bodies in the turrets at all times lest the fighters change their minds and make a run. Had to keep people getting food, drink, and rest time. Had to give the *Jumper*, at some point, a chance to recharge its batteries.

How to make a plan?

Sometimes, you wing it.

"If we're going home, there's a back way we can take," Vi said. "There's a chance it's defended, but . . ."

"Whatever's there, we can blow it apart," Davin said, clustered together with Phyla in the cockpit.

"Eden's gonna come in like a swarm of hornets if we head right to Vi's house," Phyla said. "You have a back door, I say we take it."

"They're gonna come like hornets no matter where we

go," Davin replied. "We arm up, we go in." He tweaked the comm, sent the message across the *Jumper*'s speakers. "Anyone object to crashing at Vi's house tonight?"

"Was great last time around," Merc shot back first from his berth in the upper turret. "So long as the popcorn's still there, I'm in favor."

Agreements peppered in from a crew all too enthusiastic. Being under the gun and unable to do anything about it had a way of messing with the Nines, getting them all twitchy. A characteristic Davin didn't mind encouraging.

Where they were going, after all, would require more than a little guts, more than a little crazy.

"Anyone ever try to break into your house, Vi?" Davin asked.

"All the time," Vi replied. "Richest people on the moon. Dad had a bunch of defenses put in place."

"Odds they've been turned off by Eden?"

"Davin, I don't know what Eden's done with my dad. Whether he's taken their offer or not. Sandeer seems to think he's swapped sides, so if you want to go attacking my house, I'd go in expecting the worst."

Davin laughed, put a hand on Phyla's shoulder, "Do we ever expect anything else, Phyla?"

The pilot, the love of his life, sighed, "With you, Davin, no, no I do not."

17

———

REJECT ROW

If Vi's parents had done one thing right in planning their private dome, it was choosing to nestle it among meteor-made mountains. The craters blew up around the dome, giving it privacy. Giving, too, a chance for a trick.

Davin, Mox, Vi, Riley, and Merc suited up for the infiltration, gathering gear and filling slim tanks with oxygen. Opal and Phyla would keep the *Jumper* flying, evading Eden for as long as they could.

"A crap job, Davin," Phyla said.

"Either that or we abandon the ship," Davin replied.

Both knew there was no way they'd ditch their home. That's what the *Jumper* was, would always be.

"When Eden comes after us in force?" Phyla asked. "What happens then?"

Davin pointed to the weapon Vi had made, the one that'd so devastated the rebel fleet with its sneak attack. Using comm frequencies, the transmitter encased in a whirling globe would send a digital disease to just about anything listening in the area. That disease would do plagues proud and kill any computer smart enough to parse it. Smart people were designing mitigation measures, but . . .

"What're the odds Heath 'I'm only thinking about androids' Swane has his people equipped?" Davin said. "Once you get him good and riled, use this to buy yourself some time."

"Some free shots too," Phyla muttered.

With the plan established, Davin's quintet—not quite the same as nine, but what could you do—hung near the hatch and waited for Phyla's evac order.

Armed up now with Melody, a couple pistols, and some novel explosives Vi threw together, Davin felt whole. Looking at Mox—no cannon, big assault rifle—all armored up and Merc with his spinning discs of glory good to go, well, it almost felt like old times again.

Until Davin reached the last two. Riley looked at his own pistol like it might jump out and bite him. Vi kept her pistol holstered, putting her faith in the floating bot always near her shoulder. Puk, a shiny silver ball hatched with different tools, hovered on tiny microjets.

They all chattered, and Davin didn't have the heart to tell them all to keep quiet. Sure, they were about to embark on a spontaneous assault on a defended compound, and sure, they could've used every second to plan, but the Wild Nines ran better on instinct.

And bets.

"A thousand extra for whomever gets to Vi's parents first," Davin said, drawing the team together.

Mox laughed. Vi scowled. Riley didn't understand.

"So in," Merc said.

The *Jumper* gave them thirty seconds. Davin's group only needed fifteen to scurry through the hatch and land on

Ganymede rock. They stood shadowed beneath a deep crater's spear wall, pressing themselves into the stone and dirt until the *Jumper*, and the trailing fighter pair, zipped off.

"Good luck," Davin whispered.

It seemed unfair that he'd reunite with Phyla only to say goodbye to her a couple hours later. Seemed worse still when he considered the time, that he hadn't slept in far too long. Davin's banged-up body begged for more rest, a request barely sated by a hasty shower and some caffeine infused nutrient goop.

Ah well. He'd had enough time to sit on his hands during the cargo-hauling years. Time to make up for it.

Vi's bot lead the party, the small orb zipping up high enough to see where they ought to go. Vi didn't expect defenses this far out from the compound, figured there wouldn't be any until the crew made it inside the family dome.

"Which means walk fast, people," Davin said. "No threats and limited oxygen says we go."

Nevertheless, he hung back to join up with Vi and Riley. Mox and Merc moved to the lead, hopping side by side through a narrow, boulder-strewn pass between crater ridges. Despite it being early morning on Ganymede, the moon had its standard golden-yellow cast from Jupiter's light.

At some point, Davin figured, the moon would slide to Jupiter's far side and put everything in a permanent shadow. Just not there yet.

" . . . recently, but until now it's been so boring, Vi," Riley was saying, the words coming into Davin's suit comm as he came within their few meters. "You dropped in for like a hot minute, made everything cool, then vanished to Eden and left us."

"Left you?" Vi countered, Davin watching her sharp-eyed look through her visor. "I did this thing called following my dreams, Riley. You ever try it?"

"Sure did, when I went to work for your father," Riley replied. "Love what I do and I don't have to leave my friends behind to do it."

"Good for you."

Davin whistled, as much to let them know he'd entered their little bubble as anything else.

"No fighting when we're on a mission," Davin said after they both went quiet. "You don't want drama when the shooting starts, trust me."

Vi snorted, "This from the guy who makes drama with everyone."

"Noticed that," Riley added.

"Hey, no criticizing the captain."

"You came back to us," Vi said. "You stepped in it."

"Because I know Merc and Mox can handle themselves," Davin said. "Neither of you are exactly prime time material."

Riley didn't argue the point, a mark in his favor, but Vi's eyes shot wide.

"Excuse me? Not prime time material?" Vi asked. "What's that supposed to mean?"

"Means you two get to hang back. Advise from afar. When things get hot, I want you both to head for the objective."

"My dad?"

"Or the code he's protecting," Davin said. "You both know your way around this place best. Mox, Merc, and I will draw the attention. You two use it."

Riley coughed, "So you're giving the people you just called not ready for this mission . . . the most important job?"

"It's the captain's responsibility to put people where they're going to succeed, Riley. Just be happy I'm not sticking you on toilet cleaning duty."

"He'll do it too," Vi said. "So you're using me to get to my father?"

"Way I see it," Davin replied, "you're using you. Without you here, we'd have to go in hot and hope we found him before a stray laser did. Good?"

"Not like we have a choice."

"Glad to see you're coming around."

Davin skipped ahead, leaving the two to get back to their childhood memories or whatever. He stood a little straighter, his hands felt a bit stronger, the pain receding after the conversation. Felt good to act like a captain again, give the orders, have 'em followed.

Then again, if everything went like it did in the old days, this mission was sure to go sideways.

Davin caught up to Mox and Merc in the crater's far shadow, Vi's family dome sprawled out below. Inside its glass shell, greenery abounded. Trees flowered, coiffed gardens flourished. Water sprayed from embedded sprinklers throughout, creating rainbows in Jupiter's light.

The house itself took advantage of Ganymede's gravity, using thin supports to send walkways between three large spherical hubs. Painted over in an easter red, blue, and yellow, Davin figured the hubs were at least four stories. Each one bracketed by Eden drones.

"Thought they weren't supposed to be here," Mox said as Davin caught up.

"Pull the humans, leave the machines?" Merc asked.

"If Heath's taken over, there's no sense guessing at a plan," Davin said. "The man's aiming for other things."

"That's what Phyla said," Merc replied. "How's it we always wind up with the weird ones gunning for our asses?"

"Because all the sane ones have more important things to do," Mox said.

Trailing Puk, they followed a shallow edge along the crater's outside before dipping into a bowl. Dust and rock shifted with every hop and footfall, small avalanches bounding away. Enough dust rose up Davin figured anyone paying attention at the house could see'em coming, but no attack swooped out to greet them.

"Attention's inward," Merc guessed when Davin mused about their lack of cover. "Who's gonna expect a bunch of people coming over land on Ganymede?"

The man had a point. Davin kept one eye on his shrinking oxygen meter, only one obstacle of many. If they'd tried to zip a speeder across Ganymede's landscape, the up-and-down pits, the atmospheric changes, the certain death if any equipment failure stung them . . . Eden could be forgiven for not dedicating a watch to the least plausible attack avenue.

"Davin," Merc said, "you regretting getting back into this?"

"You mean the guns and all that?"

"What else?"

Davin skipped once in silence.

"No," he said, "and I'll tell you why: purpose is hard to find. All that time running cargo, Phyla and I told ourselves that was the point. Healthy bank account, no new nightmares." Davin tapped his helmet. "Thing was, the old nightmares hung around just fine, and with nothing to replace'em, they were all we had. Demons and drudgery."

"But you had time."

"For what? Movies? Books? Arguing with each other

about both of 'em? Yeah, we had that time. Almost tore us apart."

"Yeah, sure."

"Get the sense you don't agree with me."

Merc laughed, "Look at Mox here. Guy's been hanging out on the Moon, keeping it stable, and he's fine. So maybe it's just you."

"Could be, but it's Phyla too. And lots like us. Those punks who gave you a lift back there being some of them."

"We're all caught in the circle, that's what you're saying, Davin?" Merc asked. "Round and round we go till someone blasts a hole in our head?"

"It's why I try to have as much fun as I can while I'm going," Davin replied.

Maybe not what Merc wanted to hear, but giving the guy some other idea didn't make any sense. By this point, if either he or Opal wanted out, they'd have escaped. This was the life they'd chosen, might as well live it.

"You two done?" Mox cut in.

"Point's been made," Davin replied, looking away from the dome towards Mox, who in turn had stopped where Puk hovered near a blasted off patch.

A sheet metal cover sat there, dusted over sure but otherwise kept up.

"Emergency escape," Puk said. "In case of intruders, we could get out this way and hide."

"Didn't seem to help much," Davin said, looking at the hatch.

"Because my dad built it for me." Viola and Riley joined the circle. "He would never run."

Davin nodded, pointed at Mox. "Crack it open, would you?"

"If it means we can get out of these suits . . . " Mox

replied, bending down to get his gloves beneath the hatch's grooves.

Mox pulled, set his feet against the ground and worked his metal-latticed fingers around the lip. The hatch didn't budge. Mox's boots dug deeper into the dirt, grunts abounded. The hatch didn't budge.

Vi laughed.

Mox glared, stood up.

"Puk, mind entering the passkey?" Vi asked her floating bot.

"Of course!"

The bot hovered over the cover and, without further ceremony, the hatch popped its seams, hissing and opening wide to reveal a ladder. Lime green lights circled the lip, giving the entry an almost jaunty appearance.

"You let me pull on that and you could've opened it?" Mox said.

Vi pointed at Davin, "Captain gave you an order. He told us to do what he says."

"Okay, smartass," Davin replied. "New order: be a team player."

Vi stuck out her tongue, barely visible through the dust-smudged visor. The engineer did, though, decide to lead the group into her own home, taking the first steps down the ladder. Davin followed second, with Riley in the middle. Merc, Mox, and Puk covered the rear.

Sneaking into another fight. Felt just right.

The ladder wasn't long, a scant ten rungs delivering them to a cylindrical tunnel just wide enough for two people to walk next to each other. The lime green lights continued, dotting the ceiling in a line as far as Davin could see, shadowed patches appearing like markers between the lights every few meters. The sloping walls bore a different character, one it took Davin a long stare to put together.

Vi's childhood must've been so different from his own.

Doodles covered the primed-over walls, metal beneath coated with white stuff perfect for holding paint, crayon, marker. Rambling colors danced along the tunnel, broken up here and there by a hung picture. Some sections seemed like the free-wheeling whims of a youngster, while others bore schematic-like sketches, the first real ideas popping free from Vi's head.

"Spent a lot of time in here," Vi said as the group gathered at the ladder's base. "Dad wanted me to free hand before a computer took over everything. He told me to do what I wanted."

"How many afternoons did we spend messing around?" Riley asked.

"Too many to count," Vi said, a wistful smile dying quick into concern. "You think Dad kept all our toys?"

"Our mistakes, you mean?"

Both Vi and Riley shared another look, a furrowed brow confusion that had Davin drawing Melody.

"Just what kind of mistakes?" Davin asked.

"Vi's dad didn't want to waste anything," Riley said. "So he'd give us tools to build what we wanted, and if it worked . . ."

"He'd stuff it back here," Vi replied. "The security code I gave to Puk should keep us safe though. It'll identify us to the house." Vi shrugged. "Ready?"

"Lead on," Davin replied.

What kind of mistakes were Vi and Riley making? What parent gave their kids anything that dangerous?

Only a few steps later, they found out. Behind, the hatch swung close with a hard click. Before, with Davin next to

Vi, the lime lights flickered, changed color to a dark blood-red.

"That's ominous," Merc said.

New sounds echoed up the tunnel, classic grinding, whirring, shifting as doors opened.

"And that's even more ominous," Merc continued.

"Quiet," Mox grumbled.

"You be quiet," Merc shot back.

Davin raised Melody, Vi brought up her pistol.

"The code should've worked," Vi muttered.

"Maybe dad's changed the passwords on you," Davin said as they eased forward another step.

The winding, grinding sounds stopped almost as one. Nobody spoke, the quiet, save for the distant hum of life preserving oxygen cyclers, dominating.

The lights went out. Save one, just over Vi's head.

Riley swore. Davin took a slow breath, his aim forward. Waiting for a charge that didn't come. After a long, tense minute, fingers came off triggers, held breaths released.

"Maybe Eden killed them all," Vi said, starting forward again.

The tunnel's floor had a gripped surface, perfect for controlled hops and walks. At least, that's what Davin figured, an opinion held until the red light's fringes moved ahead.

"Stop," Davin said, reaching out with an arm to keep Vi's next hop from carrying her far. "Something's right there."

"Shoot it," Riley suggested.

"Yep. Blow it up," Vi replied.

"No chance it's a—" Davin started, found himself stopping as the thing emerged, trundling towards them.

Looking like a half-baked child's toy, the robot planted two waist-high wheels on the tunnel's ground, notches holding onto the floor grips to keep the machine level. Between those wheels punched out six separate beams, each ending in a blue-glowing flame.

"A dynamic welder," Vi said. "Kill it, please."

The girl backed up as the welder rolled forward. Davin pressed down on the trigger, Melody blasted out a blue-green energy ball. The shock flew towards the machine, burst against those welding beams as they jutted a meter away from Davin's face.

Melody's burn melted away the welder's controlled tips, exposing the bot's gas feeds and igniting them in equal measure. The fire burst out large, covering the tunnel. Davin and the others flew back as the expanding gas pushed them, heat slamming their suits, charring their visors.

And the robot? The robot kept coming, wheels now blanketed in fire as they churned towards the group.

"Kill it!" Merc shouted, firing his rifle into the flames.

Davin couldn't see the machine's body, couldn't see anything in the blinding blue-orange glow. Then again, the tunnel didn't leave many options.

Melody unleashed hell once again.

This time the shotgun's release penetrated deeper, found the robot's gas tanks. Or maybe it was Merc's rifle, or Mox's or Vi's spastic pistol shots. Either way, the spray hit something soft and the bot exploded, burning shrapnel flying everywhere.

Davin turned, curling in beneath his heavy coat. Metallic dings echoed to his right and up the tunnel, followed by one more expansive fireball as the robot's gas blew out. Heat ran up and down Davin's body, the suit's integrity failing.

Just most pain to add to his collection.

As fast as they emerged, though, the flames receded.

The group's suits, designed to resist fire, among more other things, proved poor food. Vi's hung papers and drawings served better, but the thin pieces turned to ash fast, dwindling the tunnel into darkness. Only the red light remained, the diodes made of strong stuff.

The tunnel, too, looked unharmed. Only smoldering ruins marred the surface, the primed metal otherwise fine. No busted holes to Ganymede's earth or the vacuum beyond.

"Everyone alive?" Davin called, rising up and looking around.

To his left, Vi crouched with Puk before her. The round bot had scratches from the shrapnel, its shape blocking the steel slivers from striking Vi. Mox had cloaked Merc, using his own exoskeleton as armor.

Riley, alternating between swearing and crying, hadn't been so lucky. One of the welding beams stuck out from the man's left leg, a red stain marring the silver suit.

Vi was on him in in instant, followed by Mox. The Centurion had a med kit slotted away on his back, and he unlimbered it, the pair rushing into slapdash care.

Davin, with Merc coming up to join him, kept his focus down the tunnel.

"Suits are compromised," Merc said. "No going back now."

"We weren't going to," Daviin replied. "Where would we go?"

"Point." Merc shook his head. "Bad luck to lose a guy this early."

"No," Davin said. "It's an opportunity."

Merc gave a one-eyed squint, "You're becoming a cold bastard, Davin."

"Bosser shot Lina right in front of me. Heath made me

watch as they blew up Phyla," Davin said. "Not hard to see why."

Merc put a hand on Davin's shoulder, "Just remember we're your friends, and we're gonna help you get back at Eden. So don't get us killed first."

A good mantra, not getting your friends killed. Davin repeated it to himself as they moved off, heading further down Vi's tunnel of terror. Riley couldn't walk, but he could hold on, so Mox volunteered himself as a horse, taking Riley on his back.

Davin asked Vi what other awful things might be waiting, but Vi couldn't answer. They'd apparently made so many whacky inventions down here that she couldn't remember them all, couldn't tell which ones would still work.

"Or what my dad might've put back together," Vi said. "What I still don't get is why they'd activate at all? I gave the code?"

"You're dad's paranoid?" Davin replied as they once again led the group one red light at a time. "Maybe Eden's already cracked it."

Vi didn't answer. She'd been quiet since Riley's injury. Riley himself hadn't: the man, with drugs killing his pain, speculated endlessly about how close he'd been to death.

Davin was starting to see why, when Vi had skipped off the moon, she'd gone alone.

The next bot to come their way didn't match the welder's horrors. Instead, the treaded terror looked made for make-up, its numerous arms ending in hangers, in brushed and mirrors.

"If you need help getting ready in the morning," Vi said by way of explanation.

This time, when Davin fired Melody and turned the

robot's core into molten sludge, nothing exploded. The tunnel, did, however, pick up a rather nice lavender aroma.

From there the bots came fast and ridiculous. Household horrors, meant for things like folding laundry or washing dishes on the fly surged forward. The machines did their level best to attack the group, but the Nines had faster trigger fingers than the robots had functions, leaving the tunnel coated with Vi's old, blasted ideas.

Exactly how long they spent in the tunnel, Davin couldn't say. Several hours seemed the right mark, a cautious creeping and shooting adventure made bearable thanks to the tunnel's great ventilation. A cool breeze tamped down on the sweat while air recyclers cleaned out the smell of busted circuits. Even those red lights, their crimson guides, swapped from ominous to surreal, a movie's backdrop for bot-blowing action.

By the tunnel's end, a bland hatch at a narrowed point, Davin looked around and noted a crew tired but alive, bereft of serious wounds save the pallid Riley. Melody's power pack was running low, but she had a few bomber blasts left in her. Mox and Merc's rifles were the same, but they were about to enter a place with ammunition aplenty.

If their weapons went empty, they could just take one from a downed Eden goon.

"Puk," Davin said to the dinged bot, "after seeing all those things, I'm glad we got you."

"After seeing all those things," Puk replied, "I'm glad I got me too."

"The door's unlocked," Vi said, turning to face the foursome. "If I remember right, it'll open into my rooms in the basement. What Eden would want with them, I don't know, but they might be there."

Davin pointed at Puk. "Send the bot through first. Eden might not get itchy fingers with it."

"I object to being used as bait," Puk countered.

"Better you than one of us," Mox said, still holding Riley on his back. "Someone takes the piss out of you, we can put you back together. Us, look at what I'm carrying."

"Hey," Riley objected, albeit without much energy.

"Viola?" Puk rotated her way, shined the bot's small blue light towards her face.

"Guess what," Vi said, putting on a smile more tender than any Davin had seen her give a human before, "you go take a peek for us, and I'll upgrade your laser to something real nasty."

Puk beeped. "Really?"

"Really."

"Better than Davin's shotgun?"

"Whatever you want."

Puk floated over to the door. "Then I won't let you down."

With the rest of the team drifting back into the dark, Vi opened the hatch and stayed behind the door as it swung open. Beyond, what Davin could see, looked like a silver-blue hallway. Off-white diodes laid out a clean view.

Puk trilled, drifted through the hatch. The bot rotated around as it entered the hallway. Davin kept his hand on Melody, ready to raise and fire, but nobody shouted anything. Nobody shot.

Puk completed its full circle, beeped a single low note. Rather than waiting, the little bot jetted off to the left, leaving their view. Vi, turning to peer around the hatch at the noise, saw Puk jet away.

"Wait," Davin hissed, seeing Vi's stance change, but the woman ignored him, dipping out after her bot.

Signaling to Mox and Riley to wait, Davin struck after Vi, making it all of two steps before one of Puk's loud squawks echoed down the hall. And, after, a bright orange flash.

Followed by a hard thump as something hit the floor.

Davin, cursing Vi for not sticking to the plan, dashed through the hatch, turned after his engineer and her bot, and found the view not at all what he expected.

18

OFFICE POLITICS

Davin's instincts pulled the scene together like so: three people, two standing and one on the floor. A sole bot, Puk, adrift near the right side where the rounded hall expanded into a bubble-shaped room. One weapon visible, a pistol held in Vi's hand and vaguely in the direction of the floor-bound body. The non-Vi standing person had his arms held high, like a stick-up in a cliched robbery.

The scene thus established, control firmly in Vi's hands, Davin let his fingers off Melody's trigger and wheeled the opposite way, confirming an empty hall curling to the left after another couple meters.

"Cover the back." Davin dispatched Mox and his clinging, wounded Riley towards the curl.

When Davin returned to the scene of the crime, about three seconds after his first glance, Vi and the other scuzzball—so identified by the man's Eden-green overcoat —crouched over the fallen third. Vi let loose some choice expletives while the other guy apologized. Puk maintained its respectful distance.

"What've we got here?" Davin asked, drawing up and looking down at the damage.

Vi's aim needed some work: her rapid shot had hit the target right in the thigh, as unlethal a grazing as Davin had seen in some time. Yet here this ninny moaned, despaired as if Vi had given him a fatal nuking.

"Two stupid people getting what they deserve," Vi muttered.

The guy not on the floor looked up at Davin's words, and in all his years, Davin had never seen a face go paler. The man's already sun-spared skin went ghostly as he placed Davin's scowling mug with Eden's propaganda.

"You're the killer!" the man said, taking hands away from his friend to jab a finger at Davin. "You're the one they're all looking for."

"Thanks for the reminder," Davin said, and, just for fun, he let Melody's nozzle linger in the man's direction.

With a distinct squeak, the man abandoned his friend and scooted back across the floor, putting a few meters between himself and Davin.

The shifting target gave Davin a good chance to take in the room itself, not that he was surprised by what he found. The center held a long workbench, nearly as long as the one on the *Jumper*. The room's rounded walls sported hooks aplenty, all racked up with instruments of intelligent design. The whole thing glimmered with well-kept attention, buttered up by a pearly light ring in the ceiling's center.

Vi's old workshop, nice one too. Put all the haphazard junk shacks back in Vagrant's Hollow to shame.

"They're Eden," Vi said, shaking her head as she stood up from the injured man. "Co-workers of mine."

"Co-workers?" the coward barked. "We were hardly that.

Accessories to genius, that's all we were. Nothing. You might as well forget we existed!"

Vi sighed, rubbed her forehead.

"Should I, Vi?" Davin asked. "Forget that they exist?"

The question whisked away Vi's sarcasm, brought back the hardscrabble determination the engineer had shown ever since arriving on Eden Prime way back when.

"No, you absolutely should not." Vi angled the pistol at the wounded man. "Not until they tell us what they're doing here."

"Easy." The wounded one on the floor this time, his teeth all knotted against each other. His partner, the coward, scooted behind the workbench. Davin might've been concerned about ambushes, except they were both unarmed, and about as far away from fighters as Davin could imagine.

"You're brilliant, Vi," the injured guy continued. "Eden didn't like you getting away, so we were sent here to find what else you'd done. Unlock the key to your mind, or something."

"By ransacking my childhood?"

"Studying, more like," the wounded man sat up. At least he could meet Davin's look without flinching. "You don't know what a bind you put us in, coming up with so many good things and then just disappearing. What were we supposed to do?"

"Blaming her for your own problems isn't the way to go," Davin said. "Is it just you two nosy ones, then?"

"Just us back here," the man's lip trembled. "Please, do you have any painkillers?"

"Don't ask them for anything, they'll just as soon shoot you as give you help," called the other one from behind the bench.

Leaving Vi to intimidate the hurt one, Davin stepped over and around the workbench's side, looking right at the man's back. The coward had his right hand tapping away quick on his left wrist, a tiny computer whirring away.

"Just what are you doing?" Davin said, kneeling behind the man.

The coward jumped, hit his head on the island, and fell over. Davin raised up one foot and stamped down on the man's left wrist, felt the computer crack and break.

"Talking to somebody?" Davin asked.

"Wasn't talking, no way," the coward replied. "Just writing my will, seeing as you're going to be killing me any second now."

"Don't tempt me," Davin grumbled. "But, seeing as you asked, I might have a way to save your skin."

"Anything!"

Davin winced. Eden really needed to find some stiffer spines.

"How about you tell us what's waiting in Vi's house back there? If you're right, I won't turn your face into a smoking crater."

Given a mission the man could accomplish, with suitable motivation, the coward, with the wounded man contributing commentary, laid out a decisive and disturbing map.

Vi's parents had been split, the mother confined to the house's bedroom while the father spent his days in the home's main office. Eden wasn't interrogating them so much as keeping them under constant surveillance and control.

"We're sure they'll side with the rebels if they get the chance," the coward explained. "This way, neither one'll pull anything because of what might happen to the other."

The guard detail, though, had been lacking lately.

Thanks to increasing problems around Ganymede—good one, Sandeer—drones had been given the major responsibility, with only a couple humans watching over every shift.

"Guy like you shouldn't have any issues," the wounded one said. "Total cakewalk."

At least they knew how to suck up.

Merc eventually killed the description by poking his head in, reminding Davin that this wasn't story time. Vi took point, setting Puk on guard duty and warning her two former partners to keep their hands to themselves.

"You're not letting us go?" The coward tried as Davin and Vi turned to leave.

"We get out of this alive, Puk'll let you free," Vi said. "We find out you lied, Puk will fry you well before help arrives."

"Absolutely," warned the bot. "You'll be totally cooked."

Davin laughed as they left the room. Vi'd done a nice job there, and he told her so. Wasn't often a greenie like her found the guts to turn on an interrogation.

"I'm not a greenie anymore," Vi said as they passed the hatch, heading around the corner to catch up with Mox, Riley, and Merc. "I'm not the same girl you met on Europa."

"Don't I know it," Davin said.

The curving hall didn't give them the best view, the best hint. Instead, the clue their little moment was over came with a warning call, came with flashes, and pounding feet headed their way.

If the hallway offered an advantage, it lay in the lack of cover. Merc, Mox, and the clinging Riley spewed lasers down the arched corridor at the advancing Eden squad.

Of course, that missing cover went both ways. Return fire streaked in, forcing Mox and Merc to backpedal into Davin and Vi as the two came running to reinforce. Both Nines already sported laser burns in their outfits where shots came in too hot. Riley, covered by Mox's fat exoskeleton, stayed safe.

"Close quarters," Davin said. "Should be right up your alley, Merc."

"If you can buy me a second," Merc replied, swapping spots with Davin.

The laser exchange had Eden approaching with caution. Davin risked a peek, nearly lost his eye to a quick shot, but confirmed the Eden squad had their firing lines layered, a four-across, two deep formation heading their way.

"Melody?" Mox asked.

"Too slow." Davin grimaced. Counted down the several seconds they had till Eden rounded the curve. "By the time I pulled the trigger and the burst went out, I'd be a pyre."

"Not necessary, boys," Merc announced, his rifle replaced in its shoulder holster and his hands holding two plate-sized discs. Each one had a grip along the back, a copper outer ring and a bulb in the center. "Get ready for the follow-up."

"What're those?" Riley asked.

"Just watch."

With Vi retreating back a few steps with Mox, Davin pressed himself to the hallway's inner wall. Merc took the outer, wheeling himself up for a sidearm sling.

The first disc spun out from Merc's left hand, catching along the outer wall and zipping along it, momentum carrying it around the corner and out of sight.

"One, two," Merc counted, listening to the alarmed calls from the Eden squad. "Three."

Merc whipped the second disc at a higher angle, so the saucer skimmed up the outer wall and wrapped onto the hallway's ceiling as it sped from view.

A crackle-bang, teeth-rattling and hair-raising in equal

measure, cued Davin to roll around the curve with Melody up and ready.

Lightning arced from the first disc, jumping at the Eden soldiers, most of whom grabbed at eyes blinded by the bang half of the disc's arsenal. Those few who'd managed to adjust their goggles or avoid the flash found their weapons shorting out, their nerves spasming.

All that before the second disc dropped into their midst and repeated the salvo. Davin raised his arm to block his eyes, let the bang wash over him. The ears still rang, but otherwise Davin had a clear firing lane at eight disabled, disorganized, doomed troops.

To kill or not to kill?

Davin went the pacifist route. When Merc, following, asked why Davin wasn't shooting, Davin's answer came as the lightning died, as he slammed Melody's stock into the closest Eden trooper.

"Saving ammo," Davin said, laying out the man and continuing into an elbow-forward back-hand at the next one in line. "Mox, get in here."

The metal man made the right call, ditching Riley with Vi for a hard charge up the center. Just as Eden's players were pulling themselves together, minus the three socked out by Davin and Merc, Mox barreled into their middle. With the exo-skeleton, Mox picked up troopers and slammed them into each other like a kid playing with his toys. One flew into the ceiling, only to land on a hapless colleague dumped there as Mox struck his way through. Others mashed into the walls, the seventh found himself ground into the floor with a hard stomp.

Only the eighth, the squad's last, pulled herself together enough to turn and run.

"Down," Davin said, letting Melody hang and drawing

his pistol. He squinted with one eye, looked across the bodies, Mox and Merc confirming them out, and squeezed the trigger.

The white-orange bolt laced out, landed right between the fleeing trooper's shoulder blades. Dropped them right before another hatch, this one already open. The trooper's momentum sent them sliding through the doorway, an introduction to whatever lay beyond.

"Nice shot," Riley said, leaning on Vi as the two brought up the back.

"Easy when they're running from you," Davin replied. "Take what you can, quick now."

While the Nines kept the *Jumper* stocked with some arms, the Eden troopers offered an arsenal buffet. Grenades, charged rifles, close range stun batons. All useful and all snatched fast.

"We're going to leave them here?" Vi asked as Davin whistled for the group to get moving.

Eden hadn't pressed an attack, which meant they'd be walking into another trap. The less time Eden had to prep it, the better.

"If we're still in this place when they get up, we're dead," Davin replied. "Merc, go take a look."

The Viper pilot obliged, heading towards the doorway with rifle drawn. The man only had two of those discs, and he'd collected the used up pair, slipping them back onto his belt. Eden's own supplies made up for the loss, shock and frag grenades now dangling next to the empty discs.

How much of Vi's house were they going to destroy?

Davin grinned. Something felt good about sticking it to the hyper wealthy. Galaxy Forge could afford to pay any repair bill dumped at their feet today.

Even Vi, with Riley on her left shoulder, looked as determined as ever. No second thoughts shooting up her childhood home. Then again, maybe all those broken bots they'd left behind in the tunnel snuffed out those emotions.

"Looks quiet," Merc said, glancing back at the Nines from his vantage, left shoulder pressed against the arched hatch's left lip. "Maybe that's all Eden had here?"

"For the moment," Davin said. "Something tells me our friends back there called for help. Clock's ticking."

The main atrium rose several stories, bracketed by curling ramps on either side. Glittering chrome layered on the ramp railings, framed pictures on the walls, lay in strands hanging from a central chandelier. The metal might've been tacky save for it, being, well, everywhere. A bold decision, and a recent one.

"They've changed up the place," Davin said, joining Merc and looking out. "Interesting."

"If you wanna call it that," Merc replied.

Merc had missed the first visit, spending the time near-dead in space. Now he looked appropriately bemused at what people with little limits did with their decor.

"The office is to the left," Vi said, her voice hesitating. "Davin, you get my dad."

"What?"

But Vi didn't wait. With the atrium looking clear—Eden must've swiped the furniture—the engineer broke past Davin and Merc, sprinting out and angling for the ramp up. Every lunge carried Vi several meters in the low gravity, turning the run into a loping leap series.

One drawing out the dangers.

Eden drones buzzed down from the ceiling, swept in through the open, wide front doors. Each bot, a slender tripod with every leg ending in a slim needle gun, mixed deadly precision with fragile speed.

"Cover her!" Davin shouted, stepping himself into the open to try and draw fire.

The drones didn't notice, speckling Vi's route with hot white blasts. They cascaded in sheets, peppering the area around Vi, on Vi, with fire. Davin saw several bolts strike home, saw Vi falter but keep going till she reached the ramp's top. Only then did the drones adjust, catching on to the fact Vi wasn't firing back and the trio on the ground very much were.

Leaving Riley behind in the tunnel, Davin, Merc, and Mox advanced into the atrium, blazing up at the drones. With fresh Eden rifles—Davin left Melody alone, waiting for better opportunities—the trio could spray just like the drones, blanketing the air with red laser. Strikes melted drone jets, burst and broke power packs and batteries. Molten shrapnel drifted down as the two dozen drones shifted their attention.

If Vi had accomplished one thing in her suicide sprint, it'd been to draw the drones in after her. The bots clustered, making them easy targets for a laser.

Easier targets for grenades.

"Pop'em," Davin said. "Mox!"

Davin and Merc, dropping their rifles, didn't bother pulling the pins on the frag and shock grenades, instead swooping them up and throwing them towards the clustered drones.

As all those glittering needles oriented on their new targets, Mox adjusted his aim, kept up the fire.

Did Mox hit one grenade or all? Didn't matter. One exploded, triggering bangs, bombs, and lightning from the other three. The cloud enveloped the drones in a smokey, burning, sparking disaster, one that dropped its wreckage all around the atrium. Pulling up their rifles, taking scattered fire from drones on the fringes, Davin, Mox, and Merc played clean-up as metal rained.

With hot sparks infusing the air, quiet took hold as the last drone crashed to the ground. Davin's finger left the trigger, where it felt like it might be stuck forever. Sweat greased the captain's forehead, and laser burns laced his legs, his right shoulder. Merc and Mox weren't much better, with the latter lurching leftward with every move, his exoskeleton damaged. Merc sported a new haircut, smoking strands fried up, and had one hand near his stomach where his armor had burned through.

"But we're alive," Davin said, standing amid the ruin.

"And they're not," Mox agreed, though his strained face showed less victory, more stress. "Let's hope we don't join them."

"Which means getting the hell out of here," Merc said. "That the office?"

The pilot pointed with his rifle to a single door left of the main entrance, arched like all the others. The only clue it didn't lead to, say, a closet came from the hatch's ornate appearance and a keypad on the right.

"Let's find out," Davin said. Vi could've confirmed, but the engineer had disappeared. Given the shots she took, she might be dead. "Riley, what—"

Davin's ask died as he swept back to look for the injured mechanic. Riley, though, wasn't in the hall. In fact, the man had used the railing to pull himself all the way up to the second level, pistol dragging along in his right hand.

"Going after her," Riley called back down. "Just like your plan."

"My damn plan said you two ought to get her dad, not run off and die," Davin countered, but Riley didn't stop moving. Ripping off a sigh, brought upon both by the growing aches and his disobeying crew, Davin turned to Mox instead. "Feel like breaking down a door?"

"Always," Mox replied.

With Merc moving to cover the house's front entrance—no immediate assaults incoming—Davin followed Mox to the closed office hatch. Riley, for his part, disappeared after Vi, his repeated calls for her name echoing throughout.

Mox gauged the hatch, built, like all the others, to handle a vacuum break in the surrounding dome. You had to be able to survive no matter what room you were in, and these metal-and-rubber seals did the trick.

"Not easy," Mox said, studying the hatch.

"Unless you know the passcode," Davin glared at the keypad and its numbers array, "brute force is what we've got."

Nodding, Mox shifted back a step, took a deep breath. Davin readied an Eden rifle.

"Go for it, big guy," Davin said.

Mox stepped into the haymaker, a solid swing going right at the hatch's left joint. The metal rattled, something groaned. The door didn't fall apart. Backing up, Mox swung again, and again. The hatch grew dents, the joint twisted.

The door remained shut.

"Okay," Davin said, steadying Mox before the guy wasted more energy. "New plan."

The keypad had a speaker, another common safety feature. Davin pressed the little red button and made his short and sweet speech.

"Friends, we've tried knocking a few times, but our hands are sore and our patience is gone," Davin said. "Next up comes the big boom. We want you alive, but we'll accept you dead, so here's your chance. Open up in five, or regret it for eternity."

It took till three.

The hatch clicked, bars thunked as security measures gave up their holds. Davin kept his trigger finger ready, the rifle up. Mox had his own knees bent, shoulder in charge position. A one-two punch: Davin would clear the way with an opening salvo while Mox made it inside to ensure no coward managed to close the hatch again.

Three Eden flunkies stood inside, hands up. Rifles lay on the floor. A floor, Davin whistled, that shed the usual tile for wood. Actual maple, a type Davin only recognized from a bad 'Hero of Earth' sponsorship ad campaign for . . .

Stay focused.

Beyond the soldier trio, the maple found itself covered by a single arched desk—must everything in Vi's home be curved?—of similarly light wood. Two chairs, upholstered in Galaxy Forge red fabric, sat to the room's sides, beneath walls blazing with big screens. Even in his first second, Davin parsed the wraparound glow: Galaxy Forge production progress, numbers and stats from everywhere on Ganymede.

Talk about a workaholic.

"Out," Davin said as Mox planted his arm against the hatch to hold it open. "Lest you want to wind up like these drones over here."

The soldiers didn't ask questions, wisely realizing an Eden paycheck wasn't worth their lives. Maybe, too, they saw Davin's face, his wounds, and realized the most wanted man wasn't to be trifled with.

Merc took up escort duty once the soldiers hit the atrium, leaving Davin and Mox to head into the office. A sole figure remained, seated at the desk, eyes tight, mouth frowning as he glared at Davin.

The president of Galaxy Forge, one of the wealthiest,

most powerful people in humanity's stockpile, had given Davin a friendly welcome before. Now, Davin had the sense Vi's dad wasn't so keen on his mercenary self setting foot on that pretty maple.

"Ready to go?" Davin asked, jerking his head over his shoulder to make it clear.

"Go where?" Vi's dad talked like the powerful tended to, every question accompanied by a sneering curiosity that someone had dared ask him anything. "This is my home."

"Know that," Davin replied. "'Cept it's not your home any more, is it?"

"It's a mess, if anything. Thanks to you."

Davin blinked. Vi's dad hardly seemed a willing escapee. Sandeer wanted him freed, but the man looked all too willing to stay in his little prison.

A loud curse, the hiss whine of rifle fire from outside saved Davin from having to think up another line.

"Merc's getting shot at," Mox growled.

"Those three had more weapons?" Davin asked.

The answer came from Merc himself, the man hustling through the hatch and yelling at Mox to close it behind him.

"Eden's here, and they're not fooling around," Merc said between breaths. "Those three goobers went out the front door and when I checked to make sure they were still walking, I just about ate laser."

Bright hot flashes followed Merc, several lacing into the office, leaving burn marks on the big screens. Mox threw some bolts back with his own rifle, huddled behind the hatch's door.

A bad choice: shutting the hatch would trap them inside the office. Not shutting it would let Eden overwhelm the trio, cook 'em quick.

"Close the damn door," Davin shouted, and Merc spun

back, gave Mox covering fire as shadows moved in the atrium.

The metal man did the deed, slamming the hatch shut and sealing it tight. Three large bolts on the hatch's backside clicked into place, helping form the vacuum seal.

Merc sat down, Mox leaned against the door, and Davin was about to turn back to the frustrated goal of this particular crap shoot when the captain felt a cool barrel touch the back of his neck.

Aww, hell.

19

DEADLY DECOR

It wasn't the gun that irritated Davin. He'd been held at barrel-point enough times now that it felt a little cliche. No, the annoying feeling twinging Davin into a headache as he stood there in that screen-filled office came from the stupidity.

"You know they're going to kill you right?" Davin said. "Once Eden figures out how to keep you from breaking their new toy?"

"They won't," Vi's father replied.

"They will," Merc shot back. "Your daughter put together an amazing weapon and they figured out an antidote real quick. They'll get you too."

Something hit the hatch hard. The battering bang of a breaching ram. Another couple hits without action and Eden would turn on the screws, drill a hole.

No way they'd blow it apart and risk their prize.

"I'll take the chance," Vi's dad said, and Davin had to give the man credit: not a waver entered his tone. Not easily shaken, this guy. "Open the hatch or I shoot."

Davin flipped through his mental card deck, throwing

out ideas and discarding most. The rules of the game said when you couldn't win, you tried to lose the least. Davin figured there was one card that could give him that.

"How about a deal?" Davin asked.

"You're in no—"

"Shoot Davin, we kill you," Mox growled, rising to his full height.

Davin couldn't name any sights more intimidating than that metal-clad monster of a man glaring at you. Vi's dad seemed stunned into silence, so Davin continued.

"As I was saying, a deal. We go out there and you offer Eden a bargain: me, without a fight, if my friends there get to go out the way they came in."

"How did you get in here?"

"Not important," Davin replied. No way he'd hand that info to Vi's dad and, by extension, to Eden. "Deal?"

"Why would Eden agree to that?"

Davin sighed, "Do you, just, avoid the media?"

"I'm a busy man."

"Suffice it to say I'm their public enemy number one. My face haunts their nightmares. My name makes their squads turn and run. I'm—"

"I get it," Vi's dad said. "I'll offer you to Eden. If they don't bite, I lose nothing."

"That's the spirit," Davin said, ignoring the protests coming from Mox and Merc. "Gents, I know this looks grim, but think of it this way: vengeance is a great motivator, and I fully expect you both to trash Eden in my name after I'm gone."

Merc squinted, shook his head. Mox kept glaring at Vi's dad.

"Not funny, Davin," the big man said.

"Yeah, but realistic."

A third and final bang hit the hatch, and when the sturdy circle didn't crumple, a new whine spun up. Sparks and shrapnel would start flying momentarily.

"Time to go," Vi's dad said. "Open the hatch."

Mox looked to Davin, Merc cursed and swapped out his rundown rifle for another charged Eden one off the floor.

"Do it, big guy," Davin said. "It's the best shot we've got."

"It's a crap plan," Merc muttered, but the pilot didn't stop Mox from flipping back the bolts, pulling the hatch open right into the spinning breacher's teeth.

The two Eden soldiers manning the breacher pulled back, clearing the way for six others to point their rifles right into the Nines. Standing with them, looking utterly cool and composed, was Aya.

"Drop the weapons," she said, nodding at Mox and Merc, who, with another gratifying look towards Davin, obliged.

Quite nice to know the two would've gone out in a blaze of glory for him.

"Aya," Davin said, stomping over Vi's dad. "Nice to see a reasonable person here for a change. Want to discuss terms?"

Aya cocked her head at Davin, noted the pistol held to Davin's head, "I believe he's the one I should be talking with."

"Correct," said Vi's dad. "I'll offer you a simple deal. Davin Masters in exchange for my freedom."

"And their lives," Davin said.

"Ignore him," replied Vi's dad, and he shoved the pistol's end into Davin's neck. "You'll take these three and leave my house forever."

Mox turned a new look at Vi's dad, a look that held not

so much anger as a flat-faced promise of doom, in this life, the next, and all the ones after that.

Davin had seen that look once before, given to the man who'd killed the only woman Mox had ever loved.

"You really screwed this one up," Davin said.

"I accept," called Aya. "Please come out, and do refrain from moving your hands or legs in a dangerous manner. We wouldn't want you to die for nothing, now would we?"

Vi's father nudged Davin with the pistol. "Out you go."

"C'mon boys," Davin said, leading off the death march. "Let's see how they want to kill us."

Aya's squad spread around the atrium, cutting off the stairway ramps, the tunnel exit, the front door with their glistening green-black rifles, their padded armor. Helmets and visors coated every face, deep green gloves every hand. Like the shock troops outside the comm building, Eden turned their killers anonymous. They acted like it too, raising their weapons in synchronized fashion to cover the Nines trio.

Could these all be androids?

Unlikely Heath could get so many going if he'd put so much effort into Mecha-Phyla, but who knew. If Aya's squad was all murderbots, no trick Davin could come up with would matter.

Better, then to hold to the cocky belief that these were the same slapdash troops serving on Heath's frigate, the ones more concerned with dessert than details.

Aya stuck to her ethereal qualities, eyes half closed as she watched Davin, Mox, and Merc approach. She had on the same Eden uniform, her visor pulled up for the occasion. Sweat marred an otherwise clean face, dust and dirt clung to her uniform, a likely holdover from the comm center scramble.

Mox and Merc stayed off to the right, standing beneath the huge chromed chandelier. Davin received the face-to-face treatment, a bemused staredown, as if he was a student about to take a class he was in no way qualified for.

Better reset those expectations.

"Where's good ol' Heath?" Davin looked around. "Captain too scared to come?"

Aya's wispy smile grew, "He's dealing with your other half. You have an impressive crew, Davin."

"Secret to looking good? Surround yourself with people better than you," Davin replied. "Might be a lesson you could learn."

"I'll consider it." Aya finished by sweeping her pistol free from its holster and leveling at Davin's face. "You can back away now."

Davin blinked, then realized Aya was talking to Vi's father. The man obliged her, dipping a few meters towards his office. Davin didn't bother looking back, the main event would be Aya's fingers and that trigger.

"What about dying for something?" Davin asked. "Don't think blazing me here is going to help you any."

"Have you ever made propaganda, Davin?"

"Guess you could consider some of those Earth Hero ads that, not sure what side I was talking up, though," Davin meandered his way through the words, taking his time to study the surroundings, see what options presented themselves.

The answer: not many. Mox and Merc didn't have weapons, stood in the same death circle as Davin. Mox was about the only one who might escape, use that exoskeleton to take some hits en route to a charge out the door or, hell, through the wall.

Meanwhile, Davin and Merc would shuffle off their souls on the tile.

"The best persuasion comes from real life," Aya said. "When a, as you put it, hero makes a point for everyone to follow. We've been trying to deliver that point clearly. Unfortunately, you've been difficult."

"Because I haven't let Mecha-Phyla kill me?"

Aya's smile didn't change, those placid eyes locked on him. Until her wristlet beeped, which prompted Aya to snap her glance to her forearm and nod.

"Showtime," Aya said. "Please look frightened."

She aimed down the pistol. Davin tensed his knees, waited for the right moment. If Eden wanted an execution, he'd give'em a mess instead.

Aya's cheeked tightened, the slightest ripple ran down her arms, and Davin dove right. The pistol shot blazed over his left shoulder, cracking into the atrium wall. Davin hit the ground, expecting a second shot to torch him, but instead he heard a shout, a disembodied voice coming from all around them.

"Get your guns off my friends," Vi said through speakers nestled throughout the atrium.

Vi ended the sentence with four names: her father's, mother's, her own, and 'Kitty'. The confusion crossing everyone's faces morphed to curiosity as buzzing, hissing, creaking and groaning filled the atrium. Similar sounds echoed in from the front door.

Aya shook her head, refocused on Davin, even as the chandelier above her unfolded like a flower. The chromed bars shifted, breaking their synchronized flow to focus on . . .

Eden's troops.

"Watch out!" Vi's father yelped, the Eden soldiers

already noticing as the chromed portraits receded, revealing nasty turrets.

Vi's father started to say something else, started and stopped as Mox clapped a hand around the man's neck. Eden should've shot right then, should've lit Mox up, but the atrium exploded instead.

Aya's follow-up shot started things, a plug striking Davin in the shoulder as he rolled. His thick coat took most of it, another burn otherwise added to his collection.

From there, the Galaxy Forge defenses took over. The chandelier lanced out with a dozen shots at once, each one blasting into Eden's armored troops. Five turrets lit out at their nearest targets, spitting hot green fire.

Eden didn't take it sitting down: the troopers countered, the chandelier breaking into glorious purple-orange flames as lasers smacked its hidden power packs. Three turrets were reduced to slag in as many seconds. Smoke suffused the room as misfires lit up clothes, rifles blew up in hand as they overheated.

And Aya kept coming, ignoring the chandelier as it delivered a strike to her right arm. Aya flipped the pistol to her left as Davin curled back to his feet. Lasers, screams, smoke, shrapnel blew up around them.

"Not very sporting fighting a man in cuffs," Davin said as Aya took aim.

Her eyes were wide and focused, no more sleepy soldier here.

Staying still meant a swift death, so Davin went for the unexpected: he charged. A meter apart, Davin didn't have much time to gather momentum, but he could duck his shoulder forward. Aya was a good enough shot to hit Davin's chest anyway, filling Davin's lungs with a burning, wheezing agony.

Adrenaline, coupling with the pain-suppressing drugs Sandeer provided, kept Davin on his feet.

The captain's right shoulder hit Aya's shooting arm, knocking the weapon up as Davin barreled on through to its owner. With Ganymede's limp gravity, Davin's hit knocked Aya onto her back, the top-heavy strike causing her to float for a half second as she flew across the tile.

Davin didn't stop running after. Hopefully, somewhere behind him, Mox and Merc were getting Vi's father to safety. That bastard.

On his right, Davin saw an Eden trooper go up in smoke, the chandelier acing the man with three bolts at once. His run caught a boost when a grenade exploded behind him, the shockwave giving Davin's feet an extra kick.

Aya brought her pistol back down, just in time for Davin's outstretched hands to grab it. The captain's momentum carried him past Aya, his grip on her pistol's scorching barrel enough to push it from his face.

The shot singed hair, slammed into the wall above the atrium's front door.

Aya, proving she had some moves, let the pistol go. Davin's run kept going without resistance, the pistol barrel in his hands as he lurched himself into a somersault. Dipping his injured shoulders, ignoring how damn much it hurt, Davin rolled in the air to land on his back, looking across the floor towards Aya.

The Eden soldier stared right back at him, second pistol in her own hands.

"Draw?" Davin tried to say, rasped instead, the effort burning his throat.

Aya's face tightened. Davin pulled the trigger.

The shots beamed out, Davin's careening over Aya's shoulder while Aya's burned above Davin's nose and out the front door. Davin adjusted, Aya lowered her aim, then cursed and pushed herself up, scrambling as a turret sent a laser line scorching through where she'd been. Davin added to it, but his upside-down accuracy was lacking, the shot instead vanishing off into the gray-black smoke.

Curling up, ignoring the tugs from his body telling him time was up, Davin stood and snapped off another shot Aya's way. She'd been moving to his right, Davin's blast, by luck more than anything else, torched near enough Aya's hand for her to drop the pistol.

She kept running, angling towards the atrium's curving entry wall. Davin drew a bead, looked to put an end to it, and felt hands grab him, tear away the pistol.

Davin threw an elbow, bought a half-meter gap between himself and the Eden trooper, a man on fire in a couple places, laser damage scarring his armor. A wide circle on the man's left side glowed orange where a rifle must've blown.

No matter, the man drew a half-melted knife from a sheath on his thigh.

Davin dropped into his brawling stance, letting his coat's ruins fall around him. The trooper came on, weaving the knife through the air as if carving a big letter in space. Davin let him work, taking a step back, very much aware Aya would be changing her own course.

A couple seconds.

The trooper made a cut, a slash forward that, on Earth, would've been fast enough to tear Davin's face apart. On Ganymede, the swing took a hair longer to get going, gave Davin a chance to hop up, twist his left arm.

Snaring the knife on his coat's collar, Davin used his right to dish the soldier a jab to the goggles. Those tight-fitting things would send a hit to the eyeballs. The soldier tried to yank the knife free, succeeded, but earned a second whack from Davin for his troubles. Two hits to the head had the soldier stumbling, had the soldier clearing a meter from Davin.

The chandelier found him, lighting up the poor punk from above.

Not that Davin had time to celebrate.

Aya, flying in off a wall-kick, a killer move far easier in low gravity, crashed into Davin's back and bore him to the ground. She arm-barred Davin's neck, grinding his face into the tile. Grit nuzzled Davin's cheek, his ears ringing from the impact, from all the curses, the calls, the threats. His whole body protested.

"If nothing else," Aya said, "I will have you as a prize."

Her words cut through, gave Davin an idea. His left hand, mashed in next to his waist, found a looted sphere, found the pin.

"Last one you'll ever collect," Davin wheezed.

He jerked, pulled the pin free, slid his arm up so Aya could see just what he'd done.

As deaths went, at least this one would be quick.

Life takes measures of the living. Opportunities unplanned for bring judgment, by others and oneself, about capabilities, about willpower, about sacrifice.

Aya was not willing to sacrifice herself.

Cursing, Aya released Davin's neck, swung her arm wide and batted the grenade away. The flashing orb bounced out the atrium's front door, and in that moment, his life restored to him, Davin sent his head cracking back.

He'd been accused of having a thick skull. Davin took it as a compliment.

The shot hit Aya's chin, rolling her back. The grenade crackled, blew just outside the front door. Tile and dirt swept in, the shockwave cutting Davin a hundred times, throwing both him and Aya end over end into the atrium's center.

Davin hit first, a gentle landing on some trooper's scorched body. Aya crumpled near him, groaning. Davin tried to think of something witty to say, if only because everything else seem scrambled. His vision swam in red— something must've cut his eye, or his brow—and sticky warmth pooled beneath his legs.

Would be real nice if the fight ended now.

But no, like some villain in a bad horror movie, Aya pulled herself up. Her uniform lay in ruins, burned and blasted skin exposed. Hair scorched, no doubt like Davin's own. But, like the other Eden trooper, she still had a knife and Aya pulled it free. A job to do, a mission to accomplish.

Read the room, Davin wanted to say, because as the ringing subsided, the captain noticed something else: quiet. Not absolute— the groans and cries for help from wounded troopers rang out—but the booms had ceased. The laserfire no longer whined.

Aya took one step.

"Drop the knife," Merc's voice, bladed, came from beyond Davin's feet. In the direction of their old entry. "Or don't and let me blast you, I couldn't care less."

Aya growled, glanced away from Davin. Despite the blur, Davin read the calculation. How far could Aya get with a single jump, could she slice Davin and make it out the door before Merc landed a shot?

A whine, a click, a warning came from above. Davin shifted his head, saw the last two spokes remaining on the chandelier angling Aya's way.

"You heard the mercenary," Riley's voice, now, over the intercoms. "Knife on the ground."

Aya closed her eyes, straightened, but didn't drop the

knife. Davin saw the tightness flow through her muscles, the legs tense.

She was going to go for it, and he couldn't raise more than a finger.

The helmet, Eden-green, flew hard from the side and struck Aya like a baseball, slamming her head and knocking her to the ground where, finally, she lay still.

"Helluva throw, Mox," Merc said, voice carrying in the atrium's silence. "Still think it would've been easier to shoot her."

"She's valuable," Mox said, and Davin saw the big guy walk into view. Mox looked Davin's way, frowned, then went to check Aya's pulse. "Get the captain."

FOR A VICTORIOUS PARTY, the scraggly group leaving Vi's family home held nothing but grim looks. Vi's mother, coupled with a limping Riley, carried a patched up and barely alive Vi down the stairs and out. Mox lugged Aya, keeping one arm free and armed just in case Vi's father, whose will to resist seemed to dissipate with his daughter's devastated appearance, wanted to try something stupid.

Which meant Merc won the draw to carry Davin, the pilot doing his best to bring Davin outside without much damage. An effort that succeeded in getting Davin into open air, but failed in making it anything other than a painful exercise.

At least the reward proved worth it: an Eden speeder, one designed for swift strikes, parked outside. Able to hold a couple squads, the speeder sat ready, though the Nines didn't have the keys.

Davin tugged on Merc's sleeve as the pilot settled him into the speeder. The craft's sparse inside had a center corridor bordered by long benches. A hatch at the rear led to a single turret, with a lavatory door to its left. One long white light gave the green-colored everything its shine.

"What's up, captain" Merc asked at the tug. "You're not dying are you?"

Davin wanted to joke that a few laser blasts, punches, and a grenade couldn't kill him. Instead, mustering up enough air in his burnt lungs, Davin gasped a single word, "Puk."

"The bot?" Merc blinked. "Oh, right."

Vi's little machine packed emergency meds, not enough to patch Davin up, but enough to dull the pain and keep him from going into shock. The little black orb stuck Davin —a few more holes he wouldn't notice—as Vi and her family loaded in, Mox glaring at them the whole time.

"Get me the comm," Davin said as Merc settled into the pilot's chair, trying and failing to find an emergency override.

"It's open," Merc replied. "Who do you want to talk to?"

"Leave it on Eden's frequency," Davin said, "and help me up there, or do you expect me to shout?"

"Normally?" Merc asked, scooting back, then lifting Davin into the speeder's chair.

Davin, his hand feeling vaguely alien, as if all the fingers weren't there, broadcast a simple transmission.

"Heath, you coward, I have a deal to make." Davin stopped, heaved in a big breath. "Aya's alive, and I'll give her back to you, if you let us leave."

A preposterous deal. One that'd only work if Davin read Heath right, if the man cared about his passions more than raw numbers.

The reply shot back fast.

"You have your deal," Heath replied, the man's stilted

voice seeming as in shock as Davin felt. "We'll leave your ship alone until you're on it."

"Good," Davin replied, "and one more thing, we'll need the codes to this speeder of yours."

"Stand by for them," Heath said, then the man actually chuckled. "You're doing me a massive favor, my friend."

"How's that?"

"You'll see. When this is all done, and your legend is laid waste, you'll see," Heath said. "Or perhaps you'll be too dead to care, but I hope not, Davin Masters. I hope not."

20

LAST LINES

The *Jumper* picked the Nines up at a small spaceport on Ganymede's developing side. They left Aya there, cuffed and stuffed in a side room. Riley and Merc offered the spaceport employees a bribe—Eden gear left in the speeder, namely—to leave Aya alone till the *Jumper* left. Soaring through Ganymede's cloudless sky towards Jupiter's bulk, Davin, surfing a high from a strong painkiller cocktail, sent Heath Aya's location.

Then came the real work.

The Nines captain lay in his bed, wrapped and bandaged. A slapdash IV stuck in one arm kept him flush with fluids. Phyla, no doctor, and Vi's mother had played emergency medics, helping both Davin and Vi crawl back from the brink.

Vi herself lay in her own quarters, knocked out by stronger stuff than Davin let himself take. She needed rest. Davin needed to negotiate.

"The terms are simple," Davin wheezed, his torched lung refusing to play nice. "You shut down Galaxy Forge and we let you leave."

Vi's father, with Merc standing behind him, glared down at Davin. The man's wife frowned, her hands running up and down her forearms, moving various bangles with every swish.

"Do you even know what you're asking?" Vi's father replied. "Shutting down Galaxy Forge isn't like turning out the lights. It's not a simple switch. There are a billion billion mechanisms at play here. Livelihoods get stopped, people don't get paid. Shipments are left in orbit or thrown away."

"Shipments that, right now, are going to Eden and being used to hurt the people you live with," Davin countered.

"Not all of them. We make passenger transports, delivery speeders. We build the generators used on Saturn's moons to keep them warm. All of that ends with what you're asking." Vi's father pointed a finger at Davin. "All those lives will be on your hands."

Merc snorted, "You chose to let Eden run the show instead of shutting down. You could've fought back, but you chose not to."

Vi's father shook his head, "Your side lost. I chose not to lose everything."

The worst negotiations were when both sides had valid arguments. Much better when Davin had a moral imperative he could leverage. Instead he had to hope that shutting Galaxy Forge down could end the war. *Could* end the war. Not *would*, not *will*.

Lot to risk on a word.

But maybe they didn't have to risk anything at all.

Credit Vi for the inspiration, that and her family's ridiculous house.

"You've got a key to Galaxy Forge," Davin said, dropping the anger from his voice, letting back the sly scoundrel.

Draw them in, make 'em believe they're partners, not enemies.

"Vi told you right," her father said, not bothering to deny it. "It's a safety valve, meant to keep Galaxy Forge in our family. Anyone tries to tear it away, I break it all."

"You don't think Eden's trying to tear it away right now?"

The man took a deep breath. "They can't play that hard. Not while they need Galaxy Forge making their ships."

"So what if you keep making them," Davin said, "but you put in a little insurance?"

"Insurance?"

"Add your key to the software you're dumping on all these ships. Tweak the AI so that if you give the word, all these new Eden toys go dark."

"They'll find it," Vi's father shook his head, "they'll scan the code and figure out what I've planted there."

Davin grinned, "And do what about it? If they ask, it's your new policy. To keep Galaxy Forge's products from being used the wrong way. If Eden doesn't like it, they can go suck a supernova."

Vi's father blinked, didn't say anything for a long moment, until her mother spoke up. Like the dad, Vi's mother ditched any nerves for a boss's attitude, those rubbing arms going instead to her husband's side.

"Do it," Vi's mother said. "It's an easy addition. You have every right, and Eden won't say no. They're weak."

"It means I'll have a shutdown code implanted into every ship we sell," Vi's father said. "Nobody will buy from us. They'll be suspicious."

Vi's mother smiled, a shark's grin, "They don't have any choice. Not now. And these horrible people are going to end the war, right?"

"Horrible people?" Davin asked. "That's a bit harsh."

"Answer my question."

"That's the idea, ma'am."

"Then it's settled," Vi's mother announced. "We'll adjust the software. If Eden makes war using ships we build, we'll shut them down. Then, when this all wraps up, we can delete our little switch."

The three men in the room stared at Vi's mother, who didn't look so much satisfied with herself as confident, impatient.

"Now then," she said, "how are we getting back home? I let Vi make quite the mess, and I don't trust our bots to clean it up."

Davin shouldn't have been surprised, but Vi's parents approached their daughter's recovery with efficiency in mind. Once Vi had left imminent death behind, her parent's view turned to their daughter's right to make her own choices. She'd run away from home, joined up with a group of, as her mother kept saying, disreputable pirates, and then ditched out on a good gig with Eden to, once again, run around with riffraff.

Davin heard all this with a strange laughter horror blend swirling in his drug-addled head, Phyla being the one to recount the conversation as the *Jumper* wrapped around Jupiter.

"I wanted to shoot them just for being so callous," Phyla said, sitting on Davin's bed and changing a dressing on the captain's shoulder. "Our parents would've never said that to us."

"We were all our parents had," Davin replied.

"Oh yeah, because that's an excuse." Phyla rolled her eyes. "You should've seen their eyes when the pickup came by."

The screwball quartet that'd punched a whole in the

Jumper made up for their raid by serving as the taxi between the *Jumper* and Ganymede, intercepting Davin's ship and taking on Vi's parents for a return trip. According to Phyla, Vi's mom took in their would-be fliers and demanded to be delivered back to Ganymede via the *Jumper*'s escape pod.

"I told her she was welcome to jump out the airlock any time she liked," Phyla said. "Opal suggested I go back to the cockpit after that one."

Riley, at least, stayed on. With Vi incapacitated, the ship could use a mechanic. Given the option between returning to Sandeer's minor league resistance and joining the Nines, Riley hadn't hesitated.

"I get the feeling he's been looking for a way off Ganymede all his life," Phyla said, "but he's never been able to pull the trigger."

"Might say the same thing about you."

Phyla sat back, thought for a second, nodded.

"It's hard to leave. Easier when someone gives you a little push."

"Speaking of, find Alissa yet?"

"Can't reach her," Phyla frowned, "the frequency only pinged back a standard message saying to try again later."

"Still from Earth?"

"Still from Earth."

Davin tried to throw up a smile, "The Hero returns."

"As a wanted villain."

"You're saying you want me?"

Phyla ran a finger down Davin's chest, traced the bandages running along the burns, the stitched up shrapnel holes. What started as play faltered partway through, the spark withering under the ridges, the valleys, the railroad tracks carving their way across Davin's skin.

"This wasn't what I meant back then," Phyla said, "when we were fighting."

"You didn't want me shot up? That's comforting."

"Davin."

The captain leaned his head back against the pillow. Tiny strings kept the cushion tied to the bed, same with the blankets and everything else in the *Jumper*'s microgravity world. Couldn't float away, no matter how hard they tried.

"We left this life once, right?" Davin asked.

"We did."

"I almost forgot what it was like, feeling all this," Davin said, closing his eyes. "It's worse now that we're older. Don't recommend it."

"If I'm racing, you won't have to worry."

"You'll still have to worry about me."

"Some things will never change."

Phyla kept her hand on Davin's chest, sleep coming close, sleep almost there, until an angry buzzing popped Davin's eye's back open.

"Sorry, lovebirds," Fournine said, the ship's AI cheery as ever. "We're catching a hail from your favorite Eden stooge."

"Not now, Fournine," Phyla said, only for Davin to lurch up.

"Don't listen to her," Davin said. "Put the moron on."

"Why?" Phyla asked.

"Because I need to know if he's learned his lesson or not."

A small screen on the room's far side flickered to life. Meant for movie watching, the flat rectangle didn't do the best job pulling in Heath's grumbly visage, but Davin considered that a positive. The only stubble he needed to see was his own.

"Captain Masters," Heath said, "my sensors tell me you're slingshotting out of Jupiter's system?"

"And you believe them?" Davin said, only for Phyla to repeat it, loud enough for Heath to hear.

Damn lungs, ruining Davin's style.

"I do, because I believe I know what you're up to," Heath grinned, an unnatural leering smile. Someone who'd spent too much time admiring their toys. "Your little ship has some speed to it, Masters, but you will stop eventually. When you do—"

"No," Davin coughed, forced the words out loud enough. "You don't get to make the threats. We're the Wild Nines. We threaten you."

"From your bed? I don't think you're threatening anyone," Heath replied. "Rest up, Masters. I'll be there when you wake up."

The transmission blinked off, the screen going dark.

"Crap last line," Davin said to Phyla.

"Yours was better."

"All the same," Davin looked down at himself, grimaced, "get us to Earth as fast as you can. We'll need time."

Phyla's eyes glittered, "Have I ever let you down?"

"Well, if we're—"

Phyla pressed a finger to his lips, then replaced it with her own.

Read on for an excerpt from *LUNAR GAMBIT*, book six in the Wild Nines, available soon!

AN EXCERPT FROM LUNAR GAMBIT

Follow the light. Easy enough. Davin tracked the cherry glow with both hands, cupping the dot as it drifted up and down, left and right. Curls and sudden dips, the captain had'em all. At least until a long descent had Davin flipping over himself, floating as he was in the Jumper's middle bay.

A modded out old freighter with its share of stories, the Jumper provided an even-keeled float from Jupiter's red-gold domination to where they were now, somewhere about interstellar kissing distance from Luna, from Earth.

Its hero would look a little different this time.

Davin completed the flip, did a mock bow to his physical therapist, a black-and-silver orb named Puk. The bot, not much larger than a basketball, blinked the red light off.

"You're progressing," Puk said, injecting some of that AI cheer. "I estimate you're at—"

"No estimates," Davin said, lunging for one of the handles spaced throughout the ship. The *Jumper*'s greasy gray-and-green panels embraced the function over form argument, as should anything built for space travel. "I'll be good enough."

"Good enough for what?" Phyla, the Jumper's primary pilot and Davin's squeeziest of squeezes—a term, if he said it aloud in her presence, would get him a hard slap.

"Adventure," Davin said, reversing his push to the floor and instead kicking off the wall to head straight towards Phyla.

The kick came with a new sensation, a buckle and extra press as the leg braces boosted him along. The jolt came as a disconcerting reminder. Davin had, over the several weeks travel time from Jupiter to Earth, come to ignore his braces. Their constant pressure no longer threw him off, instead adding mass to his movement, helping his fried and fractured muscles jump, kick, and hold form like they used to.

"Forever?" Davin had asked Riley when the mechanic first slapped them on. "I gotta wear these things all my life?"

"Don't know, Davin," Riley replied. The guy still sent his eyes everywhere, bumped into things as he learned how to roll with zero g. "I'm not a doctor."

"But you built these?"

"Because Fournine said we should," Riley put up his hands as he saw the frown slide over Davin's face. "Look, the AI's right. It's what all the videos say when you're recovering from hits like the ones you took."

The argument had about as much spice as the nutrient goop wallowing in the *Jumper*'s freezers, but Davin accepted it for one reason: Phyla told him to stop being a baby.

Less easy to get over were the hardened patches along his chest and side. Stitch covering seals slowly repairing laser and shrapnal marred skin from the last awful hours on Ganymede. Those would come off sometime, when the patches themselves turned green and popped off.

Until then, anyone lucky enough to get a look at a naked Davin would see a patchwork man.

Thankfully, the only person with that kinda luck stood right before him, reaching out to catch his floating approach.

"I think we should try again," Phyla said when their hands gripped, she standing, as much as anyone could without gravity, on the walkway as Davin hovered over space.

"Getting a little old for kids, Phy."

She sighed, but smiled in that patient way.

"Alissa." Phyla dropped the delight. "Eden's all over Earth. I don't want to stay here a second longer than we have to."

"You're just being nervous," Davin said. "Once I flash this smile, the whole planet's going to be begging for my time."

"Says the man currently marked as the top terrorist in the solar system."

Davin whistled, "The top spot's mine?"

"Since they took Alissa off it, yeah."

Now there was a question. No big broadcast the Nines had caught during their trek mentioned Alissa's capture, death, or other horrible fate. She'd simply disappeared off the list, a rebroadcast one blasted along standard comm frequencies every time a ranking changed. The only explanation Davin had found was, well, that she hadn't done anything awful for a while and Eden had bigger priorities.

Because Eden controlled just about everything now. Not all that long ago, the company had just been large. Just been a usual mega-corp doing its part to own humanity. Now, with its grip over military, space, and most colonies off Earth itself, Eden was the de facto ruler of modern civilization.

Which made 'em, naturally, the bad guys.

The big expansion wasn't met with flowers and kisses from everyone. Alissa Reinhart, already a plucky fighter for the outer colonies, swept up the discontent and morphed it into actual resistance. Armed pushback on Eden's grasping hands.

David and Goliath stories tend not to work out the way the first one did. Alissa's people had pluck, hell she had a few Nines working for her, but moxie couldn't shoot lasers, couldn't build battleships. Outclassed, outgunned, and tricked—Davin like to forget his own played part in all that —Alissa's rebellion found itself blown apart.

And Alissa herself? The shining star meant to guide billions to freedom from corporate crap? She'd gone ghost, while her lieutenants took to guerrilla tactics and made Eden's life miserable.

So miserable the big boy wanted to talk truce.

Alissa still didn't show. Eden wouldn't accept anyone else's signature on the proverbial dotted line, leading to a slow sliding back into the knife fights on moons around Jupiter and Saturn.

And, eventually, Davin's crew getting stuck with finding Alissa. Find her, get her to sign the peace agreement, return things to sanity. Just the usual job for a bunch of mercenaries turned cargo haulers turned, now, into branded criminals.

They had, at least, proved Alissa still lived. Talked to her, even, before they'd blasted away from Jupiter. There, after performing some skullduggery on Alissa's behalf, the Nines used their good graces to extract a promise: get to Earth and Alissa would meet with them, explain the whole song and dance.

Except Earth wasn't, you know, an exact address. The planet crawled with cities, and those cities with people. Davin wasn't about to bop from one creaky mall to the next hoping to spot Alissa standing in line for coffee. But if she didn't reply, what other options did they have?

"You can't bail," Phyla said as the pair floated into the *Jumper*'s four-seated cockpit. The two-by-two affair had that lived in coziness, padded seats soaked in sweat, stress, and a few celebrations. "Opal might just shoot you."

The old-school sniper might just do that. Opal packed more baggage than Davin in this fight, having done some devious death-dealing back in her Eden employ. She leapt at a leadership role in Alissa's rebellion only to find her ships blown out from under her. Hard to roll with a bad turn like that, but Opal feasted on vengeance like Davin feasted on scrambled eggs. She'd be fine so long as Davin helped get some Eden goons in her crosshairs.

The easiest way to do that would be getting Alissa on the comm. Anywhere she happened to be, Eden would be too, or trying.

A call out the cockpit brought back the same nothing as before. A static hiss. Davin and Phyla stared at the console, willing it to change. Beyond, out the sloping glass shield, Earth's blue shape spun thumb-sized. At the moment, the sun lay off to the left, its blasting light always annoying going towards the inner planets.

Like trying to fly with a flashlight pointed at your pupils.

"If she doesn't answer, what do we do?" Phyla asked. "With your friend chasing us, turning around won't be easy."

"We could duck him."

Captain Heath Swane, an android apologist and Eden scuzzball. Despite getting turfed to the turgid assignments after Davin and the Nines proved androids were more dangerous to keep around than dump on the scrap heap,

Heath nursed a grudge into a retread. When they'd met outside Jupiter, Heath sought to use Davin's execution-by-new-android as a PR stunt, rescuing his career and ridding his nightmares--Davin assumed, anyway--of the nines captain in a single shot.

Things hadn't quite gone Heath's way, and now he trundled after the Nines at busted old frigate speed.

"I didn't get back into this life to be hunted again," Phyla replied. "If Alissa can't give us a way to stop Heath, I say we take it into our own hands."

"I love it when you get aggressive."

"Hope those hands are ready to fire a turret, because we'll need your best, hotshot, if we're going toe-to-toe with an Eden frigate."

A suicide mission, that, and they both knew it. Now, the Nines had one functioning version of Vi's secret toy on board, a ship-disabling miracle device with a simple counter. If Heath didn't know the dodge, the Nines might be able to score a sneaky victory.

If the Eden captain read his mail, though, the Nines would be toast.

"Team meeting," Davin said. "We get the group together, like we always have, and pick a path."

"This was easier when it was just you and me."

"Yeah, but our decisions were generally around which nutrient goop packets to eat."

"There wasn't a good choice then either."

A full seven, eight with Puk and nine if you counted the *Jumper*'s AI, meandered into the *Jumper*'s middle. Like Davin, Vi floated in tentative, her middle and left arm still wrapped up in heavy, ointment-soaked bandages. Her eyes wore the puffy smear that came from pain-killing drugs.

Riley wasn't much better. Both had been lit up by lasers

—much like Davin—during the raid on Vi's homestead. Riley at least kept the wounds to his extremities, aqnd the legs at that, two of a human's least important bits in zero-G. If Vi could barely carry herself, Riley lugged a toolbox in with him, as if proving his place in the crew with its presence.

Merc and Opal drifted down together from the mess where they'd been enjoying a meal nobody envied. The two had fast tracked their romance, dialed up their relationship to its heights thanks to constant near-death days. Davin respected their back-and-forth dialog, also the way both could turn an enemy to ash and laugh about it later.

Mox had already been in the center when Davin called the meeting, working out his exoskeleton's joints. All the carbon fiber weaved into his muscles looked cool until you realized how much work it required to keep functioning.

A greasy hinge was one thing, an arm that wouldn't move was quite another.

"That's the situation," Phyla concluded, holding serve with Davin's lungs still raw. "We give Eden the business, or we go hunting for Alissa."

"Do we have any leads?" Riley asked. "Back on Ganymede, we'd get big ideas all the time and realize we had no idea where to start."

"The frequency," Phyla replied. "We can track where we hooked into it last. It's not exact, and Alissa might've moved in the, oh, three weeks since we spoke. But that's what we've got."

"I'm all for knocking out some Eden teeth," Merc said, ditching an Opal handhold to scratch the back of his head, "but even I think we're going to die fast running up against Heath's ship."

"Seconded," Opal added. "You're saying he runs a ragged

shop, but he'll have us outgunned twenty to one. You fly back at him, you drop us first."

A harsh start, but that's why the team meetings existed. Davin didn't run a dictatorship. The Nines had always been come and go as you please and as you profit. Also, trying to hold Merc and Opal against their will would only get Davin killed.

"That leaves Earth, then," Phyla said. "We try to get to the ground where Heath can't find us, then dig up Alissa's last known location."

"And pray," Mox grumbled.

"And pray," Phyla agreed.

Vi coughed, winced. "Do we know she's even alive?"

Silence. Eyes meeting each other, surfing the floor. Davin tried to think of something inspirational to say, but nothing bloomed. He blamed his own painkillers.

"Don't be dumb." The voice came from everywhere, lancing out from the *Jumper*'s loudspeakers with a sardonic slant only a bodyless robot could provide. "Your odds against Eden's frigate are basically zero. Your odds of finding Alissa, while not much higher, are not zero. The answer is obvious. But perhaps not to humans, who seem so incapable of smart decisions."

Davin pointed a single finger up towards the ceiling, "You heard the android. Objections?"

"I'm here to end this war," Mox said. "Getting killed by an Eden ship isn't going to do that."

Nods, murmured agreements followed.

"Done then," Phyla said. "I'll try to get us to Earth. You all think of back-up plans in case that doesn't work."

It didn't work. Back in the cockpit with Phyla, Davin watched as she beamed out a permission request. Earth's flight control rejected it immediately, beaming back that the *Jumper* and her crew were wanted for all manner of nefarious crap and they should turn themselves in at the nearest Eden station.

Phyla had Fournine draw up a digital middle finger and send it back.

Throttling down the *Jumper*, really just flipping the ship around so its engines would slow their arrival, Phyla put her hands behind her head and looked Davin's way.

"Told you," she said.

"So the obvious is out," Davin replied. "We can be clever."

"If 'clever' means flying through Earth's defense force, then I think you're using the wrong definition."

"I think there's more than one way to get down there, is what I'm saying."

Back when Davin had first met Mox, the hulk had only just acquired his metal machination. Spurred on by vengeance, Mox had broken the rules and made some risky moves, ones Davin took as a sign Mox matched the Nines temperament. Part of the deal to bring Mox into the fold, though, meant realizing that revenge.

And the target had snuck onto the Moon through some more subtle channels.

"Not going to work," Mox said, still in the *Jumper*'s center, still greasing up his rig.

Phyla elected to hang in the cockpit, keep an eye out for any harassing patrols. Since contacting Earth, the local space would likely know sooner rather than later the *Jumper* and her wanted crew were around. The need to jet off or fight back might be imminent.

"You're about to tell me Luna's tweaked their procedures,

right?" Davin asked. He lay on his back, floating about a meter off the ground. Almost like being in his bed. "That they're so good at monitoring traffic now any sneaky play is foolish."

"You got it."

"So foolish a Centurion couldn't get us through?"

Mox threw a narrowed glare Davin's way. "I want a life to go back to, Davin. Not sacrificing that."

"If you don't, then we have to dive down Earth-side. You know those odds aren't good."

"You're pinning me."

"It's what I do best."

Mox grumbled. Squeezed some oil onto a cloth and rubbed it along his left leg.

"Lucky you have friends like us," Mox said as he finished.

"Luck, or design?"

"I'm gonna design a new shape for your bones if you don't float your ass away."

"Appreciate you, Mox."

Luna's foremost former Centurion came through with a series of tight-band calls to the Moon. Thankfully, if there was one thing Lunar folks despised more than anything else, it was Eden. The company had ravaged the lunar economy, removing its gray plains as the kick-start to space travel by building orbital stations everywhere.

All because Luna wouldn't allow Eden to buy up vast swaths of its dusty regolith.

Mox took the conversations private, refusing to deliver names and oodetails to anyone. Phyla and Davin waited outside the cockpit, sliding door shut, for Mox to appear with coordinates, docking codes, and a new name.

"Whiskey," Mox said. "That's what we're calling her while we're on Luna."

"Not much of a change," Phyla replied.

"It'll be enough," Mox said. "We land, we leave, they'll keep her sealed off."

Now it was Phyla's turn to issue one of her patented suspicious stares, "Sealed off how?"

"Evidence," Mox said, a slow grin. "We're criminals, right? Luna's gonna keep our stuff locked away until we get caught or turn up for a trial."

"And if we want to leave?"

"We gotta clear our names first. That's our ticket in, and out," Mox replied. "Either that, or give Eden enough trouble Luna thinks we've earned it."

"Phyla," Davin whispered an interruption, "this is the only deal we've got. We take it."

"You're telling me to leave my ship," Phyla said. "I'd better get it back."

The pilot's words took on a sharper edge when she repeated them two days later when Phyla and Davin were the last two hopping down the *Jumper*'s ramp into a dusty, near-abandoned docking bay on the Moon's dark side.

A motley bot collection waited to greet them, a remote-monitored skeleton crew meant to keep the two berths available for emergency landings. Tight ovals hollowed out in the gray sand, the berths lit themselves up in orange for the *Jumper*'s approach, and now shifted their spectrum to a pleasant blue-white as the Nines moved into the bay proper.

Davin told the crew to pack light--as if anyone on board had enough stuff to do otherwise--and the shambling collection looked more like wayward tourists than a hardened mercenary company on a mission.

At least if you ignored the hidden holsters, the long backpacks just large enough to store a rifle or, in Davin's case, a particular energy-blasting shotgun.

Mox's Centurion subterfuge served not only to get the Nines onto Luna, but also to secure them transport. The enclosed rover would be picking them up shortly, then would ferry the Nines to one of Luna's couple cities. From there, find a way to forge some IDs and sneak onto Earth.

Simple.

So simple, Davin actually napped while they waited in the bay's small terminal. The vending machines here, so isolated, held only water and, yes, nutrient goop. A disappointment so profound Davin could do nothing else save find one of the soft plastic benches and spread out. The rest seemed more interested in stretching muscles so long without even a hint of gravity.

To each their own.

Phyla's hand squeezing his shoulder pushed Davin back from oblivion. It'd been a nice oblivion too, free from stress, pain, dreams, anything. The look on Phyla's face said there'd be plenty of stress, at least, in the waking world.

"Our ride's close," Phyla said as Davin blinked sleep from his eyes. "They brought friends."

When Davin was the one making snap changes to plans, things were good. When someone else did it, well, Davin snapped open his bag and hauled out Melody.

"Any coffee in this place?" Davin asked as Phyla checked her rifle's power pack.

"Powdered," Phyla replied.

"I'll take it."

"Then get it yourself, captain." Phyla nodded back towards the doors to the *Jumper*'s bay. "I'm getting back on board to get her ready. Have a feeling we might need a quick exit."

The other Nines had themselves hustling too, gearing up for a fight that hopefully wouldn't be necessary. Then again, Davin's history tended to be filled with unnecessary fights.

This one turned a whole lot worse when, powered coffee in hand, Davin saw Phyla stalk back from the *Jumper*'s bay, raw anger etching lines across her face.

Davin called the Nines together with a whistle and Phyla gave the unfortunate update: the docking bay doors were shut, the Jumper sealed in.

"Can't blow our way through?" Merc said.

"These aren't thin," Phyla shook her head. "We'd need artillery."

"Then we're assuming those speeders coming in aren't friendly?" Opal asked, her look angling towards Mox. "Thought these were your people?"

"They are my people," Mox replied. "They're also Luna's people."

"They're cowards then," Riley said. "The only people after us are Eden, which means they're rolling over for—"

"For their lives and everyone on the Moon," Davin finished, putting a hand on Riley's shoulder to stop the kid talking. "It's a bad call, but I get why they might be making it." His crew leaned in a bit to hear the whispered words, prompting Davin to clear his throat before he started in again.

This was supposed to be inspirational, and a captain gasping his way through a chat wasn't exactly that.

"We set it up right," Davin said. "Positions. Make sure these Centurions know a fight's going to cost them, and while they're thinking about it, I hit 'em where it hurts."

"You will not shoot them," Mox said, the tone brooking no argument.

"Don't worry, big guy," Davin replied. "Shooting's not what I have in mind."

Thanks for reading! Find Lunar Gambit and other adventures at www.blackkeybooks.com!

ABOUT THE AUTHOR

A.R. Knight spins stories in a frosty house in Madison, WI, primarily owned by a pair of cats. After getting sucked into the working grind in the economic crash of the 2008, he found himself spending boring meetings soaring through space and going on grand adventures.

Eventually, spending time with podcasting, screenplays, short stories and other novels, he found a story he could fall into and a cast of characters both entertaining and full of heart.

A.R. Knight plans on jumping through to other worlds and finding new stories to tell in the limitless borders of our imagination.

Thanks, as always, for reading!

For more information:
www.adamrknight.com

To Dad

9 7 9 8 8 8 8 5 8 0 2 5 7